The abbot's eyes narrowed angrily. "Glorifying the gods is quite different than hoarding power for ourselves. You are mistaken about our motives."

"Then why doesn't the Church support Rawn, under a Winstow Regency, as the best way to prevent a brutal civil war?" Dex tried to sense the currents swirling about the man. Was he venial, or merely misguided? Was he looking to boost his own power in the Church, or was he playing a part in a dangerous political game?

"We do not trust any of the prinzes to do what is right. If Rawn were our ward, we could ensure the best for the world, for the people." The abbot leaned forward. "Are you going to be a problem, Dex?"

Other titles by the Author

Doors into the Dimensions series:

The Barton Street Gym
Chicago
The Twin Cities (2014)

Fantasies:

Demi God

Demi God

Zoey Ivers

Iron Ax Press

Houston

To all the marvelous horses, dogs, and people who have enriched my life, and touched my soul with magic.

Yeah, yeah. There've been some pretty amazing cats as well. But do *they* care what I think? Nooooo . . .

Demi God

Chapter One

"...forty horses and sixteen men," Nevrille looked at the stone ceiling as if scanning the sky. "I wish they'd hurry, I can't risk the storm moving off to the east, which it really wants to do."

Dex kept chopping carrots and mumbled so none of the other kitchen shift would hear him. Not that it really mattered, they all thought he was slow and talked to himself all the time. "Will it be a bad storm?"

"Oh yes. Snow drifts over your head and at least four days of very deep cold."

The door slapped open, and Abbot Sherin marched in, swept the busy kitchen with his eyes and marched straight through Nevrille without so much as a twinge or shiver.

"Damn Bookeeper," Nevrille glared down at the man.

Dex kept his face straight with an effort. He agreed with Nevrille, of course, but it wouldn't do to show disrespect. Actually he was glad that the head of the local order hadn't a sensitive bone in his body. It made life so much easier for him.

Nevrille was just a minor god, one of the Younger Siblings not even named in the liturgy, but none-the-less dangerous when he was given a reason. Now, however, he limited himself to a rude gesture at the abbot's back. Nevrille was reasonably good with Fire and Air, useful with Water and flat bad on Earth, but for all that he was powerful by human standards and conscientious about caring for the region that bore his name (more or less, given the history of border squabbles with neighboring counties before the previous Emperor put an end to it.) Nevrille County prospered in a modest way that kept envious eyes away from them, and the deity prospered similarly. Ambitions and wars were strictly the provenance of the Elder Siblings.

The abbot, having seen that everyone was working hard and not slacking marched back out, through the Deity again, and left the students to finish their chores in peace. Dex scraped his board full of chopped carrots into a pot and grabbed a basket of scrubbed potatoes to cut up next.

"Better see if you can get them to make extra," Nevrille said. "Those travelers are going to very cold when they get here. I've got to turn loose the storm. Merd will kill me if I let it mess up the last of the

Northern Plains harvest." He gave Dex a quick hug that Dex could almost feel, and faded.

"Bye, Dad," Dex whispered, reaching for another potato.

***

Stevan followed Captain Reddeer right into the barn before dismounting. He flexed his stiff cold hands and tried to brush the snow off his cloak but the wind had already done the job. The storm had held off most of the day, but had come down sudden and hard to make the last three hours a frozen misery. The holy brothers were scampering out to take the horses, and he surrendered the reins gratefully and followed the captain through a covered walkway to the nearest of the stone buildings.

The smell identified it as the refectory, and the fire at the far side beckoned. Reluctantly he stopped to meet the men waiting for them.

"I am Abbot Sherin, of Meadow Green Abbey and School. With the late hour, we thought you must have stopped at Kun to avoid the storm."

The captain bowed respectfully, "I'm pleased to meet you, Abbot. May I present Vizconte Stevan

Longbow of Merd. I am Captain Arlo Reddeer. I see you got the conte's letter."

"Indeed," The abbot swept an arm in invitation for them to sit near the fire. "I'm afraid that this will probably be the last stop you will make on time, these early storms can be fierce."

Stevan's conscience suddenly pricked him and he turned back to check on Bartli. Fortunately Gaspif was seeing to the man, and was helping him to a seat. The valet's dislike of the secretary hadn't extended to cruelty. Stevan flushed in shame, unable to not hope the man was so sick he couldn't continue the journey.

Surveying the rest of the room, he saw the monks of the order were at the closest tables and the students at the further. The older boys had apparently either finished dinner or ate late. They were clearing the tables while the younger boys still ate. He looked carefully, but none of the children appeared to be under ten. Not surprising, being a school and all. His escort, twelve of his Father's light cavalry with their sergeant, were dropping the packs they'd brought in along the wall and joining Gaspif and Bartli at the last table. More boys, in their knee length student's robes were bringing bowls and mugs to them. Stevan sighed quietly. He and the captain would no doubt have to wait for the kitchen to prepare them something grander. When his father had chosen him to go to the Imperial capitol as a living token of the conte's loyalty to the Emperor, Stevan had rather hoped his hostage status would result in his being treated like an ordinary teenager. Possibly even mistreatment and suffering. Instead he was getting treated even *more* nobly. It just wasn't fair.

Fortunately a rather thin but hot soup showed up before he died of starvation, tortured by the sight of the obnoxiously proper Bartli picking at his stew. The soup was followed by beef, potatoes and gravy, fresh vegetables and preserved fruit. Captain Reddeer kept up conversation with the abbot, mostly the latest news from Merd, and the plains counties, and about which Contes favored treating the Islander's incursions as piracy and which wanted to declare war and hold the various island governments collectively responsible. Stevan had heard it all before. His father wanted to tread carefully, and some of the others were convinced that the incidences were being blown out of proportion as a ploy to raise taxes. The Plains weren't interested in a war.

Stevan scoured his mind for a memory of the map this trip had been planned on, then gave up. "Is

Letfor Harbor in Nevrille County?" he jumped into a breach in the conversation.

The abbot blinked in surprise, as if not used to being questioned by children. "No, My Lord, while the county encompasses the eastern and northernmost parts of the Great Shake Bay it's too shallow for ocean going vessels. Letfor is on the south side, nearer the mouth of the Bay, in Hastur County."

"Good fishing, both inside and outside the Bay, as I recall," The captain added. "Plus crop and grazing land inland. Good stewardship, there. By both Gods."

The tall boy bringing plates of cake dripping with caramel wrinkled his nose at that, but said nothing. Was he a heretic? How someone could doubt the existence of the Gods was beyond belief. Well, perhaps someone from an area that didn't have a Little God. But what would such a person be doing here? The west part of the continent of Easterly was populated enough to have attracted plenty of gods.

He studied the boy's face, so he could recognize him among all these brown robed people. Curly black hair, and broad shouldered for all his lean gawkiness. It could be interesting to talk to a real heretic.

The abbot sniffed. "Historically that area was part of Nevrille County, so most likely He's still in charge."

Oh. Competing Gods. Or at least jealous advocates. Not nearly as interesting as a real heretic.

"Has this Northern coast suffered from the Islander attacks?" the captain steered the conversation back toward the trip.

"One village was raided, but everyone assumed it was just ordinary pirates taking advantage of the fleet's absence." The abbot smiled. "Of course the wind and waves put them on the rocks."

Stevan blinked. Little Gods weren't actually supposed to do things like that, were they? To the best of his knowledge Merd hadn't ever so much as rained on a bandit.

One of the monks approached and whispered in the abbot's ear. The abbot turned to Stevan politely, "I understand your secretary is ill? Our hospital here is quite good."

"Thank you, sir." Not that the abbot has actually offered... "I would be glad of your physicians' treatment. Bartli has been coughing for three days now and has a fever."

The abbot nodded to the monk, who left and

Stevan saw Bartli escorted off by yet another brown robed man.

The abbot left shortly thereafter to get ready for evening prayers, leaving a miscellany of servants and older students to escort his party to their quarters.

Like all religious orders, a sizable portion of their operating funds came from housing travelers, so the quarters they were shown to were comfortable and well furnished. This apartment must have been specifically designed for the highborn traveler, as it included a common room for the guards that all nobles and rich merchants found necessary on the roads.

Stevan got the largest chamber, Captain Reddeer the small room next to him. Gaspif had gotten there first and unpacked a change of clothes, and heated water over a cozy fire.

"I though it was a bit cold to take a bath, but you should clean up before turning in, m'lord."

Stevan rolled his eyes. Gaspif tried hard to keep up the appearance of snobbish Roma manners despite the thief brand on his right wrist. He'd never stolen anything from the Longbows, and they'd never enquired as to the origins of the brand. Stevan had wrangled some lessons in dirty knife fighting from him, so he was willing to—for now—forgive him the hoity-toity airs, especially since they kept slipping.

Bartli was something else again. A genuine Imperial City scribe. His parents had hired the man to put some polish on their tribe of wild children. His attempts to graft court manners onto Stevan's roots had been unremitting for the last six months. Guest or hostage, Stevan had realized he was going to be stuck "doing the pretty", probably for years, so he'd worked on the silly stylistic eating, greeting and dancing. But he didn't have to like it. Nor getting saddled with Bartli as a part of his personal household. He'd rather wondered if his parents hadn't been delighted to send the stuffy little pest away. Now maybe he could send him back.

A brief knock at the door was followed by the entrance of a stack of firewood with legs. Dumping the wood in the rick uncovered the older student that had served them dinner. "If there's anything you need, just jerk that cord." The boy was taller than Stevan but looked no older. "Someone will be on duty all night."

"You're a student here?" Stevan asked, "Why do you want to be a priest?"

Gaspif growled "Manners!" under his breath.

The boy just grinned. "Oh, not me. I'm just here for the education, and the abbot is going to have to let me go eventually. I figure I'll probably join the Imperial Army."

"The army?" Stevan brightened, "Don't I just wish I could! Well, the heavy cavalry, probably. I guess you don't ride?"

"Oh, I get a bit of practice in. The abbey keeps some extra mounts for travelers whose horses go lame and I sneak out nights sometimes and ride them."

Stevan politely refrained from mentioning that that was unlikely to be good enough. After all, the boy couldn't have had any sword practice here and that was even worse.

The boy's head twitched around at the sounds of a bell. "Excuse me. Evening prayers."

As he headed out the door, Stevan called, "What's your name?"

"Dexter Fiz Ambalia." Then he was gone.

"Hmph." Gaspif sneered. "Some lord's blowby."

"Ambalia. Isn't that the family names of the Dukes down in, umm," Stevan gave up. "Somewhere?"

"Ha! So you have been listening to Bartli's lectures." Gaspif let a faint smile cross his lips before resuming a properly blank expression. "The Dukes of Leston South. The current Duke is elderly. He has three sons and four grandsons in the Book, so this boy is probably a bastard fifth grandson."

"We're stopping there, aren't we?"

"Yes, the ship will put in there for supplies and to pick up more of the Emperor's guests before crossing the Formian Ocean. No doubt one of that lad's cousins, plus probably a youngster from at least one inland county."

Stevan crouched down to poke the fire, and added another faggot. "Why'd the Emperor suddenly decide he needed hostages?" He spoke in exasperation, not ignorance.

"You're not hostages, you're guests." Gaspif pressed his lips together disapprovingly. "This is a valuable opportunity for youngsters from all the contes' and dukes' families to meet the Crown Prinz and see how the Empire is governed."

"And has nothing to do with repressing any possible rebellion when the Emperor dies."

"Not to mention," Gaspif continued remorselessly, "the social opportunities. Dukes and

Contes that have no young unmarried male heirs are sending their eldest unmarried daughters or granddaughters. This is an incredible opportunity for all the younger sons to advance themselves. Even though you will inherit the county, you might want to consider an advantageous alliance."

"I'm sixteen. I *don't* want to get married."

"You are nearly seventeen, and don't think I haven't noticed you noticing some of the young ladies around Hastin, lately."

"Yeah, well," Stevan squirmed a bit, "I still don't want to get married." He peeled out of his travel stained and horse-smelling clothes and washed quickly, before crawling into the chilly bed.

***

Dex delivered the pot of soup to the hospital, trying to be silent and respectful. Old Father Berndis didn't look to survive the night. According to the records he was just two months shy of having lived a century.

Jeri and Mic carried in the rest of the meal, and scurried back to the kitchens where they'd scarf any extra pie before finishing the dishes. Today was their tenth day serving in the kitchen, so they, like Dex, would be getting assigned to different tasks tomorrow.

With visitors in, Dex rather hoped he'd be assigned to Brother Wrangler. He always enjoyed working with horses, or even cattle, when that was his duty.

Tonight, though, he lingered. He could tell Nevrille was here, but not showing himself. The Brothers who were drawn to the healing arts tended to be sensitive, and might see him talking to Dex.

Dex knew why the god was here. Brother Berndis. Nevrille didn't usually attend at deathbeds. Souls, freed from their bodies, remembered where to go, knew instinctively what to do.

Or they had until recently. The drastic drop in the births, the appalling numbers of stillborn babies, seemed to point to a problem.

"I know Berndis's soul." Nevrille's voice whispered in his mind. "It's a fine old one. I'll follow along and make sure it finds its way to its next body."

Dex nodded, and slipped back into the kitchen and quickly washed the few remaining dishes. The Cook was finishing preparations for breakfast bread, and looking tired.

"Would you like me to fetch the dishes from the hospital and wash them Brother Karst?"

It wasn't the first time Dex had done extra work. He was one of the reliable boys, in the eyes of most of the brothers. He just hoped he wasn't getting himself volunteered as full time cook's assistant.

Brother Karst nodded. "Thank you, Dex."

So in peaceful solitude he slipped back to the hospital and sat quietly in a dark corner and felt for the flow. Earth, Water, Wind and Fire, all braided together in human form. The flow of the elements was rather bumpy and rough here, not surprising, he supposed. Little discordances all over that he could smooth and comb carefully out straight, and larger breaks that he winced away from, dark kinks and the fading of age and grey masses of cancers.

Father Berndis was nearly faded away. There was nothing he, or even Nevrille could do about that.

The sick visitor was just the other side of the wall. He had a touch of lung fever. Dex eased through it, soothing the cough and pulling away the fluid in the lungs. Water manipulation was easy. Then he sank further, looking not at the glow of the Elements, but at the matter it appeared to be on the surface, looking smaller and smaller, until he could see the cells. He could see the infection, bacterial not viral, and he combed through at that level, separating the bacteria, and with an effort, shifted just partially to see the Elements, and pulled the Fire from the bacteria. He shifted back upwards, carrying that tiny spark, sifting out a bit of Fire from all the background of the World, and added it all to the Fire in the man's flow, to give his system the strength to finish off the remaining bacteria.

He pulled back out, and extended his awareness over the whole of the hospital. He winced away from some sharp edges, wishing he were stronger.

"You will be." Nevrille whispered, "You are getting stronger every year. Last year you wouldn't have been able to see those bacteria, let alone kill them so carefully."

Dex nodded, and turned his attention to Father Berndis, watching over his father's shoulder, so to speak, as the old man slowly faded.

And after a long quiet interval, all the color was gone and a clear colorless *something* slipped away. Dex's awareness followed the colorless bubble as it moved away. And when it reached the limits of his ability, he watched his father's greater glow trailing it. Traveling so smoothly it concealed the speed, it headed west. Then something swooped for it, a diving falcon of darkness that pulled up and sheared off suddenly as Nevrille moved in. The soul sank suddenly and disappeared. Dex had a brief sight of a village, a house... then he was back in the hospital.

"What was that dark falcon?" Dex barely breathed the words.

"I don't know." Nevrille answered, wholly in Dex's mind. "I have never seen or heard of such a thing. Is it a predator of souls? I shudder to think of the existence of such a thing. I will talk with the others siblings, and find out if they know of such."

Nevrille was the oldest god on the continent, or at any rate he'd gotten here first, with one of the early explorers. To the east, Merd was a very young goddess, filling up an empty area that hadn't had a deity until she moved in. Almost half of Easterly was godless, but then that was to be expected of a frontier. Hasto was to their south, and Lesto beyond. Dex had spoken to both of them; they weren't terribly strong, but they might have knowledge of some sort of soul predator.

Nevrille faded, and Dex stood and stretched and gathered the pots and dishes for the kitchen.

A predator swooping down upon souls,

plucking them as they sought their next home. Dex shivered, even in the heat of the kitchen, up to his elbows in soapy water. A predator would explain a lot.

***

He wasn't one of the boys called early for kitchen duty, nor was he called out for the barns. Dex took full advantage and slept in as long as possible, sliding into the breakfast line at the last moment. After warm porridge and fruit, the Proctor read out assignments. Dex frowned as duty after duty passed without his name attached to it. At the end, the proctor lowered the list, "Dexter Ambalia, see the abbot."

Had he been seen out too late last night? He certainly hadn't thought so, and he was used to dodging notice.

He took himself off to the abbot's office, and stood politely, waiting for the abbot to arrive.

"Ah, Dex, good." The abbot frowned down at him suddenly, "How old are you? Well, close enough to the vizconte. The young man's secretary is in the hospital with lung fever, and he needs a bit of assistance, and would probably not mind a bit of a tour as well. Go see him, and make yourself useful."

"Sir." Dex bowed and backed out of sight before scampering off toward the guest quarters. Talk about a plum assignment, and exactly the sort of opportunity he'd been considering for years.

***

The bells woke Stevan at midnight, and again at dawn. He heard the rattle of hard snow against the window and decided to snuggle down and sleep more.

Gaspif was already up, poking up the fire. "Breakfast will be served in about half an hour. I passed a request to the Proctor that he assign you a secretary, so that you can write your parents. And perhaps give you a tour of the school. I suggested the boy that brought the firewood in last night."

Maybe he didn't need any more sleep, now that he'd thought about it.

He spotted Dexter at breakfast, eating rather than serving. One of the monks read off what he thought were assignments and all the students scattered. Ugg. One more problem with church school. Chores before classes.

Dexter showed up at the door minutes later. "So, what do you need first? A guide or a secretary?"

Stevan caught Gaspif's eye and sighed. "Let's get the letter out of the way first. I could write it myself, but Mother says I have to be a Gentleman, and Gentlemen have other people to write their correspondence."

The boy nodded. "You'd think nobles would show off their brains and schooling, wouldn't you. Instead they hide them." He grinned wickedly. "Or maybe some of them are hiding something else?" He pulled out a nice case with a quill, ink bottle and sheaf of good parchment.

"Dear Mother, You'll be glad to hear that I still have all my fingers and toes after getting caught in an early blizzard halfway down the mountains. Bartli has lung fever, so we'll be leaving him here at Green Meadows to recover. The troops will pick him up on their return trip and get him home to you."

Stevan scowled. "Surely that's enough? Well... Please give my warmest regards to Father and the Pests."

"Do you really want me to say pests? And it's Meadow Green, not Green Meadows."

"Yes, they're my brothers. Definitely pests. Isn't Meadow Green backwards?"

"No it's actually the name of a little flower." He scribbled for another minute, then blew on it as he handed it over.

"Oh, nice! Once you get out of here you won't have any problem getting a job, if the army doesn't work out." Stevan grinned at his horrified look.

"Just because I have pretty handwriting doesn't make me a secretary. I'm certain I'd be in trouble, full time. C'mon. I'll give you the inside tour, then the outside, we can check on your horse and all."

Dex led him off through tunnels to the Hospital to check on Bartli, who was sleeping peacefully, then through the maze of buildings. "This is the School. The library is hands down my favorite room. The upper classmen take classes up stairs, the little kids are down here."

"Are you nearly done?"

"Yeah, I can leave anytime. I should have left in the spring, I suppose, but there always seems to be a reason to stay."

"Sounds as bad as parents. Until the Emperor's request came, they were talking about maybe in four years I should take a world tour. I haven't figured out yet whether I'm grateful or not. But I sure wish everyone would stop treating me like I was my father in a bad mood. Yes, sir, can I help you sir, and eating dinner with the abbot. Ugg."

"I understand. I think I know what I want, but I won't really know until it's too late to crawl back into my comfortable little hole here."

"Comfortable?" Stevan looked around the wintery landscape as Dex led him into the octagonal sanctuary.

"My safe little baby bed. I've outgrown it, it's high time I left."

Stevan eyed him challengingly. "You should come with me."

Chapter Two

"M'lord Abbot, my schooling is complete. It is time for me to leave." Dex managed to keep his voice steady.

The abbot sat up and frowned. "I have always thought that you would take orders. You have lived so content among us. All the brothers praise you."

"The school has been a home to me, since my mother died. I will miss you."

The abbot's frown deepened. "It is not that simple. You are destined for the Church. Your mother gave you to us."

"I beg your pardon, sir, but she didn't. I believe the Bishop has the paperwork. I was to be educated, with no obligations, at my mother's insistence."

The abbot's lips thinned. "You are the result of an unfortunate lapse on the part of your mother. The mark of shame on an otherwise holy and reverend woman. You are, under the Decree of 4593 the property of the church."

"That decree addressed the children born to women who had taken vows. Nuns. My mother was a Saint. Quite different. The Church served her, not the other way around. I am free, and acknowledged as such."

"Saint Vythis is dead. Your Grandfather gave you into our keeping."

"None-the-less, the contract the Bishop has, as regards my disposal, is quite clear." Dex stood his ground. "If you are uncertain, ask him."

"Better yet, I'll send you to him. As you say, you have finished your schooling in any case, and are more than old enough to have joined the Brotherhood." The abbot frowned at him a bit uncertainly, probably doubting that he was remembering Dex's age correctly. "Actually, this is a good time to return you to Devon's Gap Cathedral. The vizconte's group will be passing through Devon's Gap on their way to Letfor Harbor. You can travel with them. You will assist in the kitchens until you leave."

Dex bowed his head submissively. Which also hid a great deal of glee.

Nevrille was satisfied. "About time you were out of here. I was beginning to think I was going to have to get nasty."

Dex pressed his lips together to retain a reply, and at the abbot's wave, bowed himself out of the room and the old man's acute hearing. "I know it seems like a long time, but I still look too young."

The god sighed. "Yes, sorry, but that's how demi-gods grow and age."

"Yeah, I know. You and Mother both warned me I'd be slowing down even more. But now I'm almost big enough to pass for old enough to make my own decisions, and it's time to get some experience out in the world. Do you think I should try to stay with Vizconte Stevan beyond Devon's Gap?"

The god narrowed his eyes in thought, as he paced beside the boy, passing through the occasional furniture without effect. "That might work well. It would certainly give you a good look at the world."

"All I have to do is survive the Bishop."

He turned into the kitchen and glanced around. Bread was rising, and by the smell, some was baking. Lunch would generally be vegetable or bean soup, fresh bread and perhaps cheese. With guests...Visconte Stevan was a lad and his escort not highborn, but Brother Karst was probably out getting some sort of meat, none the less. Dex knew who would be scrubbing and chopping the vegetables on the big table, and set to it.

He had three big pots going and was

contemplating removing the bread from the oven when Brother Karst swept in, bringing the outside chill on his snow covered shoulders and hood. "Excellent Dex! The snow's so deep I had to send some boys out to shovel to get down to the barns. Pluck and clean these, won't you?"

Dex took the proffered chickens and ducks and stepped out to the porch to handle the messy part. Fortunately the womb blight didn't affect birds. Nor sheep or cattle, that he'd heard. Only horses among the hooved animals. Cats and dogs that he knew of. That dark falcon spirit shape, was it the cause? If it wanted the souls of smart creatures, humans, dogs and horses made sense. Cats? Less so, yet they had a strength of will... Perhaps that explained their inclusion. If it was a predator. . . He needed to do some research in the archives of the library, but that would depend on the weather and when they were going to leave.

Brother Karst took the first chicken immediately, no doubt for the guests' lunch. The ducks would probably be their dinner while everyone else had chicken. Dex finished up the rest, then cleaned up and ate a late lunch himself.

Afternoons he had classes. Geography and

Math, his two favorites. He'd had them often enough that his current instructor used him as an assistant and gave him assignments to tackle alone. Today though he was sent back to the Guest House.

He tapped and walked in, as was customary in Neville. The captain of the escort glanced up, and then rose.

"Are you this Dexter who is traveling with us?"

"Yes, sir."

"I'm Captain Arlo Reddeer. As we travel, I'll expect you to follow my orders. You are going to need riding clothes, and a bedroll. We have plenty of tents and I'll take care of the food and provisioning. Abbot Sherin suggested that as the vizconte's secretary is too sick to travel, you should take his horse and leave it at Devon's gap. Most of the escort will not be traveling on the boat from Letfor, so they will pick up the horse in Devon's gap and the secretary here on their return trip."

"If that is what you and the abbot wish, sir." *And I might borrow him a bit further, too*, Dex thought. "I'll collect my gear and be ready whenever the weather breaks."

"Hey, you're coming?" Stephen stuck his head out of his door. "That's great. You'll get some extra

27

riding practice, and I'll show you some sword work."

The captain frowned at his charge.

"He wants to join the army." Stephen informed him. "He needs all the practice he can get."

"The abbot seems certain that he's bound for the priesthood." The captain slid a glance at Dex.

"No. They all want me, but that is not my calling." Dex braced himself, but no further comments were made before he headed back to the dormitory.

He, like all the older students, had a semi private tiny room. There was no door to conceal whatever Bad Things any given boy might take to trying, so he kept all of his accumulated possessions in a dry tunnel under the Old Chapel. As far as he could tell, he was the only person who knew about all the tunnels. The doors were in out of the way spots and seemed to shed attention. The dorm had been built on older foundations. When he woke as usual in the pre-dawn, he just slipped down the stairs into the basement baths and through the door behind the old furnace. The stairs led to a tunnel floored, in this weather, with a thin coat of ice. He walked carefully until he got to the dryer areas. He hesitated over his neat stack of worldly goods, then left the old saddle.

He'd use the ailing secretary's, until they took ship, and then buy a horse and tack, when and where he needed to. He wondered if he could talk his way onboard, or if he'd get left behind.

So. The clothes he wore for riding, boots and warm cape. And of course, the swords. Both of them. The old sword was securely wrapped against the damp, for safe storage. It was still too long for him.

"You'll grow into it." Nevrille nodded reassuringly, "You'll be a very tall man when you finally get there."

Dex sighed, wishing demi-gods grew at the same rate ordinary children did. His mother had kept him with her, and out of early school. Everyone had assumed, as she had been dangerously old when he was born, that he was one of those slow children. When he'd finally started school, he was the size of children two years his junior, and had, at his mother's insistence, hidden that he already knew his letters. After his mother's death, the Bishop has shifted him here to finish his schooling 'before entering the order'. The school had looked at his innocent smallness and placed him with children five years younger. And he'd still kept quiet, acting shy, never showing what he knew... some of the teachers had caught on to his brains, and noticed him enough to realize he'd been in school for rather longer than most students, but even they didn't realize his actual age. He was twenty-seven and looked a decade younger.

He drew his other sword, the one he used all the time, in practice and in sparring with Nevrille. He'd found it during an attempt at feeling the natural harmonies. It, and the small horde of coins buried with it, had caused a break in the smooth flow of the natural Earth. He'd tracked down a number of disharmonies since then, and the drawstring purse he hefted was impressive, or would have been if it weren't for the lack of any way to replace it as it was spent. He split it up now, with a generous supply of coppers for his belt purse and the rest into a saddle bag, along with more clothes. The old sword was going to be a problem.

"Take it down to the barn, and your saddle bags as well." Nevrille said. "They've got pack horses, get both swords packed before the abbot brings you down, lecturing all the way about how you are meant to waste your life locked in a monastery."

"Ah." Dex grinned, "And the storm is clearing and we'll go after breakfast."

He carried the lot through tunnels to the

basement of the refectory, and then wound around the food stored off the kitchen and through the back door. He cut around the corner and found the main barn already busy. Two of the brothers were feeding the horses, so they'd have time to digest a bit and be happier on the road. Stevan's escort was up and about, checking tack and supplies. He spotted the sergeant and carted his stuff over.

"So, lad, up early for your adventure?"

"Yes, sir." Dex shrugged off his saddle bags and unslung the two swords. "May these go on one of the pack horses? It's my father's sword, and the one I use now, but the abbot doesn't approve."

"Ah. Well, and if they just get packed, there won't be any recriminations." The sergeant grinned knowingly. "I think you're a smart lad to avoid vows, myself."

"Thanks." Dex grinned back. "I'll be getting more than enough recriminations from the Bishop in Devon's Gap, when we get there."

"Oh, ho! Want you bad, do they?"

"They know my Grandfather will settle a deal on them to be shut of me." Dex shrugged. He hadn't seen his Grandfather in ten years, but he'd spent several summers there before that. Grandfather wasn't going to be happy to see him.

The sergeant snorted his opinion of greedy churchmen, and tucked the two swords in with several other long parcels in a pile. "Well, we'll just skip one problem." he frowned down the central corridor of the huge barn. "And move on to the next. Mr. Bartli's horse is an ill tempered brute."

"I've handled horses quite a bit. Bringing them in from pasture is one of my summer jobs." Dex followed to the stall of a mid-size heavily built black gelding. The black pinned his ears and tossed his head.

"This is Cliffside. Got a pedigree as long as my arm. Rockhead would be a better name, if you ask me."

Dex nodded thoughtfully, picked up a halter hanging on the wall and slipped into the stall. "I'll just get to know him for a bit."

"Call if you need anything, lad." The sergeant walked away, glancing back dubiously.

Dex slipped on the halter and stroked the unwelcoming neck. He sank into the relaxed state his father had taught him. Like people, every plant and every animal had a rhythm and flow. And Cliffside's rhythm was badly bent and unharmonious. Dex ran a hand down the straight shoulder, the just-barely puffy knee, the stiff and sore tendons and the upright, stiff pastern. "I'll bet your trot is rougher than the hills." Dex told him, smoothing his hands down the leg, over and over. He picked it up and massaged the tendons and pastern, smoothing harmonies as he rubbed. He repeated with the other foreleg, massaged the gelding's stiff neck and back, and was working down his hind legs when the abbot loomed in the stall doorway.

"You missed breakfast. We thought we'd give you one last chance to stay with us." The abbot frowned, "There's a problem with your paperwork, it claims that you are twenty-seven years old. That can't be right, yet I think you are of age to take vows on your own."

"I'm very sorry, Father Sherin, I was busy packing and then getting to know the horse I'll be riding, and I didn't even hear the breakfast bell."

"Don't ignore me, young man."

"I will not take monastic vows. This is not how I am called to serve the Gods."

"Oh? If you think the Gods are calling you, why do you turn your back on the church?" Sherin pulled himself up to his full height, which was nearly enough to tower over the young-looking student. "Do you expect to be a War Champion? Perhaps a Protector of the Realm?"

"Eventually." Dex told him. "Right now I need to see a bit of the world, learn other things and establish myself…"

"You arrogant puppy! You should at least try to redeem your mother's fall by dedicating yourself to the church that has paid the of raising you."

"The Church milked the world for all the money Saint Vythis' presence, miracles and artifacts could command. Educating her son without a leash was part of the deal."

"Deal? You think the Church *deals*?"

Dex sighed. "Father Sherin, you are a good man, and much the happier to be out of the politics of the Church leaders. It's a pity I didn't like you." He could feel the disharmony from here, being already attuned, so he reached out and tapped the abbot gently beneath one cheekbone, and pulled the rhythm straight around the infected tooth root. "Goodbye." He led the horse out, jostling the old man, who stood there, stunned, one hand to his face.

***

Halfway down the hill, Stevan pulled his horse back beside the church boy's horse. "Good morning, Dexter. The abbot seemed to not want to lose you, for all he doesn't seem to like you. He was practically raving when he gave that letter to the captain."

"Letter?" The boy looked over at him, warily.

"To the Bishop. All about you, apparently. What did you do?"

"Showed them how valuable I am, more the fool me."

"Oh, c'mon, Dexter. You said you hadn't given them your vows?" The very thought of vowing to spend your life inside walls and away from the world and well, girls, was enough to curdle his stomach.

"Call me Dex. No. No vows, ever. My mother paid for my education, and now they are going to have to let me go, whether they want to or not."

"Good." Stevan eyed the other boy, "You ride a lot better than I thought you would. Cliff seems to like you. I'm afraid Bartli chose him for his flash, not his gaits."

They chatted about horses all through the cold morning, walking the horses all day on the treacherous frozen roads. Their lunch break was brief. Not even the horses wanted to stand around in the cold, so they mounted up and continued, slowly, downward and southward, and camped on the first thawed and sheltered ground they came to in the late afternoon.

Stevan groomed his own horse, and joined the captain as he walked a round, checking that all men and horses were taken care of and setting up a watch schedule.

He felt a bit left out, and figured Dex felt the same. So when he woke in the pre-dawn to hear the cook getting rousted out, he groaned and wiggled out of his warm bedding. Dex, bedded down near him, poked an eye out as well, and then joined him.

The private told off to cook breakfast, Jeffis Blackrock by name, agreed that more firewood would be useful, and after that they helped feed the horses. Feeling virtuous, Stevan grinned at Dex.

"Now how about some fun. Would you like some sword instruction?"

"I've done quite a bit of practicing, but not much sparring with real people."

The camp was stirring now, and to Stevan's surprise, the sergeant approached Dex with two long bundles. "I reckon you'll be wanting one of these, then?" he asked.

"Thank you, Sergeant." Dex took the bundles and grinned at Stevan. "My sword and my father's."

The captain joined the group, asking, "Your father's?"

Well, it wasn't that unusual for a bastard to be acknowledged, but he'd gotten the impression that Dex *wasn't*.

But the other boy unrolled the oiled leather, and then the oiled cloth and exposed a blade over three foot long with a waving pattern to the metal, the crossbar brass, the handle almost long enough to get two hands on it. The golden pommel was cast into the Nevrille crest.

"That's beautiful." Stevan breathed, wishing instantly for one just like it.

"Looks like Western work." the captain said, "You don't see much of that anymore, what with the blast furnaces."

"Dad says this is stronger, but takes much longer to make. Not really economical, any more." He wrapped it up again and picked up the shorter bundle.

"It's a dying art," The captain agreed.

The second sword was disappointingly ordinary; its scabbard shared belt space with a knife and belt purse. Dex belted them on with practiced ease

Stevan saw the captain and the sergeant swap glances, then the sergeant brought out two of the weighted wooden swords they used for training.

Stevan was used to the older men beating him—and he was getting used to their approving looks when they couldn't. He knew he was fast and accurate, and was growing into strength and reach. Dex was faster, deadly accurate and trained *very* well. He beat not only Stevan, but the captain as well. Twice.

Then he had to show them some of the moves slowly, and coach both Stevan and the captain in them.

"Clearly I've underestimated those Church schools." Stevan told him, once they were back in the saddle.

The roads had refrozen over night, but after the sun had been on them a few hours they were able to pick up the pace and make up a bit of the time they'd lost yesterday. It was still nearly dark when they reached the town of Hastkew. The captain had sent Private Fontaine ahead to secure beds, so they were warmly if not opulently housed, Stevan, Dex and

Gaspif in one room, with beds, everyone else in the common room on straw pallets.

The third day they made excellent time. Now on the flats of the Miscow Valley the towns were close enough that they slept under a roof every night and they were spared Jeffis's uninspired cooking.

The sixth day they started climbing, the heights of the Transverse Range peeking out of the cloud cover now and then. The temperatures started dropping again, and the early morning wakeup and warm up sparring had spread through the group as the best way to face the day.

They walked the horses to warm them, then, the footing being good, Stevan challenged Dex to a race.

"You always win," Dex complained, then booted Cliffside into a gallop.

"Don't get too far ahead," the captain called. No doubt he'd be sending a couple of men after him.

Stevan caught Dex and passed him on a long gradual climb, then pulled up and stopped. A trio of wagons was ahead of them the teams slow on the climb. Stevan was eyeing the rough hillside climbing steeply to their right and dropping steeply to their left to see which side they should pass on when the first arrow took the driver of the lead wagon in the neck.

Dex kicked his horse forward and Stevan flinched as a scream marked an arrow finding another drover, and then a dozen howling warriors were pouring down the hillside.

Stevan grabbed his sword, wheeling to form up on Dex who booted Cliffside into the middle of the charging bandits.

Despite the screaming, the bandits had fair discipline, keeping a line, and with groups assigned tasks. A pair of axe wielders were obviously designated to immobilize the wagons. Dex ignored them and hit the center of the charge, using his horse as a weapon, deflecting a man's hooked halberd with his sword and trampling him.

Except the stupid horse jumped over the man once he'd knocked him flat, and Dex vaulted off the horse.

Stevan wished he had a longer weapon as he leaned and chopped, and finding himself spending more time protecting his horse than inflicting injury, he spun him out of the melee and jumped off. He went after the ax men, ducking a swing and lunging as if he had a rapier. Against the unarmored bandit it was effective, and he jerked the sword loose. He twisted away from a sword, and slashed awkwardly across the man's belly. The man fell back screaming. Stevan staggered back his own stomach twisting. Dex jumped past him and parried a thrust, then kicked and broke a kneecap. He lunged and stabbed through another bandit, front to back. Stevan got a grip on himself and when a pair of bandits jumped them, he shoved the blade away and kicked, grabbed and thrust his opponent down the steep slope. The man got his feet under him, but took a look back and then kept going. Stevan looked around. Two bandits were running away, back up the hill. The rest were either dead or too badly injured to run.

A footstep behind him was Captain Reddeer. "Well, I'm glad I decided to catch up with you two." He looked Stevan up and down for injury then relaxed. "Good job lads."

The injured bandits received rough aid, mainly from Dex.

"I've helped in the hospital," he admitted. The bandit Stevan had gutted was stitched together.

"Good enough to get him to the hangman," the merchant growled.

The captives were loaded into the wagons, for delivery to the guard at Durant's Gap. The merchant's lead driver had been killed, and he had taken an arrow in the shoulder. Dex drew the arrow and bandaged the wound.

The town of Durant's Gap was on the far side of the pass itself, and after two more days of climbing up and down ridges they finally, according to the well-traveled Sergeant, started down the last decline.

The thin fog, or low clouds they were riding through burned off at mid day. Even from this distance the white spire of the cathedral was visible, dominating the picturesque town.

"It's smaller than I thought it would be." Stevan said. "Merd's Bishop is in Hastin and it's a huge town."

"Durant's Gap is just a waypost on the road to the coast. Conte Baldur answers to the Bishop, of course, but the conte himself lives down on the coastal plains, so only local troops are stationed here. The Bishopric employs most of the people in town, secondhand if not directly." Dex frowned, "I think it moved here because of some Bishop with allergies or something. The old cathedral in Gradin burned down, so he figured he might as well build the new one here."

Stevan nodded. "I suppose it doesn't matter, so

long as the Bishop and Conte get along well."

"Nevrille has a habit of backing up which ever one is right, so neither usually gets too out of line."

Stevan boggled a bit. "But, how can you tell which one the God is favoring?"

Dex grinned. "Cathedrals burning down around a Bishop's ears tends to get the message across."

"Oh." Stevan hesitated, "I thought only the Elder Siblings interfered directly like that. What do you know about the Gods? They teach a bunch about that in Church schools, don't they? The Gods and the Kingdoms? I understand what's going on with the Emperor, but then they start in on all the gods, and that I don't get at all."

"Huh. It's the politics that I don't understand."

Stevan shrugged. "The Emperor is old, he's got three brothers, a bunch of adult nephews, grandnephews, sons-in-laws and grandsons. His only living son is a sickly youngster. Eight years old. One of the older relatives will be regent, Prinz Winstow is at the moment, but he's not much younger than the Emperor. But with all those possible claimants to the throne, that sickly boy is pretty much written out of the Book already, in most people's minds. All the nobles are backing one or another of the herd."

Dex nodded suddenly. "Oh. I see. The Emperor is collecting hostages to try and save the sick Prinz. I can understand that."

"Yeah. But what about the Gods? Do they have anything to do with this, or do they sit back and do nothing?"

"Ah," Dex frowned. "Politics and wars and ambitious backstabbing maneuvers like this are the province of the Elder Siblings. They're above caring about mere people, like our County Gods do. They get called Siblings, but that's just a metaphor."

"Well, if they're all children of the Creator…"

"All souls are the children of the Creator. The Younger Siblings are like souls that are so old they don't reattach to bodies anymore, but they still care about people. At first they can barely control Fire." Dex raised his eyebrows in query. "Have you studied science?"

"Yes. What does science have to do with Gods?"

"Well, you know there are four states of matter? Solid, liquid, gas and plasma?"

Stevan nodded.

"Or Earth, Water, Wind and Fire, the way the Church puts it. It's all the same thing. New Gods can barely manipulate Fire, then as they grow, they learn to handle Air, then Water and finally Earth. Once a God is strong enough to work all four, he or she is powerful enough to have a place among the Elder Siblings, caring for whole continents or oceans or whatever takes their fancy."

"I thought you said they didn't care?" Stevan challenged him.

"They don't seem to care about ordinary people, or the crops or anything." Dex said. "They care on the level of contes and dukes, kings and emperors. They care about the wealth and prestige of their regions, compared to the other gods. Will they speculate about who'll be the next emperor? It makes them sound like they're a bunch of gamblers at a horse race. They just want to win, and who cares how many horses are lamed or jockeys thrown."

"How do you know that? Sounds pretty heretical to me." *I was hoping to meet a Heretic. Found one.*

Dex grinned. "Just watch. The Elder Gods are betting on their favorite horses in the Imperial Race, and there aren't any rules for them."

Stevan suppressed a grin at the thought of contending Prinzs being nothing more than horses running for the Gods' pleasure.

"And the rest of us need to mind where the hooves are headed and get out of the way. Because there aren't any rules about them interfering."

"Yeah, but how do you know?"

Dex sighed, staring up at the town walls as the approached. "My mother was Saint Vythis. She talked to Gods all the time."

***

As he'd expected, Dex was separated from Stevan's party as soon as the staff realized who he was. He abandoned his packs and swords, and followed the acolyte to the Bishop's office.

"So, Dex." Bishop Jurdis hesitated, frowning at him. "You haven't grown much since I last saw you." his frown became thoughtful, his eyes drifted toward a beautifully embellished calendar, giving away his thoughts.

Dex braced himself for the worst. If it occurred to the Bishop...

"Your Mother always did look thin and waifish, and younger than her age. Not surprising that you do too. Now. This matter of you not taking vows.

You've received a valuable education from the Church, don't you feel that you should pay for it?"

"Your Eminence, I believe my mother paid for it. Was I mistaken?" Dex was nearly limp in relief. If the Bishop had even thought his father might be Nevrille, he wouldn't have a chance.

The Bishop frowned, turned to the papers on his desk. "Your grandfather has informed us that…"

A sudden brisk wind whipped through the window and dislodged a small stack of papers on the sideboard. Dex leaped to stop them sliding to the floor, snatching one persistently slippery one—"Oh, here is the contract with my mother." He smiled artlessly, skimming the single page quickly. "Oh yes, it is quite clear, any and all children of hers are to be raised and educated by the Church, but be legally free souls, without obligation to the Church."

The page was snatched from his hands. The tight lipped Bishop glared at him. "You've had a great deal more than that from us. You are twenty-seven years old."

"I believe I pointed out my near adulthood before you sent me to Meadow Green."

The Bishop smiled serenely. "Perhaps we should ask a judge what you owe the Church." He sat down behind the polished desk.

The two candles in their tall holders quietly lit themselves. The Bishop paled.

"If you wish, your Eminence." Dex said, "But I would prefer to take my leave of you in a friendly fashion. I think I'll travel further with Visconte Stevan, if I can, perhaps visit my Grandfather."

The Bishop pulled his eyes away from the tiny flames. "Do you think you will be welcome there?"

"I doubt it, but I would like to say goodbye to him."

The Bishop opened his mouth, glanced at the candles and forced a smile onto his face. "You will always be welcome here, Dexter. I wish you a pleasant trip."

"Thank you, your Eminence." Dex bowed politely and let himself out. Out of earshot of the Bishop, he muttered, "You don't play fair do you?"

"He wasn't playing fair either. Now perhaps he will stop stepping over the line. You are not the only youngster he's pressured." Nevrille showed as little more than a glimmer, but led Dex off to the side, to a small walled garden.

The lifesized bronze statue in the center was of his mother. Dex blinked back tears. "He did a good job. Whoever the artist was."

Nevrille nodded, solidifying, or at any rate *looking* solid. "She was a brilliant and independent woman. Your Grandfather couldn't wait to get her out from underfoot, but she refused all three marriages he arranged, and refused to take vows when he tried to give her to the Church. She wanted to attend the University in Imperial City. They do allow women students, if they try hard enough to get in and can pay. Your Grandfather was outraged—again—and refused."

He circled the statue on insubstantial feet. "I talked to her, I could feel her curiosity from here. We talked about everything. I steered her to where she could find some books, but sooner or later your Grandfather always found them and burned them. Then the Bishop of Leston South caught her half of a conversation with Lesto, and the Church was all over her to take vows."

"That's how she negotiated that contract, isn't it?" Dex asked.

"Yes. She got away from her father, came up here where I could talk to her more often, and she had her own rooms, unlimited access to the library and that provision for children, although she didn't actually expect to have any."

Dex blushed and looked away. "How did that happen, anyway?"

"Her mother died. She felt guilty, to have not been there. I told her she couldn't have done anything, but she wouldn't listen to me. She locked herself in her bedroom, wasn't eating. She wouldn't *hear* me. It was the hardest thing I've ever done, to work with solids like that, so complex." Nevrille grinned, "She couldn't ignore a naked man appearing in her room like that."

"Naked?"

"Didn't think about clothes. Or how to stand, or walk. Or talk. Or undo it. Well, most of it I remembered quickly enough. But she had her hands full keeping me hidden for a couple of weeks while I tried to figure out how I'd done it in the first place, so I could reverse it." He hugged Dex. "We loved each other. I guess it was inevitable, given the opportunity, that we'd love each other with our bodies as well."

"So…it's been twenty-eight years. How are you doing at solids? Why are you still a Younger God?"

"Because I never managed to do it again, and I can't shift rocks and things." Nevrille shrugged, "Twenty-eight years isn't very long, for a god," he flicked a swift glance to one side. Dex looked but couldn't see anything. "Besides, she's still here. She's getting stronger all the time. I need to hang around until she's got enough control to not burn down the cathedral... accidentally. When she's strong enough, I'll move on, let her handle the county."

Dex swallowed a reply as he heard footsteps approaching. Stevan and Captain Reddeer walked in through the far gate, and he waved to them.

"So, they haven't pressed you into giving vows?" Stevan looked relieved.

"No, the Bishop was pretty gracious about it. Much better than I'd thought he'd be, but the contract was quite clear." *And he wasn't going to go against a God known to express his displeasure with Bishops by burning down their cathedrals... deliberately. Although for a demi-god in his hands, the Bishop just might have burned the cathedral himself.* Not that Dex was going to actually say that out loud. Being naturally grounded in Earth, demi-gods were in some ways as powerful as gods. In all the ways Churches used them to make money, demi-gods were much more powerful than Saints. "I can go anywhere I want to now."

Stevan lit up. "You can come with us!" He

eyed the captain hopefully. "I need a secretary, right?"

The captain snorted. "Some secretary. You do need a bit of an entourage, though. A friend, I think, would give a bit of prestige, and yes, Dex, we will pay your way."

"All right." Stevan thumped him on one shoulder, and Nevrille on the other. The God faded out and left him to the young man.

Chapter Three

Gradin was another five days west and down hill. The conte's seat was a large town. It had outgrown its protective wall a century ago, and stretched down various roads. They were expected. Late, in fact. The conte was about to send his son off without the Merd representative when they trailed in. They had only a short break there, and spent most of it trying to remember peoples' names.

Vizconte Durant ed'Secke of Nevrille County, second son of the conte, had two servants in addition to his valet and secretary. He had a Captain of the Guards, two Sergeants and two dozen mounted troops. Five friends were traveling with him, the sons of minor nobles and major merchants, each with a servant and groom. They managed with only fifty horses because the conte had sent 'everything else' ahead on wagons.

Stevan shook his head in disbelief, but was secretly pleased to have Dex, in his best clothes, exaggerating the supercilious manners of Durant's friends at dinner. They got an early start the next morning, and Stevan found himself riding with

Durant.

"So, I'm not familiar with *Merd*." Durant had apparently decided that a Plainsman Noble should be patronized. Or was that, put in his place?

"We're mostly grain farmers," Stevan told him, "Some fibers, a bit of mining, timber and so forth."

Dex leaned forward, and added, "Merd's the largest exporter of grains on the continent. They ship most of it down the Draven to Saint Portersburg for shipping worldwide."

Stevan hid his surprise. He knew that, but he hadn't thought Dex would.

Durant wrinkled his nose. "I was speaking of your God, actually."

"Oh, she's fairly young." Stevan told him. "Came with my great great grandfather, when they steaded the northern plains."

"Ah, so your family is young as well." He looked smug.

"Recently elevated. The Emperor didn't create us out of nothing," Stevan agreed, failing to elaborate further.

"Your family has been holding the county for, what? Eight generations now, Durant?" Dex asked.

"Yes…Dex." Durant looked down his nose

from the lofty superiority of eighteen years of age.

"Don't worry, Durant," Dex said sunnily, "I'm a bastard, so my bloodlines don't *conte*."

Stevan snickered at the emphasis, but decided to change the subject. "What are your horse's bloodlines? He's a beautiful thing."

Discussions of horses, horse breeding, horse racing and imported bloodlines kept them tolerably polite to each other all the way to Letfor Harbor.

They'd admired the bay for three days riding along it, accustoming themselves to the salty scent. The ripe fish smell of the harbor town caught Stevan and Dex by surprise. Durant laughed at them. "What did you think a fishing town would smell like?" he jeered.

The two groups descended on the local Church's guest quarters, and found them half full already. Stevan signaled the captain, and they let Durant's group take the remainder. They sent Private Fontaine ahead to negotiate rooms in a tavern by the docks.

The Widow's Lament was clean enough, despite the fishy smell, noisy enough that night to fascinate the boys and had plenty of room for their party.

"The Blue Lady has been in port for only a day," Captain Reddeer told them, the first morning. "So they're still loading supplies. We'll board late tomorrow and leave with the evening tide."

Seeing Dex's questioning look, Stevan explained, "She's an Imperial ship, an older warship refitted for passengers. We were told when to be here to meet her. The Hastur County hostage must already be here, I think, or they wouldn't be planning on leaving so soon."

"Guest," The captain growled.

"Ha!"

"So, what I was about to say was, you have today free to prowl the town, but no trouble, and you'll take Fontaine or Blackrock with you." He fixed Stevan with a beady eye until Stevan nodded.

The captain and the two privates would be with him all the way to the Imperial City on Roma, guarding him until some undefined time in the future when he returned home. He might as well get used to having a body guard.

It didn't bother Dex a bit, he promptly cornered Fontaine and asked him what else he'd seen in town, and wasn't there supposed to be a light tower out on the point?

After an even worse fishy smelling stroll along the wharves, Stevan was more than ready to saddle up and ride out to the point.

Durant was ahead of them, and escorting the Hastur Conte's daughter.

"Vizconteza Nati ed'Treliff." The girl was big. Tall, with the sturdy build many horsewomen developed. Old too. Stevan guessed she was a bit above twenty, and wondered why she hadn't married.

"Vizconte Stevan Longbow of Merd." Stevan reached across and shook her hand, belatedly wondering if he ought to have kissed it. Drat, maybe he shouldn't have been so glad to get rid of Bartli.

"Dexter Fiz Ambalia."

Dex bloody well bowed politely over her hand, neither shaking nor kissing it. Stevan made note of that, for future encounters with his 'equals'.

"I thought we'd be picking up the Leston South representative on our next stop down the coast." Nati said, sounding surprised.

"Oh, I've been at a church school inland, and am traveling with Stevan for the experience. I'm sure Grandfather will pick a more valued grandson than me to represent him to the Crown Prinz."

Ooo, smooth and polished. Stevan admired the

polish. So did the vizconteza. Durant scowled.

"Are you coming or going from the light tower?" Dex continued. "We felt the need to get a bit of exercise before we embark."

"We've just been. It's quite a climb up to the top, but well worth the view," Nati's eyes twinkled. "Not to mention the curved reflecting mirror."

"If you grease the palm of the old men that run it, they'll tell you everything about it, and its entire history. Pay them again and they'll shut up." Durant rolled his eyes.

"Thanks, we'll do that," Stevan said, reining Cedar around them.

"A pleasure to have met you, Vizconteza," Dex called back. "We'll see you aboard the Blue Lady."

Out of earshot, Stevan sighed. "I hope that isn't the kind of highly placed wife my parents are hoping I'll find at Court."

Dex blinked, "You didn't like her? She seemed smart and had a good seat on the horse."

Stevan sighed. "She was a bit, umm fat. And old."

"Hmm. I guess I haven't actually met all that many women, now that I think about it."

'That kind of happens in Monasteries." Stevan

pointed out. "So take notes. You might find one that doesn't care if you're a bastard, and she could buy you a commission in the cavalry."

"Buy...Oh." Dex looked like he was thinking about something. Or listening to the wind. "Somehow I thought the officers earned their places."

"The good ones do. Or that's what my father says. He says they start out with training at home, then buy just a lieutenancy to start with. They move up, learning all the way. At least," Stevan said. "That's how Father did it. He cashed out after the surrender of Kastle Foygrath, proposed to Mother and brought her home to Merd."

Dex sighed wistfully. "That's... perfect."

"I guess your situation is... awkward?" It was the first time he'd broached the subject.

"It was definitely strange." Dex shrugged. "After Mother died I was shipped off to the Meadow Green school, as mostly a nuisance. My father kept in touch. If the Bishop had known I even knew who he was, let alone saw him regularly, he'd have... well, I don't know. They thought they had my Mother completely isolated."

"I guess they thought she should be pure. Or something." *Right, let's insult his Mother.*

Dex just snorted. "They wanted her completely under their control, no outside influences that held other views on what God-given information should be released, what sold, and what buried. Not to mention the artifacts."

"Oh. Yeah, I guess they get a lot of money from the artifacts, not to mention how useful they are. We have a cold box so powerful it freezes meat in mid-summer. Dad paid a small fortune for it."

"Does your Bishopric have a Saint?" Dex asked.

"No, but if we really work at praying, Merd seems to be able to charm things. So the church has a good income." He frowned. "Some people say they charge too much, and own too much. Dad says the church owns so much property across the ocean, all over the continent of Roma, not just in the Old Country, that they're nearly equal in power to the Emperor."

Dex nodded. "They aren't supposed to have that sort of power. My mother especially disliked the way they owned *people*. She negotiated for the best deal she could come up with, but she had no choice beyond that. The Church wasn't going to let her get away. Between them and Grandfather she was trapped."

"I've heard of nuns running away," Stevan proffered. "But never a Saint."

"Even Dad couldn't have protected her. And really, she liked the life, the learning, all the books and so forth."

"How does a Saint talk to a god? Like prayer, and things happen more quickly than with ordinary people praying?"

"A little bit like that, I mean, the god can use the Saint as a sole focus and affect things, but Saints, or at least my mother, just talk to them like they're people. They were friends, always talking about things, especially stuff mother had read about in books. Nevrille would answer her questions about things, history and science and stuff."

"Huh." Stevan drew rein under the tower and gazed upward. "Which god made this light?"

"No gods needed, young man," a rough voice broke in. "Men can make things with their own hands, although some prefer to forget that and leave it all to the Church."

Dex dismounted gracefully. "I've heard you have one of the largest mirrors in the world, sir."

"Well, the largest in this part of the world,

that's for sure." The old man was clearly gratified by Dex's respect. "Would you like to climb up and see it?"

***

"No!" The cry was full of despair, with an edge of tears.

Stevan stepped out the back door of the inn with Dex at his heels, and saw its source trying to pick up two gangly puppies at the same time. The innkeeper looked exasperated. "I told you we should have drown them at birth, before Hily got attached to them."

His wife nodded. "I just thought *someone* would take them, and there were only the two live ones out of the litter of thirteen," she noticed Dex and Stevan. "Good morning, sirs, sorry about the noise, I'll have your breakfast in just a moment."

"There's no rush." Dex stepped around Stevan and crouched down to look at the pups. "What handsome dogs, what breed are they?"

The father answered for the daughter. "Oh, this idiot noblewoman, begging your lordship's pardon, came through with this fluffy creature, with his hair all shaved in some parts and fluffed out in others and *bows*, and he got to my mastiff bitch. The pups aren't going to be good for anything."

"Poodle and mastiff?" Stevan snickered, "Now that's got the be the most awful…"

"They're cute," Dex said. "How much are you selling them for, Miss?" He looked down at the little girl, who suddenly stopped glaring at her father.

"Dex, are you crazy?" Stevan eyed the furballs uncertainly. Cute?

"Tuppence each," the girl glanced doubtfully at her father.

Dex dug out his purse and forked over the coins.

"Puppies on a ship, Dex?" Stevan snickered as Dex had not much more luck than the girl at picking up two wigglers at once.

"Sure, it'll give me something to do."

***

"Well, cleaning up after sea sick puppies does keep you busy." Stevan noted.

"At least they're not as sick as Nati." Dex nodded forward to where the greenish tinted girl crouched against the rail. "Good thing we'll be in White Cliff Harbor at dawn tomorrow. The trip across to Roma is going to be rough on her, though."

"The captain says she'll get over it in a couple of days. Everyone does, he says."

Stevan had been thoroughly intimidated by the captain. Impressed, but intimidated. A bit over average height, well over average width of shoulder, he was the younger brother of a Bortian King and took no snottiness from mere Conte's sons. Durant had taken one look and disappeared into his cabin, with his friends slinking along behind him. Apparently the captain had made it quite clear that they were nuisances, inconvenient, hostages, and a burden, and had better not get in the way of his crew.

His attitude toward Nati was superior, when he deigned to notice her at all.

The sea sick puppies were fast asleep in a large closed basket. Dex carried it forward and perched on the rail near Nati. "Is it better out here?"

"Much, much better." Nati sat up straighter, "I may spend the night out here. Very improper, but I just can't make myself care."

"You didn't bring a maid, or anyone?"

"No. We're poor as can be, and a plain younger

daughter can just take herself off to court in the hopes of finding a rich husband all by herself."

"That seems a bit cold."

"Well, I'm the fifth daughter of six and I've got two older brothers as well. And, well, Father favors Conte Mongote as regent for the Crown Prinz."

As the new Emperor. Stevan translated that with no problem. Nati's worth as a hostage was *low*.

"I've been advised to attach myself to some well-to-do noble daughter. I can be a lady-in-waiting if nothing else." She glanced at the basket. "I'd rather be a kennel girl, or care for horses, but that's apparently beneath me."

"So you'll end up shoveling out a different kind of stall?" Dex grinned, "Have you ever read this book called 'The Harem'?"

Even green she managed to look indignant.

"It's not *that* kind of book." Dex protested, "It's a history of several generations of the Imperial Families, but all from and about the women. It's a real eye opener."

"How did you get a hold of something like that in a Church School?" Durant had come up behind them.

"Sneakily." Dex pulled the basket closer, out of

Durant's reach. "There were old tunnels, connecting basements and such all through the school. I read everything in the library at least once."

Durant withdrew a few inches as if Dex were contagious. "I preferred to learn swordcraft, to spending my time indoors."

Only two of Durant's friends were on the ship. The Emperor's invitation had apparently been clear on the maximum sizes of entourages. Of course, each of them had a servant, and the conte had sent three armsmen along.

"It must be complicated for a host to invite one and receive nine." Dex murmured to Stevan.

"Apparently that's the way it's done." Stevan shrugged. "My invitation specified a maximum of three armsmen. I think they're being careful to not accidentally assemble an army. And then two friends, and up to three servants. Total. I'm being frugal, just bringing you. I wonder if they'll stuff everyone but the guests and friends into the attics."

Chapter Four

The harbor city of White Cliffs perched on a rocky ridge south of the small bay. They had their choice of steep stairs or the more gradual road that climbed slowly to the east and then turned back to the city. The conte had sent a carriage, much to the relief of Nati. Durant and his friends, Robeir and Fridrec joined her. Stevan followed Dex up the stair. Captain Reddeer didn't comment, and managed to keep up without a problem. They'd sent their luggage on the carriage, even the basket of puppies, so they were unencumbered.

"Hasn't changed much since the last time I was here." Dex threaded an expert path through the merchant's district and out into the central plaza. "It's the second oldest city on the continent of Easterly."

"It's bigger than Hastin," Stevan admitted. "Is that the Palace?"

"Nah. The Cathedral." As they crossed the street and could see to the right across the plaza, Dex pointed. "*That* is the palace."

Stevan stopped and stared. Captain Reddeer had to nudge him back into motion. "That's, that's... "

"Colorful, gaudy, overly ornate and in incredibly bad taste?" Dex looked fondly at the building. "When I was younger, Grandfather had me down here for a couple of months each summer. I thought it was grand."

They stood and took it in for a long moment.

"The central part is over five hundred years old. Double the age of the city. The founding conte had his Roma mansion disassembled and shipped here. They built up the base and all those ridiculous steps, so it's two floors taller than it was originally. Then his son—they were both named Garon—had those spiral striped onion towers built on each side. Then a couple of generations later they built the west wing, with the flying buttresses. Then eventually the east wing with the columns and carved capitols. That pointy thing with the platform on top poking up over there is a replica of a pre-historic Garm pyramid. Except it has more space inside it. Conte, umm, Farth had archeological yearnings. It only connects to the rest of the palace through the basement."

Stomping feet preceded a curt voice from behind them. "Cursed goggle eyed tourists. What the fuck have *you* got at home?"

Dex didn't even turn around. "And *that* is my

cousin Pierre."

"What? Who the he... oh, little gods. It's the *bastard*. What are *you* doing here?"

Dex's shoulder was grabbed and he was hauled around to face a young man with curly black hair. "I'm accompanying Vizconte Stevan Longbow to Roma. Nice to see you again, Pierre."

Pierre stared down at him. "Haven't grown much have you, shrimp?"

Not a surprising observation, Dex admitted. He was three years older than his foul mouthed cousin, but now looked not much older than he had been on his last visit. Although he wasn't enough shorter to really warrant being called a shrimp.

Pierre switched his attention to Stevan. "Huh. I'm also going to be a *much* respected damned guest of the Emperor."

Stevan blinked a bit under the impact of Pierre's lifelong avoidance of manners. "Please to meet you, I'm... sure." He spotted the wagon with relief. "There's Nati and Durant." He led the way to the carriage as it stopped at the foot of the steps.

"Yow." Pierre said. "I'd heard there was going to be some prime lamb sent along." He held a helping hand out to Nati. "Looks like I've suddenly gotten lucky."

Nati flushed uncertainly; obviously she wasn't sure if she'd been complemented or insulted.

"Vizconte Pierre. At your feet, to be kicked if that's your pleasure."

Durant laughed. "I'd heard you Ambalias were plain spoken, I see I missed the irony."

"Probably happens a lot. C'mon in, Grandfather's even worse." He grabbed Nati's elbow and led her up the stairs.

Durant narrowed his eyes, but lost any verbal reposte in the rush to keep up.

"Dex?" Stevan asked uncertainly.

"Just stay in the background and watch the spectacle. I'll probably get shoved down to the foot of the table, so I'll depend on you to report on all the insults being passed at the head."

Captain Reddeer slanted a skeptical look toward Dex. "Surely his own grandson... "

Dex grinned, "There's half a dozen of us. The other ones are legitimate, and I'm not doing what he wants, so I'm both a disgrace and in disgrace."

His grandfather was in the front hall. The echoing arched roofed space was dimly lit by the slit windows in front and the massed candles toward the rear. The tall dignified gray haired man who greeted the young nobles abandoned them abruptly when he saw Dex. "You! What are *you* doing *here*. You know where your place is."

"Grandfather." Dex bowed politely. "Having no calling for the Church, I am accompanying a friend to Roma... "

"I told you, you are to take vows. Do I have to beat obedience into your illegitimate hide?" He stalked toward Dex, drawing his sword.

Dex eyed him warily, keeping an eye on the old man's guards out of the corner of his eye as he backed away.

"Stand still and fight you coward."

"With what?" Dex asked, exasperated. He grabbed a long candle holder from a side table. Why didn't they ever leave furniture out in the middle of the hall where it might be useful? "This?" His Grandfather lunged, and he sidestepped, pushing the point of the old man's weapon to the side.

Enraged the conte swung at him, cursing as Dex backpedaled and maneuvered himself out to the open where he could dodge and duck. The alarmed guards scrambled about, with the conte ordering them to stay away, cursing when Dex dodged behind them and around them. The old conte occasionally managed to get close enough to lunge or swing. Dex easily dodged and parried, and let the old man chase him around the Great Hall until the conte finally came to a wheezing halt.

About time too. The Hall was getting crowded as people ran to the sound of metal clashing. If it had gone on much longer someone might have gotten hurt. Dex spotted an uncle who appeared to be ordering the guards to grab *someone*.

"Sorry Grandfather," he said. "I am not taking vows. I'm going to see a bit of the world, and most likely not darken your doors again, so you will be shut of me, even if not in the manner you wish."

"You... you... unspeakable *brat*. Your very... existence is an insult... to me."

"Yes, I know Grandfather. Shall I change my name when I enlist in the Imperial Army?"

"Enlist! Ha!" The old man was getting his breath back. "Don't think I'll be so horrified by the idea that I'll pay good money to buy you a commission."

Dex blinked in surprise. "I haven't asked. And have no intension of doing so."

"Ha!" The conte hawked and spat on the floor.

Nati winced. None of the other observing women looked the least surprised. The conte frowned around at the audience. "Doesn't anyone have anything to do around here? No wonder this place is such a wreck. You!" His gnarled finger jabbed at a dignified man in a formal jacket of the conte's colors. "Find rooms for our guests. The bastard can no doubt find some corner to sleep in." He stalked out of the rapidly emptying hall, leaving the newcomers aghast.

"Sorry about that," Dex said. "Grandfather has a bit of a temper."

"A bit?" Pierre snorted. "Although it has been nearly a month since he went after anyone with a sword. Good to see the old boy back in form."

"You mean he does that all the time?" Nati gathered her skirts in close, as if not wanting to touch anything.

"Oh yeah." Pierre laughed. "It only get exciting when he draws on someone who doesn't know better than to hurt him, or worse, just stands there, gawping. Last year two of the guards had to grab an Ambassador and drag him all over the place to keep him from getting hurt. Even Hastings looked a bit worried that time." He grinned at the man in the conte's colors.

"I see." Nati said weakly.

Hastings cleared his throat, "If you ladies and gentlemen will follow me, we have rooms ready for you."

Dex shook his head when Stevan glanced his way. He collected the small bag of clothing he'd brought, and the basket of puppies. He did indeed have a corner to sleep in, unless someone had discovered it in the ten years he'd been gone. The addition of the Gothic wing to the main house around the back of the west tower had orphaned a small triangle of a room, complete with a window to the south and a secret door he'd made himself. A narrow bit of wooden paneling gave to a firm shove with toe, knee and both hands on its left side. The hinges creaked, unoiled for ten years. His tracings of the old conglomerated building's flows had revealed the puzzling little wedge without access. He had forced an entry, and then sanded down the wood *just* a bit and added hinges.

No one had been here since he'd left it. It hadn't even been able to get dusty. He poked through the chest of old clothing, but he'd probably grown just enough... well, he could wear his old fancy vest. And the red shirt had had awfully long sleeves. And the moths had missed his socks. With a grin he sorted through the clothing for a few other odds and ends, and then headed for the baths.

He spent a few hours in short pants and his wrists poking out of the sleeves of an old shirt, hobnobbing with the servants, feeding the puppies and polishing his own boots while the laundry maids boiled, soaped, thumped and ironed his travel and salt stained clothing back into respectability. Then he tracked down Stevan and Nati sitting uncomfortably in a small parlor listening to Pierre and Durant verbally sparring and gave them a tour. When they reemerged from the basement connection to the pyramid they were all three giggling. They stifled their amusement to observe another group that had just arrived. The conte merely greeted them stiffly and turned them over to Hastings.

"Don't you wish he treated *you* so indifferently?"

Dex startled a bit when Pierre spoke in his ear.

"Where'd you run off to with the only worthwhile person in the county?"

"I gave her the weird tour." Dex said. "Worthwhile? I can't remember you *ever* complementing anyone. Apparently the last ten years has mellowed you."

"Ha! I grew up. What happened to you?"

"Guess I'm just average height." Dex shrugged, hoping Pierre wouldn't mention his actual age in front of Stevan and Nati. Speaking of whom, they'd gone ahead and were introducing themselves to the new arrivals. He closed up with them in time to catch a name.

"Vizconteza Syvinda ed'Misiac."

"Ah, Leston North shows its loyalty to the Emperor." Pierre swaggered up and introduced himself.

This Vizconteza was traveling with two older women whose stiff looks of pro forma disapproval faded into appalled horror as Pierre chatted.

Dex turned to the two young men who hovered uncertainly beyond them.

"I'm Lord Raulf Folgat, Monte, and this is Lord Jesif et'kestle from Nefi." The county between Leston North and Hastur, and the county inland from there. Nephews, not sons, by their titles. He'd have to find out if either Conte had children before he could decide if this was interesting or merely lack of choice.

He introduced himself and pointed out the rest

of the party, then sent them off with Hastings.

He kept a low profile at dinner. Seated, as expected, as far away as possible from his Grandfather, with a very large woman to the side to minimize the possibility his grandfather might spot him. She was the local Mayor's wife, and congratulated him on being in disgrace. He thanked her, and talked about his mother, whom she'd known slightly as the Vizconteza Who Rebelled. "Really, I'd never have had the nerve to turn down my first marriage proposal without her example." She sent a fond glance up the table toward her husband. "It took Tully a while to get ahead enough to dare to approach Father."

She brought him up to date on his family and the city, and they chatted pleasantly until her husband escaped and collected her. Dex slipped out then, and into his little triangle.

***

Dex woke early and wound his way up the onion tower. Any attempts to furnish it had been abandoned generations ago. Dex settled cross-legged on the floor of the room at the top of the column. It was open to the weather and a bit dirty, but it was too high to collect anything but bird nests. The walls were high enough to keep the puppies safe, and they bumbled about sniffing through the debris.

He closed his eyes and breathed in the cool air, sinking down to where he could feel and see the elements, silvery Air flowing through and past him, a bit of Water, Fire…he followed the red and oranges inland, in his mind, tracking down the strongest streams until they pooled, glowing and hot.

"Good morning, Lesto."

"Dex." The god fire uncurled a bit. "What are you doing here?"

"Just passing through, on my way to Imperial City." Dex frowned as the Fire writhed uneasily.

"Be careful. You've never met any of the Elder Gods, they aren't like us. They're not even like Nevrille. They're powerful, more powerful." the god was silent, pulsing with thought. "They're *old*. You don't understand how we change… Be careful, Dex." The Fire slipped off, further inland and out of his range.

He slipped back slowly, scanning the sky. There was no sign of the dark falcon, but were the skies darker, cooler? Had Lesto been afraid? He wasn't as powerful as Nevrille, he tended an area less than a quarter the size and was much less involved with people. Dex pulled his awareness back to the tower and looked at the city. It sparkled with the mixed Elements of life, and yet... a dark streak flashed and disappeared. It was too far away for him to locate it exactly, but ... What was it? What had it just done?

Disturbed, he retreated to his body and opened his eyes. "Is this new, or just new to me?" he asked out loud. He knew he'd been growing in mental abilities the last few years, yet Nevrille had been watching for something new.

For something that was interfering with souls reincarnating.

They wandered the city all day, Pierre and Dex showing the rest of the bloods the sights. The captain had wanted a full day to lay in supplies. They all went back aboard after dinner, and the ship departed at midnight on the tide. Nati stayed on deck, pretending to be interested in the stars, and definitely distracted from her woes by Pierre's imaginative reinvention of constellations. Dex had been cautious in feeding his puppies, and was able to soothe them enough to avoid needing to clean up after them. Nati, he couldn't affect from a distance. Her flow blazed with red-orange fire, behind her calm exterior, and increasingly with blue and green bumps and hiccups. When they cleared the sheltering bay and wallowed through the larger swells, she turned abruptly green and barely managed to get her head over the rail before she lost what remained of dinner.

"Damn, you've got good manners. I never puke so politely." Pierre commented. "Want me to show you how to make proper retching noises?"

"If you do," Nati's voice was muffled, "I will probably puke on you, on purpose. Go. Away."

"Ah, that's so sweet." Pierre strolled over to Dex and inspected his basket. "Do those hair balls puke too?"

"They did on the trip down from Letfore." Dex shrugged, "They seem better this time."

They all four sat out on the deck all night, dozing, retching and chatting in turn.

With daybreak, Nati tried to pull herself together, disappearing below deck long enough to change into another gown, but emerging in a rush for the rail. "I was going to try and chat to Vizconteza

Syvinda, but I don't think I dare." she moaned.

"I can see where you might not make the best impression, just now." Dex allowed, feeding biscuit to the puppies. He offered her one, and she took it dubiously.

"Aww, why'd you want to impress *them*" Pierre shrugged a dismissive shoulder and offered her his tea cup.

"I've got four older sisters, and one younger one." She took a sip of the tepid brew, rinsed her mouth and spit it over the side. "So, no dowry. I need to get a position as a lady's companion."

"No dowry? That just means you need to find a potential husband with enough money to not care." Pierre dismissed her concerns with a forceful wave Stevan had to duck as he joined them, biscuit in one hand and sausage in the other.

"A woman has to be a lot prettier than me to not need a dowry. Trust me on this." Nati's color was looking better.

Stevan peered ahead and then behind them. "Five days with no land in sight? This is going to be strange."

"Five days." Nati sounded grim. "I will probably survive."

With various friends fetching biscuits and weak tea, and standing and sitting around chatting idly and pretending she wasn't occasionally sound asleep, she did indeed survive, and it was with much rejoicing that they passed in between the two northernmost of the Great Arc Islands and into the quiet waters of the Shallow Sea. In the quiet waters Nati went below and managed a full nights sleep and appeared in the morning, bathed, bright eyed and in a crisp clean gown as they approached Imperial City.

The City had been founded nearly a millennium before, on a barren inhospitable shore on the boundary of the two kingdoms whose melding started the Empire. The City had grown, stretching for over fifty miles along the shore, and now encompassing several dozen anchorages and inlets. Laboriously constructed breakwaters now sheltered the commerce of an entire world, and a substantial portion of the Empire's Navy.

The Blue Lady passed the harbor buoys and sailed on for two more hours before she slid into the Imperial dock.

This time Dex accepted the carriage ride. He hadn't ever imagined anything like the City.

Chapter Five

Stevan had been a bit overawed by White Cliff, and the Ambalia's palace, although he had worked to not show it.

The Imperial Palace complex looked about half the size of the city of White Cliff.

He gave up and gawked like a provincial hick.

Fortunately all the "guests" currently in residence were being collected in a merely huge old mansion on the palace grounds. Carriages were always available to the guests, and were very nearly necessary just to get from the guest house to the main building.

The official guests were assigned quarters whose size varied with the number of the entourage. Stevan, to his surprise, was considered to have honored his Majesty by showing up with a friend, a manservant and three armsmen. Only Durant and Syvinda were given larger suites.

The Housekeeper fluttered around Nati, apparently disturbed to have found a woman traveling alone, and finally assigned her a maid from the staff.

Stevan was surprised when he finally realized that Pierre was traveling alone.

Pierre waved it off, but since he was the second son of the third son of the conte, Stevan suddenly wondered where the old Conte and his heir's future loyalties lay.

The biggest suite in the building was already occupied by a famously beautiful younger sister of one of the best connected Dukes of Roma. She'd apparently arrived yesterday, overland, with three friends, half a dozen lady companions and a troop of armsmen. Vizduquez Fabrigel se'Marint of Moster Duchy.

Good thing he'd gotten his gawking out of the way early. The vizduquez was stunning. Soft curls that hadn't been able to decide between brown, red or gold had settled on all of them, and glowed wherever the faintest bit of light hit them as they curled from the clip on the crown of her head to her waist. Her bare shoulders were graced by tasteful jewelry, her makeup minimal, a mere highlighting of the best of nature.

***

Fabrigel waited until the new "guests" had been installed, and then rounded up for the dinner parade before she swept down on them.

Two years ago she'd been the clumsy leggy scrawny girl everyone ignored. Or compared themselves favorably to. Now her revenge was complete. Every male eye in the place was riveted on her. Merci and Gisipia and their little clique trailed dispiritedly in her wake. She wasn't hovering in *their* shadows wishing for a bit of attention any longer. The grim old biddies her brother had insisted on trailed after her. Hmph. If he wanted her looks to not go to her head, he shouldn't have disparaged her looks for her first fourteen years. The only question was, how many of her entourage could she get rid of altogether. For just a second her confident exterior thinned as she realized that every male eye really was riveted on her, and not a one of them gave a damn about anything but her beautiful body, her wealth and her political alliances.

Well, blight take them, she didn't care about them, either. She wouldn't cry in front of them.

Instead she bestowed the full wattage of her smile on the overwhelmed looking boy in the horribly dated vest and small cape. He bowed over her hand.

"Stevan Longbow." He faded back in a near panic. From his name, a recent addition to the nobility, probably a military award and land grant in Easterly. No wonder his clothes were outmoded.

"Vizduquez, a pleasure." The tall black haired boy was taller than the first, but looked almost younger. "Dexter Fiz Ambalia." But he had a calm gaze and looked her in the eyes as he spoke. She blinked in surprise as she realized he wasn't oogling, or for that matter, calculating.

The next boy slobbered all over her hand and moved closer. She dodged, of course.

The fourth boy just nodded, "Oh, Moster, the horse place, pleased to meet you, I suppose." And turned his attention back to the, umm, sturdy girl beside him.

Just for a moment she felt like she'd reverted to the mousy-haired flat-chested girl of two years before. But the heavy girl gave her a genuine smile. "I'm Vizconteza Nati ed'Treliff. Don't mind Pierre, he has apparently been truant during etiquette lessons his entire life."

"Was not!" The rude boy protested. "I just never saw any damn point to 'em."

Nati took over introductions, starting with Rude Pierre, who was the Leston South guest, Vizconte Pierre et'Ambalia. The two other young men from Easterly were ooglers and droolers, and the other woman barely nodded.

When the butler announced that the carriages had arrived, she stuck with Nati and her odd friends for the ride. Her own so called friends and duenas could take another carriage.

"Do you ride?" Nati asked. "Your dutchy is so well known for its horses…"

"Oh yes, every minute I can. I've brought my favorite horse along. I hope she'll be all right sailing down to Shingay."

"Shingay?" Stevan Longbow asked, then blushed and looked down.

Little gods, was he *shy*? "You may not have heard, we'll be leaving in a few days for the Winter Residence. Crown Prinz Rawn is there, apparently the mountain air is good for him. I think we're about the last groups to arrive, all of you because you came from so far, and me because we were close and left it late and got caught by bad weather. We were trapped in this little village by floods for over a week. *I* had fun, watching the 'ladies' deal with actual mud, but I expect the village was glad to see the last of us." She glanced back at the carriage following theirs.

"How the hell are they going to fit all of you into this Winter Residence?" Rude Pierre was going to live up to the nickname she'd given him.

She could feel herself blushing, her entourage wasn't *that* large! "Fortunately for the Royal purse, most of them won't be going any further." In an unusual burst of candor, she added, "Unfortunately I can't get rid of them all."

"That bad, are they? See Nati, you're not *alone*, you're free." Dexter grinned at the young woman.

Nati looked a bit thoughtful at that.

Dexter glanced at his cousin. "What I want to know is what Pierre said to Grandfather to get himself exiled without even a servant."

The older boy, young man really, he looked to be in his mid-twenties, made what Fabrigel assumed was a rude gesture. None of her father's people—now her brother's people—would have dared do such a thing in front of Daddy's little darling. "I, err, might have said something rude to the old boy at just the wrong time."

"What a surprise." Nati's tone was dry, but a smile quivered just under the surface.

"I figured I'd track down Uncle Gressim, he's here as the Leston South Representative on the Council and get some funds, maybe hire someone." He shrugged his indifference.

Fabrigel hid her envy. Men had all the advantages. If she wanted to 'pick up some funds' she knew *damn* well what the price would be. Fortunately her brother was not going to risk her virginity, putting her in that sort of spot. She was carrying an inconvenient amount of coin, with bank drafts just-in-case.

Dexter, a bastard cousin, apparently, who somehow didn't count as Pierre's entourage, leaned toward her. "Do you know the City? It's a bit intimidating for us country hicks."

"Oh, if you want to see the City, take a carriage. We have them at our disposal. The shopping is grand, but so are the prices. I'd recommend you wait until we get to Shingay. It's used to supplying the nobility that are on their way to the residence, so the quality is good. Lots of merchants will be bringing goods to the Residence, in fact with so many people there. I expect they'll hold a regular bazaar."

"You've been there?" Stevan asked.

"Oh, yes, my father is a regular at court, I've

been dragged along since I was ten." She frowned in memory. "And I get invited everywhere."

Pierre laughed, "Bunch of old letches?"

She snorted amusement at that. Indeed. The various nobles had gone from looking down their noses at her and toting up her worth in cash and influence to looking down her blouse and toting up her worth in cash and influence.

The carriage turned a corner around the far side of the main building and halted at yet another sweep of stairs and grand looking entry. The shy boy hopped out first, followed by Pierre, who handed Nati down and walked away with her, leaving Stevan standing beside the carriage. He put his hand out tentatively, and Fabrigel grasped it and hopped down. She tucked her hand under his elbow, and subtly steered him into climbing the steps beside her. Unfortunately they were immediately split up and assigned seats, Fabrigel to the right of the head of the table, and Stevan halfway down it. On the same side, so she couldn't even see him. Well, no matter. He was a nice boy, but her brother had more ambitious plans for her than a Easterly Nova, so she shouldn't encourage him.

The majority of the hostage-guests were male,

but Fabrigel's female entourage was large enough to almost balance the table. Beside the Easterly newcomers there were seven other young men around the table, here to personally assure the Emperor of their Father's, Grandfather's, Uncle's or Cousin's loyalty to the Emperor, and most especially to the Crown Prinz.

Then the small group of musicians played a musical fanfare, and they all stood as Emperor Ranold entered the room.

Fabrigel remembered the first time she met the Emperor. Only six years had passed, but her father's old friend looked like he had had aged several decades since then.

But despite his slow, jerky movement, he caught her eye and winked. "I was beginning to think I was going to have an issue with young Gregin. I'm glad to see he could part with his little sister."

She smiled, "I don't think he's quite adjusted to the changes of the last few years. He acts like he's afraid to let me out of his sight, sometimes."

The Emperor's eyes crinkled. "I *know* he's afraid to let you out of his sight. He's been protecting you since you were born, the baby of the family. Tried to pawn me off with a mere son. Told him I didn't want infants."

Fabrigel giggled, "Fiste is four years old, sire. Pity he's not a bit older, Rawn needs friends as well as courtiers."

"True, true." The old man looked tired suddenly. "But this is all I can think of, to help him from beyond the grave. Send me reports, won't you?"

"I will."

The Emperor turned then to the people waiting respectfully out of earshot. "Leonel, I haven't seen you for years. How is your Father?" He took Fabrigel's elbow, and escorted her back to her seat as he spread his attentions around the room.

He sat, and gestured his guests to do likewise. The servant hustled the wine, and the Emperor raised his glass to the company. "I thank you for coming. It is you, the younger generation upon which the future of the Empire depends. With your support, the reign of Emperor Rawn will be long and prosperous. I salute you."

They all drank, and Fabrigel, thinking of the thin sickly baby she'd seen years ago, and the undersize weak child he'd grown into, wondered if the Emperor could hold on long enough to secure the boy's crown.

***

Dex felt it from the street, a frighteningly strong stream of all the elements, vividly colored by the emotions driving them, but with something dark there as well, and it drew his gaze away from the graceful proportions of the huge Parliament Building. It was coming from yet another massive marble edifice. A church, by the octagonal shape.

"Fabrigel, what's that?"

She broke off her history of the Parliament to glance in surprise from him to the church. "That's the old Temple. The archbishopric moved into larger quarters a couple of centuries ago. We can go there if you want?" She glanced around the group and got indifferent shrugs.

"Never mind." Dex looked back at the Parliament Building. "Sorry to have interrupted. So, it's burned down five times?" *Surely not the gods*! *The parliament would be the business of the Elder Siblings, not the Younger. Do the Elders have just as much trouble getting points across to humans as their less powerful relations?* He looked back at the Temple. *I need to go in there.*

His opportunity came when they disembarked

at the Parliament building. Stevan's father's representative was expecting him, and Pierre said he'd escort Nati to her father's representative, an uncle of hers, before hunting for his own uncle. Dex said he'd stroll around the plaza on his own. Fabrigel frowned at him worriedly. "Tell the coachman if you take a cab back to the palace. Otherwise we'll all meet again, right here, in two hours."

Dex smiled. "Right. Don't worry so, I won't get *too* lost."

She was still looking worried as she took Stevan's arm and led him up the elegant steps.

So. Dex strolled slowly around the huge plaza, watching the currents in the elements. The currents leading into that old Temple overwhelmed *everything* else. He followed them in. In the dim light, the Elements were so thick he couldn't see, and he slowly closed his mind to them so he could study the church.

The high windows lit the walls and left the center dim and cool. The octagon was lined with bas relief scenes, a great circling stone representation that started with the faceless and nameless First Gods laboring to create the Universe across from him and proceeding to the right, became Anov placing the stars in the firmament, Pit crafting the Moon, and

Zuba cradling the world in one loving arm while she shaped the continents. As he eased through kneeling people and turned to look back at the entrance, the mural shifted to Roma, bestriding the continent that now bore his name, raising the mountains with a powerful gesture, frozen in the stone.

Dex studied the figure. Where the First Gods had been swathed in stone draperies, and the Ancient Gods had their faces turned to their work, Roma was a living God, and presumably his Priests and Saints knew what he looked like. At least Dex assumed that Roma, like Nevrille, had once been a living man, and remembered his last body's shape. Souls forgot, Nevrille said, between bodies. Only the last life was clear to the Younger Siblings.

Roma must have been a powerful man, broad shouldered and muscular. His face was almost too perfect to call handsome, arrogant as he commanded the very shape of the land.

Beside him, Formia waded in the Ocean, hands pulling islands from the water. She was said to watch all of the oceans in the world, and to care for ships and sailors. She was more of a stately type woman than a young sylph. A figure of command, rather than desire. Beyond her, Graf laughed as he threw sand in the air, funneled tornadoes spinning from his hands. Had he created the desert continent, or chosen it for its mineral wealth?

The last panel showed the Younger Siblings, looking over the fields of the world, towering over the people laboring in those fields, but less than half the size of the monumental figures of the Elders. In this light he couldn't see the deities' features clearly from where he stood. He wondered if he'd find Nevrille there, or if these were an earlier crop of Younger Siblings, perhaps now watching over continents of their own on the other side of the world.

Dex eased back to a far corner, where he could see the central altar. There was no service today, but flowering offerings covered the dais, and the people bringing them seemed inclined to linger.

He closed his eyes and opened his mind again to the Elements. The source of the deep currents were the people. Praying. Asking the Gods for help. And while he'd never been able to read minds, here the concentrated baby hunger washed over him. The women and men here wanted children. Wanted them desperately. The womb blight had started slowly, ten years ago, but now so many women were barren, or miscarried, or delivered stillborns...

He'd heard that compared to a generation ago, there were only ten percent as many healthy babies. The dark shape that had swooped down toward Father Berndis's soul... that same darkness lurked like a creeping wolf about the Temple. Were these women its prey? No, more likely its bait.

It was then that he realized what was missing. He quieted his mind and reached for the Elements. Air and Water, Earth, all mixed in this dim humid room. Fire was subdued, clinging closely to the people inside. Only a thin faint flow came or went from the building. He traced it out, but it stuttered and rambled, sluggishly stirring as people and horses walked through the streams.

"Is there a Younger Sibling that cares for the City?" he asked mentally, listening hard for a reply.

The streams of Fire twitched and cringed as a wave of dark hungry soul-stuff rolled down from the west.

"What is this?" Was there God Fire in the seething mass, so closely incircled and strongly held even light couldn't escape? Was there a hint of a face, once prefect?

"Roma?" Dex whispered in horror.

"Who are you?" a low growl, a sucking pull.

"What are you?" Dex was repelled by the putrid mass, and pulled away from it. "What is wrong? Why are there no souls for these people's babies?"

A wave of contempt, like a man swatting an annoying bug, floored him.

Dex let his awareness fade quietly. He opened his eyes on the dim old Temple, and shivered. No wonder Lesto had warned him. That was an Elder Sibling? Surely it could not be Roma. He sat quietly, warily, waiting to see if that, that *thing* could track him in the real world.

He tried to gently listen, to do a bit of tracking of his own, but it was everywhere, and hungry. He couldn't see the whole of it, or even a sizable part. Did it cover the entire continent? He stared as long as he could manage, trying to see if it actually did anything, but finally gave up as his vision wavered and a sudden spike of pain drove into his skull. He staggered back out to the Plaza, and found a seat on the rim of a fountain. Trying to smooth the pain in his head only made it throb, so he closed his eyes and tried to not see anything at all.

He really wanted to talk to his father, but he wasn't about to try it around that dark thing.

He hadn't seen any souls. Could a predator,

some carnivorous species made of soul material, have taken so many souls that few were around to be caught, either by the predator or by newly conceived babies? Was a lack of souls the reason for the lack of babies? What then of horses, dogs, and cats? Had the predators eaten all the animal souls and changed to hunting human souls, or the other way around? There was a difference, wasn't there?

"There you are!" Stevan's voice pounded on the stake. He sounded cheerful.

Dex pried his eyes open. Of course Stevan was cheerful, he was with Fabrigel.

"Have you had enough sight seeing? We were going to swing by the harbor to see the Lighthouse. It's supposed to be two thousand years old."

"Sounds interesting." Dex lied, as he tried not to stagger, following them to the carriage. He wondered if his Dad would hear him if he called. And if he'd have any answers.

***

Dancer did not like the looks of the boarding ramp. Fabrigel let her stand and look at it for a long moment. One of the other Bloods walked his horse up to it. The big gelding balked at the feel. The ramp was massively built, and probably wouldn't flex much even under a draft horse, but there was a bit of a surge this morning, so it was moving as the ship moved.

Fabrigel winced as the young man decided to make it a fight, to prove his dominance of the animal.

"Blithering idiot." Carter Ostlie muttered behind her. Her brother had sent Carter along to be her groom, silly really, since she only had the one horse.

The incipient battle was interrupted by foot traffic, and Fabrigel spotted the Easterly contingent as Stevan and his friend stopped to admire the horse. Dex said something and stroked the gelding's neck before following their friends.

Behind them the gelding dropped his alarmed stance, and walked hesitantly up the ramp and then down into the hold.

"There, sweetie, see, nothing to be upset about." Fabrigel relaxed her shoulders and advanced on the ramp. Carter was muttering behind her about it being his job. She ignored him. She'd never seen much sense in making one's self a cripple or incompetent.

Besides, the options included going below to the passengers' cabins where the four women she hadn't managed to shake would no doubt have everything all fixed up and ready for her imprisonment.

The Easterly group stopped to admire Dancer, as she lived up to her name in this very strange situation.

Dex laid his hand on the mare's hip as she skittered his direction, and she stopped instead of kicking. Not that she kicked very often, but she was really taking exception to the moving ramp. The mare looked around to see the obstruction to her dancing.

Dex extended a hand for her to sniff, "She's absolutely gorgeous."

Fabrigel nodded. "I probably should have sent her over land. She's never been on a boat before."

"I expect she trusts you enough to walk onboard." The tall boy faded back into the onlookers.

She turned to the ramp, and this time Dancer stepped daintily onto it and onto the broad deep boat. Down into the slightly moving stable below deck, where she turned the mare over to Carter.

"Thought she was going to play up a bit for a minute there." Carter received a friendly nudge from the mare. "But you didn't, did you girl?" He was still fussing over her when Fabrigel withdrew.

All the horses were off the dock, and the last passengers embarking.

"Well, Fabrigel! You finally grew up, I see."

She turned, and after a split second placed the young man. Vizduq Leonel Boje. From western Roma.

"Leonel. Are you the representative for your duchy?"

"Unfortunately. I've been working with my father's people here in the Capital, and Father decided I should be in on this as well." Leonel was going to be one of the older 'guests', he was probably ten or eleven years older than she was.

"I can see why," she replied. "We'll be meeting either the heirs or the close relatives of the heirs of every Duke, Conte and King. The people who will be your peers in the Assembly."

Leonel curled a lip, and glanced toward the bow.

"Peers? Hardly. These *children?* Half of them are novas, and the other half barely related to their lieges. Once we get to the Winter Residence, I'll introduce you to the people who will hold the real power."

"Umm, I'll look forward to that." She turned away, and stepped to the rail. Politics. Well, her brother had warned her it was going to be solid politics, and he was right. His rather vague wishes that she find a suitable husband was most likely going to go unfulfilled, though. This lot was personally ambitious, and not really focused on the good of the Imperium. She looked toward the bows. The group Leonel had dismissed as Novas and distant relatives had, to date, been the nicest she'd met. Even including the ghastly Pierre.

The Easterly gang had migrated together to the bow, and she tentatively edged up to them.

"How long will we be aboard, do you know, Fabrigel?" Nati looked a bit green.

"Three days, usually, although I suppose this boat may be a bit slower than the ones I've sailed on before. Sea sick?"

"Very."

"Umm, staying up here is probably best for you."

The young woman nodded. "I pretty much camped out on deck on the trip over—and everyone kept saying what a smooth trip it was." She shuddered visibly.

"Ah, we'll keep feeding you dry biscuits and tea."

Fabrigel blinked, the bad boy with the foul mouth was going to nurse a sea sick woman?

Apparently. No one else looked surprised.

Out in the long slow swells, Nati got greener, but didn't lose her breakfast. Various members of the group wandered off, returning with dry biscuits and tea. Their sporadic attendance at table, and early departures earned the group the nickname of 'the unmannered children'. The unmannered promptly adopted it as their own. Fabrigel was dancing on the brink of being included in the group. It was really irritating to have to fight the reasonable and sensible accustomed habits of her entourage. The middle-aged pair were both widowed and both very respectable. Merci and Gisipia were just five years her senior. They spoke with strict propriety to Lionel and his crowd, and garnered the older women's approval. They were, all four of them, rigid and inflexible. Perfect to protect her reputation from, oh, say, the gossip that would fly if *she* were up on the bow of the ship all night long with several young, unattached men.

But during the daylight hours she was up there, and she brought bread to the seasick Nati, and meat for Dex's cute puppies.

The fourth day they docked in Shingay, and the Unmannered hustled Nati off the ship. Fabrigel busied herself with Dancer, who showed no reluctance about a ramp that led to solid ground.

***

Dex sat and meditated on the water, in the quiet of the night, with the brilliance of the stars above. They'd be docking tomorrow; tonight Nati was well enough to doze a bit, so he'd moved off a bit to listen to the world.

He quieted his mind. All the bright sparks of life in the ship flared up to his inner vision. Then the deep green sea, with tiny flashes of life Fire. The shore of rich brown Earth and the multi-colored life beyond … the darkness was there. A thin high cover, now that he knew to look. He withdrew and looked out to sea. There was dark out there, too, but not the all pervasive dark. This dark darted about, dove into the water, rose again. It saw him, and turned.

He retreated as quietly as he could, but a dart

caught him.

"What are you?" Was the voice feminine? "A demi-god? One of the Young dared?"

It pulled at him, at the Fire of his own soul that carried his awareness. He jerked away, and felt the movement of darkness behind him, curling out from the shore.

He forced his body to move, to break the meditation abruptly. He leapt to his feet, and studied the seaward view. Nothing to his normal sight, of course. Nor in the other direction.

Well, Formia was supposed to be the Patron of the Oceans, so why was he surprised? He reluctantly decided that he'd better stop attracting the attentions of these beings. The Elder Gods were not what he had expected.

Chapter Six

Shingay was a small city by the standards of Roma. So it was only about double the size of White Cliff. It was also nearly a hundred miles from the Winter Residence. Wagons appeared to take all of their luggage, and carriages to carry them to a town house owned by a retired General who served as the local Imperial Representative. Fabrigel fussed over unloading Dancer, but the mare was so eager for hard ground there was no problem.

"Pity it's so late in the year," The General seemed a nice fellow, friendly and open. He circled Dancer admiringly. "The best of the horses have been sold. I'll take you others around to a few of the more honest horse traders tomorrow. They don't keep a lot of extra riding stock at the residence, and with eighty of you youngsters, plus all of your friends, you'll want your own, if you want to ride very much."

They all nodded, even the girls. Perhaps especially the girls. Nati looked wistful, and Dex diagnosed lack of funds. The next morning they headed out early. Fabrigel tagged along, saying that looking at horses was never boring or a waste of time.

Dex hung back, letting the bloods see the horses. He felt carefully, trying not to ruffle the flows and make himself obvious to... anything about. The horses the seller was parading before the Bloods all seemed healthy and sound, unlike the quivers he was picking up from down the street. He looked at his friends, all deep in discussing legs and bloodlines, and turned and walked away, tracking the nasty twist down a block and into a muddy narrow alley. In just a few steps, the character of his surroundings changed from ambitious trades to lower class scraping. The twist came from the small collection of horses tied to a large tree that dominated the knacker's yard.

"Looking for a horse, sir?" The wizened little man gave him a smile half full of stained teeth. "Got some good ones here. Some foolish gentlemen, with no horse sense, they ride their beasts into the ground and sell them as foundered. A bit a rest and tonic, and they're good as new. Just raring to go." The little man surveyed his good, but plain clothes and his smile widened at the sword. "Why, look at this big black fellow here. As fine a warhorse as you'll see south of Imperial City. Only nine hundred marks."

The stallion was actually a dark bay, but in the shadows on this overcast day he could pass for black, though why anyone would think black was better than bay... And certainly bred to be a warhorse, a solid muscular sixteen hands. But the horse's mind was a confused medley of mishandling and mistraining, and brutality that had produced hesitation rather than the aggression that had probably been some fool's goal. A good honest horse, under the confusion.

Dex made a show of running his hand down the near front leg. Yes, here was the problem. "Coffin bone's fractured. And the nerve in the pastern cut, so he doesn't show lame. Poor fellow. I'd love to be able to say I'd owned a beauty like this, but he's worth eight marks for dog meat and we both know it." The deliberate wounding, causing further damage, was why the twist was so bad. Wear and tear and accidents never twisted the flow so loudly.

"No! It's not broken! He caught his foot and cut the ankle, but he ain't been nerved." The little man didn't bother putting much effort into the declaimer. "But if you don't like him, how about this nice fellow."

Dex patted the nice fellow and glanced at his

teeth. "Sixteen, not as old as I'd have thought, but older than I want." He patted the pinto pony on the rump as he circled her to get a look at a chestnut on the far side and hesitated. The pony was a bit hungry and a bit tired of being tied up and she didn't like that man one single bit. But under the present day misery, her happy soul fairly glowed at Dex, begging to be taken away.

The chestnut had lumps and bumps all up and down her legs. "No thanks." Dex eyed the pony again. She was large, nearly a small horse. "I will need a pack horse," he ran his hands down her legs, for the show of it.

"Now, that's a nice pony. Safe for a lady to ride, drives too. A real deal at only a hundred marks."

Dex snorted, "For a pony? She looks sweet, so I'll be generous and give you twenty for her."

They haggled back and forth, and Dex let him 'win' and handed over sixty. As he collected her lead rope, he glanced at the big bay. "I have a friend who needs to be taught a lesson in horse care. For another forty I'll take him."

***

"I wondered where the heck you'd gone off to." Stevan circled the horse in disbelief. "Where did you find a horse like that, and what are you doing?"

"A knacker had him and was trying to pass him off as sound. I may have wasted my money, but I couldn't resist." Dex had the stallion's hoof resting on his knee as he massaged up and down the pastern, around the hoof, smoothing the turbulent flow, pushing the loose tip of the bone back into place and fixing it there. Working on the blood flow, compromised by both the injury and the swelling inside the hoof. The nerve he'd leave for later, when repairing it wouldn't just bring pain.

"Dex," Stevan frowned. "He wasn't stolen, was he?"

"'Fraid not," the General spoke up behind them. "That's the horse young Hoster ruined. Mayor's son, total ass, took a short cut in a race, ran him over cobblestones. Fractured the coffin bone, thought he'd gone to the knackers."

"Might be the coffin bone," Dex said, "but a bad bruise or a slight founder can be as painful. Thought I take the chance. Damn knacker nerved him, so at least he isn't in pain."

"Lad, you've wasted your money. Even if it

weren't broken, a nerved horse isn't safe to ride." A squeal from further down the barn dragged the General away before he could say any more.

"Dex," Stevan frowned at his friend's hands on the horse's hoof. "Do you have any of your Mother's healing abilities?"

Dex grinned up at him. "Good heaven! If I did they'd *never* have let me get away."

Stevan blinked. "Well, well. That's one way to save money on horses, I guess, buy them from the knackers." He wrinkled his brow. "And no matter what, that's not really a safe thing to do with a stallion, crouching in front of him like that."

"Hey Dex, where'd you get the big mud ball?" Pierre strode confidently down the barn aisle. "You look like you're proposing marriage, down on your knee with your Prinza's hand in yours. Got news for you. That ain't no prinza."

Dex removed a hand long enough to make a rude gesture. "Has everyone got mounts? I got a pack pony as well."

"What for?" Pierre wandered over and gazed into the stall. "A piebald? Gods, have you given over your military ambitions and decided to become a wandering tinker?" He leaned further over the stall door. "Oh, I see, you bought Lady Fang and Lord Blackie a pet of their own. That explains it."

Dex grinned. The puppies and the mare had taken to each other right away. "Well, actually, until this fellow's hoof is all better, I'll probably end up riding her and leading the Mudball." Dex winced as he realized his beautiful warhorse had just acquired a name. He set the hoof back on the ground and stood up. Mudball shoved him with a gentle nose. Dex could feel the horse's relaxation. He must have been gently handled as a youngster; he was responding well to Dex's subtle fogging of his recent handling. He gave him an affectionate rub around the eyes then put the stallion into the stall three down from the pony and followed Stevan and Pierre out of the barn as a line of horses clattered into the yard.

The grooms were leading three horses each, and nice beasts they were.

"That chestnut with the narrow blaze, and the bay behind him are mine." Pierre pointed. "I couldn't make up my mind. I'm going to go get my saddle and ride again." He dashed off, dodging aside as Fabrigel maneuvered through the mansion's back door, with her own tack in her arms. Her scandalized duenas followed a few steps into the yard, then retreating as one of the horses spooked and skittered too close for their comfort. They settled down to watch disapprovingly from the steps, as the grooms took the gear. Syvinda was next out the door, dangling a bridle, silver fittings glinting. A servant followed with a saddle, and her attendants joined Fabrigel's.

Dex blinked as he realized that he alone of the gang hadn't brought tack along. Something to do tomorrow, no doubt. By the time he got to the Imperial residence, he was going to be completely and totally broke.

Pierre and Nati pushed past the collection of duenas, each carrying tack. ". . . think the bay has a better trot, but I'd appreciate your opinion."

Dex hid a grin. Pierre? Seeking an opinion other than his own? Couldn't make up his mind, so he bought two horses? How could someone with so little practice be so smooth?

"I don't believe these prices!" Durant scowled at his sturdy gray gelding. "This fellow is going for double what he'd bring in Gradin."

"It's the blight. The foal crop this spring was the smallest I've ever seen." Fabrigel said. "They've been poor for the last decade, and got even worse three years ago. Now they're just selling the young mares, giving up on breeding them."

"So the prices are going to get even higher?" Durant smirked. "Maybe I'll get my money back and a bit more next year."

Stevan glanced over, "Have you heard when we're being sent home?"

"No, but everyone says the Emperor has a cancer. How much longer can he last? One of his brothers, or brothers-in-law will assume the Regency and they won't need us any longer."

"That's the first I've heard about the Regency changing hands." Nati took the reins of Pierre's bay, admiring her. "There are three brothers, not to mention the two brothers-in-law. My Father's met Conte Mongote, does he have Imperial ambitions?

One of the other Bloods laughed. "Who doesn't have Imperial ambitions? Attach yourself to the right faction and you'll find yourself on top of the world."

Fabrigel sniffed from atop Dancer. "I wouldn't recommend ambitions that are against the Emperor's wishes. He's chosen his eldest brother, Prinz Winstow, as Prinz Rawn's regent."

The General marched out of the barn and looked around in satisfaction. Except for a frown at Dex. "You're not going to ride that fellow of yours."

It wasn't a question.

"No sir. I should be able to lead him by tomorrow, if there's no swelling."

"Hmph. Going to be raining tomorrow. Roads will be deep mud for two days after. You've got three days to either give up on that poor creature, or avoid meeting the Mayor or his son, who'll cut up rough over it."

Dex grinned. "I'll try to avoid them, sir."

The General snorted, and stepped out to inspect the horses all over again.

Chapter Seven

Two days out of Shingay, Dex swapped the too-large saddle from Spot to Mudball, where it instantly became the too-small saddle. With the too-short girth. Judicious addition of leather straps made it secure enough for simply walking down the road, but he was definitely going to have to find a longer girth. Mudball pranced a bit, and Dex kept him on the soft ground until he'd settled.

They reached the residence mid afternoon, climbing the last hill to find a spectacular view over steeply dropping hills to the ocean.

"Five miles, at most." Stevan leaned over as if to get closer to the water.

"If you can fly." Nati pointed. "That path is pretty crooked."

Dex, who by then was sitting carefully balanced in hopes of not over straining his makeshift girth, was looking at the mansion. "That is a very large vacation home."

Pierre snorted. "Emperor's country homes do tend to be that way. It's built back into the hill a good ways. Not nearly as noticeable as our palace, eh

Dex?"

Durant was scanning it as well. "No wall. That surprises me."

Fabrigel laughed. "And ruin the view? Roma has been peaceful for centuries."

They'd been seen, and guards and grooms trotted out from the far side, apparently where the barns and barracks were tucked out of sight.

Dex dismounted, and ran a hand down Mudball's leg. It was fine. Still healing, the gentle ride hadn't harmed it. A groom took the reins respectfully, admiring the stallion. Poor little Spot received a curled lip of disdain, but was led away all the same.

Captain Reddeer was shaking hands with one of the resident guards. Dex noted the man for future encounters. He glanced back, at his luggage in the wagon, but Gaspif shook his head. No doubt he and the other servants would sort it all out between them, but Dex did grab the basket of whining puppies. They were probably both hungry and thirsty by now. He stroked them and they quieted.

Nati and Fabrigel dismounted and headed for the mansion without waiting for the Four Fluffies, who were taking their time getting out of the carriage.

The man who ushered them in was wearing a suit in the Royal Blue, with gold piping. "Welcome to the Winter Residence of the Imperial Family. Lady Pomfreit will see to your needs."

Lady Pomfreit quickly separated Nati and Fabrigel from the men and sent them off with a maid, the Fluffies hastening to catch up. Dex kept an eye on them until they turned to the right at the top of the stairs.

The lady eyed the young men disapprovingly. "We will expect reasonable respect and reasonable decorum from you. I have no idea *why* we expect it, the rest of the young men having disappointed us so far, but hope never dies. Now, let me show you to your rooms." She led them up the stairs, but turned to the left. "You are the last arrivals, so you will be in the furthest... "

Her lecture broke off at the ear splitting shriek from behind them. Dex and Stevan were bring up the rear, and Dex bolted back to the stairs. Another shriek or rather series of screams and shrieks came from the right and he hastened to follow the sounds. A door flung open and he dodged a howling woman who fled the room beyond. He realized he was still carrying the basket, and shoved it to the side as he drew his sword and crabbed carefully into the room.

"How dare you! How *dare* you!" The red headed girl wasn't aiming the comments at him, but rather the women who were... all... standing... on... chairs.

Flummoxed, Dex came to a halt and lowered his sword. Stevan stepped through the door and stopped and stared.

"Is, umm, there a problem, Miss?" Dex asked tentatively. The girl had tears running down her face, and was breathing in great gulps.

She jerked around and stared at them, her pale face reddening with embarrassment. "They," her voice wavered. "They tried to kill my mouse." She shot a furious damp glare at the women. "It got out." She glanced sideways at a small basket on the table.

A small grey streak darted away from under the table, and Dex reached with both inner and outer hands and scooped it up. "Um, this is a field mouse Miss. They really don't do well indoors." He glanced out the elegant glass doors in the opposite wall. "I suspect he'd love your garden."

She sniffed up congestion. "It's not *my* garden." She looked back at Dex's cupped hands, and sighed.

"All right, let him go." She opened both doors and led the way. It was just a little pocket terrace, a low wall and rather overgrown with flowering plants.

Dex looked them over. "Perfect for a mouse. Roses and chrysanthemums are both edible." He opened his hands. The mouse's flow smoothed out as it leaped for the bushes and disappeared with a rustle.

"Thanks." The girl looked glum. "I really thought I might manage to have a pet for once."

"Wouldn't a kitten be better?" Stevan asked. He handed Dex his sword. "You dropped it to catch the mouse."

"Oh no, Rya, a kitten would shed." One of the women carefully descended from her precarious perch.

The next one climbed down, frowning. "Now that we've gotten that over with, I think it is time for these gentlemen to leave."

"It's not proper." The third woman clumsily stepped down, glaring. "Really! Such nonsense!"

Dex cocked his head at the three older women and slowly smiled. He looked down at the little redhead. "Actually, what you need is a puppy. A big, rambunctious puppy that will shed mud and three colors of hair all over everything."

The girl looked wistful, but shrugged. "It's a nice thought, but... there aren't many puppies around anymore."

Stevan stepped outside the door and grabbed the basket.

Dex opened it and plucked out the tri-colored pup. "May I introduce Lady Fang?"

***

The young men's corridor was older and the rooms lacked the pretty garden the redhead had rated. But their little group fit neatly into a jutting arm of the mansion, with rooms all around. Gaspif had sorted out their belongings between three adjoining rooms, with a corner nook for himself, fairly near one of the steep stairs up to the attic rooms provided for the young nobles' guards.

Dex went exploring immediately, winding down back stairways and finding the kitchens, where he begged a bit of cut up meat and milk in a saucer for the puppy, and a promise to send the same around to "the redheaded girl's" rooms.

They been hustled out so quickly he hadn't even managed an introduction, but the girl had been gleefully cradling Lady Fang and telling the ladies to choose this or a mouse when the door had shut behind them.

He hustled back to his new room, getting lost twice, but managed to follow the howls of a lonely and hungry puppy home. The hunger dealt with, he followed Gaspif's suggestion to dress in *this* please, quickly please, and followed the crowd to the dining hall.

The seating of the men was strictly in order of rank, so Stevan and Pierre wound up at the head table with the other new guest/hostages, and most of the women, while companions and merely noble friends sat lower. Dex was satisfied to sit unnoticed and unobserved, and keep an eye on the upper table. Stevan was between Nati and the redheaded girl, so he would at least learn what her name was. She said something to Stevan, and he turned and pointed at Dex. Had she asked his name? Or just who to send a crying puppy back to?

Oh well.

The old man at the center must be Prinz Winstow. Lady Pomfreit sat to his left and there were no eight year olds in sight. So Crown Prinz Rawn wasn't here. Or at any rate, not at table.

123

His seat mate to his own left introduced himself as Mores Furthering of some kingdom on the opposite side of the continent, a friend of his Conte's second son. He nattered on and provided names for some of the people at the top table. "The skinny redhead is Vizmarquez Rya Amar of Karm March. They say her mother's a demi-god and her father kidnapped her from the Cathedral in Heorestburg." He sniffed. "The girl is supposed to be eighteen, but she sure doesn't look it. Now I haven't met that stunning young woman on the far side."

"Vizduquez Fabrigel se'Marint of Moster Duchy, not far north of Imperial City I understand."

"Oh ho!" Mores sat up and studied her. "No wonder there's such a fuss about her. All those contacts, *and* those looks!"

"That's Vizconte Pierre ed'Ambalia of Leston South on the far side of her." Dex pointed out the rest of his companions. "Cousin of mine, although I actually came with Vizconte Stevan Longbow of Merd. That's him to the left of Vizmarquez Rya. And beyond him, Vizconteza Nati ed'Treliff of Hastur County." He couldn't stand it any longer. "What do you mean, her mother's a demi-god?"

"Well, the Marquez is the daughter of a woman

said to have attracted the attentions of a god. She was taken by the Church, to determine if her mother's claims were true. The Marque apparently removed her, and married her, before she gave any vows. The Church declared the marriage false, and applied to the Emperor. Who said that if the woman had given wedding vows and not church vows, she was her husband's not the church's. There was some bad blood over it, the church not producing goods the Imperial government needed, and then the army took over some church property. Eventually it all blew over. Pity, really."

"Pity?" Dex raised eyebrows.

"Might have put the church back in its place, which is *not* owning half the world."

"Ah. Yes I'd heard the church owned a lot of the old country. Thought it was an exaggeration."

Mores' companion on the other side caught his attention, and Dex returned his own to the top table. The daughter of a demi-god. *Someone like me.*

Chapter Eight

The next morning was clear and cool, perfect for a ride was the consensus of the young bloods. They could stick to the high ground and who cared that it had rained a bit last night?

Between the hostage-guests and their noble companions, there were two hundred young men on the floor, with nearly as many servants, and twice the number of armsmen packed into the attics. No doubt most of them had grooms in the barns somewhere as well. There were also about fifty women guests and their companions and servants.

Dex was impressed with the ability of the residence to absorb them all, but then, no doubt that was why the winter residence had been chosen. He tied a cord around the black puppy's neck and took him out for a lesson in manners and, hopefully, doing things outdoors so Dex would have less to clean up indoors.

There were four barns, large ones, lined with stalls, all the fine beasts of the young bloods kept up in style. A milky white stallion had pride of place. At seventeen hands he stomped and neighed, asserting his ownership of his domain above the heads of the admiring young men that paused in their search for their own mounts. Dex felt the aggressive, dominant *angry* personality and decided he didn't like the horse's pale skin and blue eyes. Blackie gave him a high pitched puppy growl.

Mudball was with the rest of their group. Late comers, they'd been shoved to the back of the third barn. Dex considered the sort of riding the bloods would probably do and declined to risk Mudball's fragile hoof. He helped the others tack up and head out, trailed by their armsmen. Fabrigel's fluffies hadn't shown at all, and he wondered what she'd done to distract them from her absence.

"Have fun, and don't break your neck!" He called after them, and turned to hunt down Spot.

She'd been relegated to the last barn, with the wagon teams, and some mules that looked to be half draft horse. He slipped a halter on her, and led her out. He closed Blackie in the stall. The pup whined indignantly as he vaulted aboard Spot bareback and took her out for a bit of exercise.

Not one of his smarter moves. The exercise area was well filled with the less ambitious riders. Young women riding side saddle in dresses, or in ridiculous puffy pants designed to hide their legs and spook their horses. Spot, with her tinker colors, might have barely been considered suitable for any of them when they were little children. As a large young man on a fat pony, he drew titters.

He sighed and rather than brave the united amusement, he steered over to the grass beside the second barn and let Spot graze while he watched the spectacle.

The boy stood so still Dex didn't notice him until he felt for the flow.

He was breathing heavily, as if he'd been running. Gasping for air, his lips tinged blue.

"Don't call the guards," the boy begged. "I only just got away from them." He gulped for breath. "I just want to see the horses, even if I can't ride."

Alarmed by the boy's color, Dex dropped the lead rope and stepped over. "You look awful, sit down. Cross legged like this." Dex dropped down and demonstrated. "Hands open and on your thighs. Take slow deep breaths."

The boy sat on the grass, looking a bit uncertain.

Dex took his hands and turned them palm up. "Relax your muscles. When you are tense they use too much air." Through the boy's hands he could feel the problem. A hole in the heart. He reached in gently, stroking the harmony smooth to pinch it shut. The cells around it needed to grow and split, to provide more tissue. He told them to do so. It would take time, but the hole could be closed.

"Why haven't they ever taken you to the Church for healing?" he asked.

"Their price was too high. My father wouldn't pay it." The boy's color was better already, he was alert, staring at Dex. "You're a healer."

Dex nodded. *You don't lie to someone you have just realized is the crown prinz.* "My mother was a Saint. I refused to take vows, and never, ever, let them know I could do things. So they finally had to let me go."

The boy nodded. "That's what they wanted, for me to take vows." He looked away. "I... sometimes I wanted to, if it would fix me, make me healthy so I could do things." He looked yearningly toward the exercise yard. "Ride horses, sword fight."

"The Church doesn't let you do much riding, and no sword fighting at all. At the Abbey. I had to sneak around for all of that." Dex assured him. He tried gently dissolving the edges of the hole, letting them attach together as a single tissue. It was tight, too thin. "I've done a bit, but I'll need to do more. I told the cells of your heart, umm, the little things that... "

"I know what cells are," the boy interrupted. "Tell me what you are doing!"

"You've got a hole between the left and right side of your heart. Have you seen diagrams about how the blood circulates?" At the boy's nod he continued. "The hole lets the stale blood mix with the fresh, so you don't get pure fresh blood. When you get excited or active, the heart pumps faster, and squirts even more stale blood into the fresh. I've pulled the tissues across the hole, but they aren't very strong. So I told a bunch of your cells that it was time to split and grow. So there will be more cells and I can get the wall really solid and strong."

"The hole is closed now?" the boy asked. "That quickly and easily?"

"Yes. It's weak, I'll need to do this again tomorrow and the next day and that should take care of it." He saw the boy's rising fury. "Yes, it's that easy, and for that they wanted your whole life. Don't lose your temper over it for a couple of days though, all right? The tissues are really thin."

The boy relaxed and grinned. "Save the tantrum for when I won't kill myself doing it?" He leapt to his feet. "I feel *good*."

Dex scrambled up and hastened over to grab Spot's lead. Not that she was planning on going anywhere. Little mare knew a good thing when she had it.

"Is this your, err, horse?" the boy asked politely. Spot whiffed at him and dropped her nose so her itchy spots were within easy reach. "She's nice." The boy, the prinz, sounded surprised as he obliged with a rub around her eyes.

"My pony. My horse is laid up with an injured hoof, so I was going to give Spot a bit of exercise." Dex nodded at the other riders. "But I didn't feel like getting laughed at, so I came over here instead."

The boy rubbed Spot's forehead and was rewarded by demands for more. "I own lots of horses, but I don't get to ride any of them." He glanced toward the first barn. "Some of them I don't want to get near."

"Oh, not that horrible pale thing? He's got a nasty personality. I prefer to ride a good friend, thank you very much." Dex knotted the other end of the rope to the halter and slung it over Spot's head for reins. "Want to see my horse?"

"Sure."

"Hop on. You're the right size for Spot." Dex boosted the beaming prinz aboard and led the way to the third barn. He dropped a few pointers on steering, stopping, and the inadvisability of gripping with one's heels unless one wanted to go fast.

The bay stallion neighed and stomped when he spotted Dex. Or maybe the mare. "I'm afraid he got named Mudball." Dex said, leading him out.

"Whoa! He's a beauty." The prinz slipped off Spot and held out a tentative hand to the big horse. Mudball whiffed it politely, most of his attention on Spot.

Enough of that, lad! Dex reached gently in to suppress the stallion's sense of smell. The poor fellow sighed. Dex could nearly hear him think "Rats! I would have sworn that was a mare."

"You should call him something fancier."

"Yeah. The name just sort of happened. He could use just a bit of exercise. Walking." Dex said. "Would you like to come along? We could probably find some tack for Spot somewhere... "

The boy glanced warily out of the barn. "Oh, if we're just walking, bareback is fine."

Ah yes. Those guards you didn't want me to find. Dex tossed blankets and saddle up onto Mudball's high back, and finagled his short cinch and straps into something that seemed fairly secure. Muddy fairly grabbed the bit, eager for the outdoors.

He managed to mount without the saddle slipping and they walked out, turning away from the exercise area without talking about it.

The ground was damp and soft, but not clingy, perfect for Muddy's hoof. A trail beyond the last barn took them through the woods to a pasture in a little valley.

"Oh, now this is pretty!" Dex said. "I thought they couldn't possibly stall all the work horses and teams."

"Actually they do, when it snows." Rawn said. "Except this year they may not be able to, because of all of you." He looked curiously at Dex. "Who are you hostage for?"

Dex grinned. "I thought we were guests? Actually, I just came with the Merd hostage, Stevan Longbow. It seemed like the best way to get away from the church school I'd been sent to. I'm a bastard grandson of the Duke of Leston South on the Easterly Continent."

"Are you having fun?" The prinz steered Spot past Mudball and up a side path along a creek.

"Oh, yeah. I've read about all these places, and now I'm seeing them. And meeting people. Girls. Women."

Rawn laughed. "I'm never going to be that sappy about girls."

"Oh, just you wait." Dex told him. "Four more years, six at the most and you'll be reduced to a drooling idiot like the rest of us. Do you know where we're going?"

"Yeah. I've explored around a little bit, when I can get away." The prinz turned his head and frowned. "I hear horses."

Dex, from his greater height, looked back. "Oy, the Wild Hunt." He reined Muddy to the side and told him to not be an idiot. Rawn joined him as a dozen of the Bloods careened around the curve, sliding a bit in the mud. Dex checked Spot quickly. She just tossed her head disdainfully and shifted a bit as the crowd galloped past. A couple of the bloods glanced at Dex as they passed, none of them seemed to notice the prinz.

"There are going to be some stiff and lame horses tomorrow," Dex said. "Running on slippery paths is a bad idea."

"Is that what happened to Muddy?"

"No, I heard it was cobblestones. Broke the coffin bone. I'm fixing it, but bones take time, especially when they have a horse this size walking on them."

"Huh. Can you do things besides healing?"

"Everything sort of works the same." Dex said. "Everything has a flow to it, like a stream, or maybe a song. You can hear where something interrupts the flows, messes it up, and then fix it, if it's an injury, or find it, if it's, like lost or buried stuff. Then there's making artifacts. You can see cells in living bodies, but in dead things you mostly, if you look really closely, see earth, wind, water and fire. And you can change the way they flow."

"So, you flow fire out of a box, and you have a cold box to store meat in?"

"Exactly. Or flow fire to the top of a stone and have a cooker."

"I heard they have water jugs in the desert. Can you get the water out of the china?"

"Huh. I expect they leave the top off, and the water in the air flows in there."

"In the desert?" Rawn turned Spot up a tiny

side path. He'd taken to riding like a natural, balancing easily on Spot's broad back.

"Yep. Everything has all four elements in it, sometimes just not very much of one or another." Dex pulled Muddy to a halt as the path ended in a tiny clearing. A stream cascaded down the rock face opposite, and tiny flowers dotted the grass. "Wow."

"The waterfall dries up after about a week without rain. So I try to escape and walk up here after it's rained."

"I see why." Dex felt for the flow of the place, and it was smooth and flawless. Damp grass or not, he felt like he could slide off the horse and nap forever here.

A drop of rain splatted on his head, followed by more.

The prinz tilted his head up, smiling. "I guess we'd better get back. They worry too much about me."

They were both soaked by the time they got back to the barns, and with a look at the shivering prinz, Dex rode on up to the mansion and dropped Rawn off where he said he could sneak back in.

**

By simple reason of proximity of their horses, Stevan found himself riding with Fabrigel and Nati (good) and Durant and Pierre (bad). Well, not *bad* but they were certainly both obnoxious and both older and better looking than he was.

Pierre looked back as their horses climbed the slope, "Oh, little gods! he's looking for his pony hurry up, in case he decides to come along."

Durant glanced at Fabrigel, "Might make a nice ladies mount."

Fabrigel, shook her head. "Not a chance. Not big enough or fast enough." She put heels to Dancer's side. "Beat you to the top!"

It was not a close race. Even with Fabrigel slowing for groups of riders ahead of her they couldn't catch up. Stevan admired both the riding and the horse, but took a hold on Granger and slowed him. He was last to the top of the mountain, but Granger was breathing better than the other horses. Well, except for Dancer. Fabrigel nodded her approval of him, which beat winning a race any day.

There was another group on the rounded, bald mountain top. Older bloods, all male.

"Vizduquez, good morning." The wretch was old, probably at least twenty-five. Muscular. Good strong face. Good manners. "I'm Vizduq Golezan se'Procopio of Matej."

The others all arrived, and names were exchanged all around. Stevan noticed glumly that all of the bloods were jostling politely to be the center of Fabrigel's attention.

She ignored them, riding about to get a clear view of the surroundings, and incidentally cooling out Dancer, who looked eager to race back down the mountain.

Stevan found that if he just walked Granger cool, without worrying about the bloods, Fabrigel would turn up beside him quite frequently. Good.

He caught a comment, "…my sister's husband, Prinz Cuellair, he's Prinz Rondeze's oldest son, tells me your family's horses are the best in the East."

Stevan looked over to find Golezan still in pursuit of Fabrigel. Talking about horses, but doing a bit of political name dropping as well. Prinz Rondeze was the youngest of the Emperor's brothers. But rather than being last in line, in a contest involving the health of the heir, his relative youth would be an asset. He would be seen as a better candidate than the definitely elderly Winstow, or Prinz Vasik who had no sons.

139

Stevan tucked the relationship away in his mind, and decided he'd better start keeping track of the factions maneuvering for power as the Emperor died.

***

Lunch was much more casual than last night's dinner. Grab food from the sideboard, sit wherever. Dex had managed a leisurely hot soak before the hordes of cold wet riders descended on the baths, so he was a bit before everyone else. There was no sign of the prinz; hopefully he was being coddled not punished.

He heaped a plate and sought a mostly empty table to one side of the dining hall.

Stevan, Durant and Pierre joined him shortly.

"Gods, it was such a nice morning," Pierre groaned. "What happened?"

"We're in the mountains," Dex pointed out. "When it rains it does tend to be cold. Did you notice the snow on the peaks?"

Pierre parked his elbows on the table and glared. "This is the *Winter* residence. I thought it would be warm."

A feminine giggle preceded Frabrigel sliding her plate into the spot next to Stevan. "They come down here for Winter Sports. Skiing, sledding, ice skating and so forth. The weather is perfect for it, unlike Imperial city that has ice storms and blizzards and gets so cold you don't dare sweat."

Nati sat beyond her, and to Dex's surprise, the redheaded girl beyond.

She leaned forward to catch Dex's eye. "I'm sorry I didn't properly thank you yesterday. My duenas are a bit on the fierce side. I'm Rya Amar."

"Dexter Fix Ambalia. How's Lady Fang doing?"

"Great! Thank you for sending the meat and milk up from the kitchens. I didn't have any idea what to feed a puppy." She blushed, easily seen with her pale skin.

Dex nodded, uncertain how to continue the conversation. *A demi-god. Like me.*

Pierre laughed. "You let Dex foist one of those whining furballs off on you? Did he tell you how big they're going to get?"

Rya blushed even more. "He said they were large, umm... "

"They're half mastiff." Dex said. "So she's

going to be big. You probably don't want to let her climb on the furniture or sleep on your bed."

"Oh." More blushing. "Too late."

"Do your Ladies in Waiting hate her?"

"Oh yes, she's already tracked in mud and peed on the rugs." Rya smirked.

"Well, then, that's all right."

Chapter Nine

The next day, Dex was intercepted on his way to the third barn by a groom who redirected him to the first. Mudball and Spot had been promoted to premium stalls on the sunny side of the barn with split outside doors. They might have evaded the guards, but the grooms had noticed. And apparently approved. Dex's saddle was polished to a mirror shine and sported a new girth. Equally shiny tack graced the rack outside Spot's stall.

Prinz Rawn was brushing her, rather inexpertly, but the little mare was basking in the attention. He looked up with a brilliant smile. "I feel great. The nannies made me stay in all yesterday afternoon, but I feel great."

Dex rested a hand on his shoulder and felt for the Earth and Water flows of the living, and then down into the organs, and even further into the cells. Rawn's heart cells had responded well, and he gently pulled muscle cells into the thin area of the wall.

"So, why don't you show me some more of the area?"

"Sure, if you'll show me how to tack up a horse." The prinz looked at him challengingly.

"Oh dear, a prinz saddling his own mount?" Dex widened his eyes and clutched his hands to his breast in mock horror. "First, you'll want to get a halter and tie your horse up. Spot would probably co-operate, but most horses will at least wander off."

After a basic lesson in tacking up a mount, during which the grooms stayed tactfully away, they led their horses out to the practice grounds and mounted. They had it to themselves, most of the young bloods having partied well past midnight.

Dex and the prinz rode a couple of laps, with much commentary about heels needing to be down, and shoulders back, when Rya flew out of the mansion and flagged them down.

"Some one told Prinz Winstow that the crown prinz was out here on a tinker's pony and he's flaming mad."

Rawn flushed, half angry and half embarrassed.

Dex snorted. "Is he mad about Rawn riding or about the tinker pony?"

She glanced worriedly back at the mansion. "Both."

Dex simply hopped down from Muddy and started shortening the stirrups. "Would you like to try Muddy's gaits, Your Majesty?" he asked blandly,

"They're a bit different than a pony's."

"Sure." Rawn sounded a bit doubtful, but let himself be boosted up.

"Walk him around a bit," Dex suggested, turning to Rya. "M'lady, would you be interested in trying my rather colorful pet?"

Rya swallowed uncertainly. "I've never actually ridden a horse." She was wearing a sweeping full length gown, but not too many petticoats, as it was morning.

Dex looked at the skirts dubiously. "How about just sort of, perching there for a minute or two?"

Rya nodded, and used his cupped hands as a step, sat sideways on the saddle. Spot looked around and cocked an ear at all the fabric, but didn't shift a foot.

"If you were to face a bit forward and sort of hook a knee on the front of the saddle…"

Rya squirmed around into very nearly a correct side saddle position, and took the reins he offered her. Spot stepped out carefully and walked in a slow orbit around Dex.

"You look good, Rya." Prinz Rawn yelled, as a crowd of nobles and officers rounded the barn and stopped at the sight of their Prinz up on a large powerful stallion.

Prinz Winstow paled. "What are you doing?"

Rawn looked at his uncle in surprise. "Exercising a friend's horse." He leaned over and slapped Muddy's neck. "Mudaf injured a hoof and needs a bit of quiet walking."

The older Prinz sputtered a bit. "You shouldn't exert yourself, Rawn."

"Nonsense, sir," Rawn sounded positive. "This mountain air agrees with me, I feel much better and need to start getting a bit of exercise." He turned Muddy and walked him up to his uncle.

One of the civilians in the crowd pushed forward to stand with Prinz Winstow. "You know exertion makes your condition worse... " he paused. "Actually your color looks very good today." He reached up and wrapped a hand around the boy's wrist. "Pulse is good. Just don't over do it, eh?"

"I'll be sensible, Doctor." Rawn turned Muddy away with a polite nod to his uncle and walked him in a relaxed circuit of the grounds. After a long moment, the tight bunch of observers broke up and mostly went away.

Dex, switching his attention between Rya and Rawn, wasn't sure how many of them actually went away, and how many were watching from the barn, but six uniformed guards, on matching chestnuts, showed up and stationed themselves in a neat line along the south side of the grounds.

Rya finally halted Spot, and with a defiant glare at the mansion, lifted her right leg over the mare's neck and sat astride, her skirts rucked up and pooling ridiculously all over the long suffering pony's neck.

"If those women dragons of yours ever see your legs showing like this, they'll never let you out again." Dex teased.

Rya grinned shyly, "They didn't exactly 'let' me come this time. I just outran them."

"That's one way to do it," Dex admitted. "Sneaking always worked best for me. Get your legs more forward and flex your ankle so your heel is lower than your toe." He adjusted the stirrups to her leg length and set her feet in them. "Keep just a little weight on the ball of your feet." He didn't mention the incredible unsuitability of her footwear.

Muddy's foot was doing well, and so Dex held a bit of a riding lesson. "Try a little bit of a trot. Prinz Rawn first, let him get a few strides ahead before you start, Rya." Muddy's springy trot threatened to throw the lightweight prinz right off his back. "Grab his mane if you think you're slipping," he called. "A little more weight in the stirrups, perhaps."

When Rya did slide off, he made them practice falling off at a walk, and then a trot. "Grab *something* so you hit the ground feet first, try to hold onto the reins, so the horse doesn't run off. Rawn, different rule with a trained warhorse. You don't want to find yourself flat in front of a horse that's been trained to strike with his front feet. Muddy had an idiot for a trainer, but even he's not safe. Hold the reins only long enough to help you land feet first, then if you can't stay standing, fall away from him and let him take himself off."

"Don't I get to ride a warhorse?" Rya teased. She wasn't much taller than the prinz.

They were both messy and happy and walking a bit bowlegged after an hour, when Dex called it quits, using Muddy's hoof as an excuse.

The next morning the grooms had three nice beginners mounts all tacked up and ready to go. Dex took a moment to feel out each animal, and make sure Rya, today in clothes almost suitable for riding, got the steadiest and took the slightly nervy mare for himself. He didn't dare touch the prinz with so many people around.

With the six troopers following faithfully, Rawn led them around the nearby trails, and then off on one he admitted to having always wanted to be able to walk. From the flat top of the nearest peak, the panorama of the coastal mountains opened up in a spectacular view. They sat quietly and took it all in, then, surfeit with sheer space, headed back down the mountain.

By the third morning half the young women 'guests' flocked to join them, along with a sizable portion of the bloods. The most ambitious portion, of course. They all had several of their armsmen along, and a few of the women's companions joined them. Rawn rolled his eyes, and tolerated the long slow and rather tedious ride, with various young men and women variously showing off their superior riding skills, looking helpless, or trying to converse. Dex and Rya tried to provide a bit of screening for the young prinz, but the huge cavalcade circled back and ended early.

Rawn leaned over as they entered the grounds. "Tomorrow, let's sneak, all right? You and Rya head for that path to the waterfall with an extra horse, I'll meet you just out of sight of the barns."

"Guards?" Dex asked.

Rawn grimaced. "Maybe."

***

"How did you do that?" Stevan slapped his plate down next to Dex's.

"Notice an unregarded Prinz while you were out hobnobbing with the rest of the bloods?" Dex asked innocently.

"Yeah. That."

Dex shrugged. "Luck, I suppose. If Muddy weren't lame I probably wouldn't have."

Stevan looked unconvinced.

"Hey, am I still allowed to sit with the high and mighty Favorite?"

"Hey, Pierre." Dex graciously waved an invitation. "Are you all right? Knowing you didn't have good enough taste or sensitivity to avoid a mass smarming like that, I was worried sick about you the whole morning."

"Up yours, cuz."

Silence started falling over the room, and Stevan looked around to find that Prinz Rawn, without any sort of escort, was helping himself at the sideboard. The boy prinz casually sauntered over to their table and sat.

"How's Muddy's hoof, Dex?" He took a bite of chicken.

"Great. I think another week of easy work, then I can start getting him back into shape. Everyone was talking about purebreds and good nicks today. I realized I really don't know anything about Roma bloodlines."

That brought Fabrigel in, as her family owned a fabulous racing stable. A few courtiers tried to edge into the conversation and were ignored. Dex was forced to admit ignorance of Muddy's breeding, and had to promise to write and find out.

"The three we were riding today are Sheners, the foundation stock is from Shener Duchy, but they breed them everywhere, because of their smooth gaits." Rawn told him. "The racers, like Fabrigel's family's bloodstock is based more on crosses between Toros from the Graf deserts and Jusstees, another Roma breed. They started out larger and a bit heavier than the Sheners, light fast warhorses, and then they started breeding them for speed, so they got a bit lighter and longer legged.

"Toros give them more endurance." Fabrigel said, "All the big breeders use some Toro blood in their programs. My father always tried for between ten and twenty-five percent. Even the heavy warhorses have a bit of Toro in them, and I've heard some of the pony crosses are nice."

So after lunch they wound up back in the barns, looking at horses and talking about their bloodlines. Once out of the dining hall, the outsiders worked harder to get near the prinz, who eventually decided he'd had all the mob he could handle, and disappeared.

"Nice kid." Dex said, and Pierre choked.

Stevan shook his head at him. "Dex, he's going to be the next Emperor. You can't just call him a nice kid."

Dex snorted. "Even if he is? And he sure doesn't look sickly to me," he glanced aside at all the listeners. "Must just be politics. His rivals don't want him to look good."

That shut everyone up. No one was going to actually, flatly, admit to a preference for another candidate. Conversation gradually resumed as they all headed back into the mansion. Stevan made a note of which of the bloods were overly concerned with the prinz's health. Especially the ones who didn't look happy.

Back in his room, he pulled out the diary his mother had sent with him, and that he had, so far, managed to ignore. He listed all the main contenders for the throne, a long list. But lumping the sons, sons-in-law, and grandsons with the fathers and grandfathers finally resulted in six groupings.

Crown Prinz Rawn, of course. The Emperor's three brother's, Winstow, Vasik, and Rondeze. The Emperor's sons-in-law, Conte Mongote of Porter County on Easterly and Marque Inacig of Henyr on Graf.

Everyone else was secondary to those six. Most were the heirs of the others. Until Rawn married and produced a son, his uncle, Prinz Winstow was his heir, and Winstow's son next in line. Stevan gave Winstow a whole month's worth of the diary for himself. Maybe he could pick up some gossip. He was pretty sure the son's name was Choa, and he was married, but he didn't know about grandchildren.

The next month went to Prinz Vasik. He didn't have any sons, but his sons-in-law were ambitious. Even Stevan had heard of them.

Prinz Rondeze was fifty-eight, hardly young,

but significantly younger than the seventy-eight year old Emperor. A whole generation younger, born when his mother was forty. Stevan added all the information Golezan had let out about relations. Yes, he'd better figure out which candidate each Duchy, March and County was going to support.

Conte Mongote and Marque Inacig received months of their own, but he had very little information about them. Would the twenty-eight other Marches of Graf support Inacig? What about Easterly and Conte Mongote? If his own father was a supporter of Mongote he hid it well.

And speaking of supporters, whom did the Gods favor? Dex said the elder gods backed contenders like gamblers at a horse race, and he was in a better position to know than anyone else Stevan knew. The Elder Gods. Roma, Graf and Fomia were the best known, the oldest living gods. The line between Elder and Younger was more of a human definition, than a reflection of reality. That Nevrille of Dex's sounded pretty powerful, but still concerned himself with a single county.

And Elder Gods did die. There had been several cycles of gods, according to the Church. The names of the First were long forgotten; they were said to be the creators of the Universe. But Zuba who made the world, Pit who created the moon, Anov who put the stars in the sky were still known. But dead. Or gone or whatever gods did.

And new gods were created from the souls of the dead. Some dead. Noble dead, the Church said, but his father had said noble of heart. Merd was a very young god.

Perhaps he should go to church tomorrow. And listen, this time.

***

Gaspif lost no time making friends in the kitchen and among the cleaning staff. Mistress Reaso was in charge of the staff, and although she left the cooks to their own business, she saw to the delivery of tea and snacks to the rooms of the guests, and cleaning and laundry for all of them.

"That must be a huge task." He was daunted by the mere thought. "You've what, two hundred and fifty people here?"

"Oh, triple that, what with their own servants and armsmen." She examined the tea trays, and nodded her approval. "This one to Vizmarquez

Fredda, and this one to Vizduquez Darline. The others will be going to the Ladies' Parlor. Such a fuss when the young women want to be pampered in their rooms. At least they don't all do it at once."

Dit, the scrub girl, sniffed. "I 'spect they don't want to fuss with all those fancy fashions when they're, err," she slid her eye toward the male presence. "Not feeling well, and won't be seen out of them."

Mistress Reaso bent a censorious eye on the scrawny thing. "It's not our place to ask why. We are hired—and valued—according to how well we serve, and we'd best keep our opinions private."

"Yes'm." Dit bowed her head meekly, and finished polishing the silver fork in her hand.

Gaspif finished Stevan's ironing—the boy was gratifyingly easy to please—and started in on Dex's shirts. Another nice boy, he seemed to notice everything, and help everyone around him. His cousin Pierre was... certainly interesting. For all his forceful and profane speech he was remarkably peaceful, and kind to Nati. More than kind. He gave every indication of having fallen madly in love with her.

He folded Dex's shirts carefully, and picked up

one of Pierre's. "I hate ironing all these fancy ruffles, and lace." He confided to the laundry maids. He taken to doing 'his fellows' laundry himself, down here, and giving a bit of a hand where needed. It had earned him quite a bit of credit with the staff. Disliked or not, he worked his way through Pierre's ruffles and then gave a quick press to the three young men's trousers. His own work done, he assisted with the rest. Fancy gowns belonging to the women, always a good source of gossip.

"Now that is a bright enough red. I'll bet that black haired Vizduquez Zora owns it." He ran the iron over the partly disassembled dress. The women's clothing, with mixed colors and fabrics were very difficult to wash without colors running or differential shrinkage puckering fabric where puckering wasn't wanted. Once clean and ironed, the lace, ribbons, embroidered panels and buttons would be restored.

Gaspif had heard that a noblewoman shouldn't be seen twice in public in the same dress. Seeing the work that went into a noblewoman's wardrobe, Gaspif was wondering if they didn't mix them up and create 'new' ones as they stitched them back together after every wash.

"Oh no, this is Vizmarquez Joya's favorite dress. Blondes look good in red too."

Gaspif looked skeptical, which earned him considerable information about which garment belonged to which woman, how suitable the colors were for each woman. A great deal of information about the woman's wealth and the industry of her attendants was available for the taking.

Along with which women went where, and when. And when their suites would be empty. Gaspift ironed petticoats without complaint and swore to resist temptation.

***

Fabrigel heaved a (silent) sigh of relief when she spotted Nati. At least there'd be one sensible person at Lady Pomfreit's afternoon tea for the ladies.

Rya's nice, too, but so young!

Nati, on the other hand, was mature and practical. If new to high society.

"I don't know anyone," she hissed to Fabrigel.

"I'll drop names, when I can." Fabrigel promised.

"I trust you've met most of the young men

here." Lady Pomfreit smiled politely around the room. "We're under very strict orders to not allow any improprieties, so let me know immediately if any of them step over the line.

You'd better not plan on locking us in. "I suspect your staff will be the ones having problems." Fabrigel made her voice sympathetic. "My father, of course, wouldn't stand for that, but you have a huge houseful of unknown young men."

"Are there any of them whose manner we should be especially wary of?" a slim blonde girl asked.

Fabrigel spoke softly so only Nati and Rya could hear. "Vizduqez Cinda ed'Fraily from west Roma, her father's a supporter of Prinz Rondeze."

Lady Pomfreit's reply was to be expected. "As long as you act like a Lady, they will treat you like one."

There was a faint snicker from the back. *Someone isn't a Lady. Or knows men who aren't gentlemen.*

"Nesser's a friend of yours, isn't he?" Vizduqez Joya turned to Lady Kari.

"Our father's are friends," Kari shrugged. "We visit several times a year. I think his father—a

Nesser, too— have more ambitions than a mere duq's niece." Her eyes slid toward Fabrigel. "Of course, there's rather a lot of competition for what they want."

Merci jumped in on that. "Oh yes, now that Fabrigel is sixteen, the letters are coming fast and furious."

Fabrigel sniffed. "I think my brother sent me down here to give him time to look over the prospects. I'm rather glad to have the opportunity to travel and meet more people, myself. Besides, Nesser's one of the western clique, supporting Prinz Rondeze. I'm not interested."

Lady Pomfriet wrinkled her nose as if she'd smelled something nasty. "I think politics are best left to the men. We have our own homes to regulate, our own spheres of influence."

Well, so much for any intelligent conversation.

"Anyway, Lord Somer is better looking than Nesser." Kari received a look of disdain from several of the other women. Admitting to realistic marital ambitions was apparently Not Done.

"He came with Winfred ed'Falconi, didn't he? Winfred is rather handsome himself, in a rugged manner." A dark haired woman sitting beside Joya fanned herself with a lacy circle that matched her peach gown.

"Lady Nui Linonier," Fabrigel breathed. "Her uncle's a Duq about halfway from here to Imperial City. Winfred and Nesser are both first sons from the west. They're making a good showing here, given the rumors floating about their father's' loyalties."

"They're both in their late twenties, aren't they?" Nati kept her voice down as well. "Are they a strong show of support, or are they scouting out the opposition for their fathers?"

Fabrigel nodded thoughtfully, "They're both old enough to act independently in their fathers' service."

Rya was all big eyed over the commentary. "You two need to learn sign language if you're going to dissect people in the open."

"I can't believe they sent someone as young as that Vizconte Stevan." Fredda caught everyone's attention, sneaking up on the object of much curiosity.

"He's a Nova. A completely unimportant child." Zora dismissed Stevan and fired her broadsides. "I think his bastard friend is simple. He just sits and looks."

Rya stiffened, but her flush was as much

embarrassment at the thought of putting herself forward as anger. She subsided without speaking.

Joya gazed at Lady Pomfreit through her downcast eyelashes. "I'm surprised you are allowing the crown prinz to consort with a commoner from the frontier."

"I think it's disgraceful how he's endangering the prinz!" Fredda elevated her nose. "You should have him horsewhipped and thrown out."

"Jealous because he's nabbed the favorite's place, Fredda?" Fabrigel smiled sweetly. "I don't think having his friend beaten will endear you to the crown prinz."

Because for all their admiration of broad shoulders, there was one bachelor here that could make one of them an empress.

"Oh, we think it's best that Rawn realize on his own that a rustic commoner is rather boring once the novelty wears off. Really, Easterly has sent a very odd collection of representatives." Lady Pomfreit sniff dismissively.

"The baby Stevan is bad enough." Fredda shot a glare at Fabrigel. "Lord Raulf and Lord Jesif are passable—well mannered and good looking, even if they aren't in line for an inheritance. The older ones, umm, Vizconte Pierre..." Several girls within hearing shuddered. Lady Pomfreit closed her eyes in pain.

Nati lowered her brows. "While his conversation and sense of humor are... unusual, he hasn't offered any, umm, improprieties."

Fabrigel suppressed a smile. "True, he has manners, despite the mouth. That Vizduq Golezan is forever trying to touch me. I've been careful to avoid being alone with him."

"Very wise of you, my dear," Lady Pomfreit nodded a decisive approval. "That whole group is heavy on arrogance and light on restraint. They are willing to take anything as an invitation. Vizmarqs Orser and Vito are also to be handled with care."

"Or better yet, not handled at all." Nati murmured.

Rya snickered.

"But Vito has such marvelous hair." Syvinda sighed.

"If you like blonds." Zora smirked. "Now take Leonel, that long wavy black hair... "

"Well, there's always Hoad the Toad." That brought a titter.

Fabrigel frowned. "Vizduq Hoad Tierald, just to the south and inland, I don't even remember meeting him."

"I noticed Vizduq Carlo is already going bald."

"Of course, on him it'll look good. Such a nice skull."

"Oh? You sound like you're planning to mount his head on the wall."

Darlin's rich laughter rang out. "Oh, I have much better plans than that."

Lady Pomfreit frowned, "On which you will take no action until you have been transferred back to your father's control."

Fabrigel frowned in turn. "Don't you think it better that we control ourselves? I have no wish to live my life under the thumb of one man or another."

"My Dear! Really! Your brother knows what is best for you."

"As recently as two generations ago, women served in the army. Some were officers. We were expected to be able to defend ourselves."

"My Dear!" firmly this time. "Anyone could *buy* a rank, but that didn't make a Lady into a war leader. Those tales like *The Death of General Songay* are just that. Tales to entertain. Myths. You need to learn to live in the world of today." Lady Pomfreit turned decisively to another woman, closing the subject. "Cherise, that is a very becoming color. We'll be having a bit of a bazaar at mid-summer. I'll have to see if any of the cloth merchants have anything that shade."

"I want to learn how to sword fight." Nati muttered. "What does the well dressed swordswoman wear?"

Fabrigel raised her eyebrows. "What an interesting thought."

"My nannies brought quite a bit of material along, in case the fashions had changed, up here in Roma." Rya said, "Let's look it over tomorrow."

"And you can teach us sign language." Nati added.

Chapter Ten

Dex settled comfortably in a pew as close to the center of the church as he could get, closed his eyes and felt for the flow. Earth through all the stone work, spiraling exuberantly off the intricate carvings in deep rich colors, and soaking into the wood, Water was the weakest here, but growing as people entered. Air, yes the air flowed with everyone breathing, a big loop coming in the high eastern windows, dancing in sparkling white and silver with bright yellow and red fire and blue and green water through several hundred lungs and hearts. There were little discordances all over, pale, faded gray smears, black ugly kinks. He worked at smoothing them away. Not the detailed, exact work he'd done with the prinz, but just... smoothing. He knew from experience that everyone would feel good when they left, bruises and strains eased, that nasty cough soothed. A mass of discordance walked in, and he surfaced enough to open his eyes and see Prinz Winstow walk by. Age mainly, starting to dim the fire, smearing the yellows and reds into grayish tones, the kinks of old injuries and a grey cancer starting in his liver. Not good. He settled down and concentrated on straightening out the discordances. Nothing he could about age, that was natural, but the aches could be soothed and the cancer... from a distance he could only suppress it.

He felt Rawn walk by, bright with reds and golds, swirling with blues, sparkling. Nothing wrong there.

He picked out a few more serious problems, and applied some smoothing to them. In many ways he was failing 'the people' by not committing himself to the Church, so that people could come to him. Yet he knew that Rawn's situation was far from rare. He pictured himself living a life of ease, healing whomever the Bishop felt had donated enough money or property to the Church.

No, this was better. Wherever the life of a warrior took him, he could heal. But he really should spend more time with that cook who always had chopped meat ready for Blackie. He should have realized her heart was weak and her arteries stiff and thickened.

The liturgy and songs poured over him, and he stood, knelt or sat with his neighbors, soaking in the beautiful fire of more than a hundred souls aligned in holy worship. With a ache of regret, he reluctantly pulled back into himself as the congregation roused itself and broke apart.

"Well, that was an interesting sermon." Stevan said. "Did you sleep through it Dex?"

"'Fraid so." *Sort of.*

"Father Puli said we all had a duty to the Church and a duty to the Imperium. He didn't say we had a duty to the crown prinz. I was expecting that, since he's *here*. What do you think?"

Dex grinned. "That the Church is more interested in its own power, and doesn't want a rival loyalty. Something as huge and impersonal as 'the Imperium' will pull a lot less personal loyalty than an actual Prinz." He wrinkled his nose, "Or maybe the Church has a preferred candidate."

"I'm trying to sort out whose backing who in this horse race." Stevan told him. "Who does the Church favor?"

"That's... an interesting question." Dex said. "From what I've heard, the Emperor has been fighting off the Church's attempts to get Prinz Rawn to take vows. Does that mean they want to take him out of the running, or that they want to control him when they put him back into contention?"

He left Stevan puzzling over his notes,

Dex changed into riding clothes and headed for the barns. The same three horses were saddled and ready.

"I don't think the prinz will be out today," he told the grooms. "Rya? Why don't you try the chestnut today, and I think I'll take Spot along for some exercise."

Spot was spotless, so he just tossed the saddle and bridle on, leaving the halter on underneath. They mounted up and rode off, without much notice. Most of the Bloods had either ridden early or attended Church and were now stuffing themselves. Dex thought wistfully of lunch, but most likely he could finagle a snack out of the cooks later.

Around the first bend, Rawn stepped out of the brush, grinning. "That worked perfectly!" He handed Dex a sack. "Food. Since we're all missing lunch." He gave Spot a rub under the eye, and scrambled aboard. "How about we eat at the waterfall? The weather's clearing up so it won't be running much longer."

Dex let them lead, calling out the occasional "Heels down, sit up straight!"

Rawn had packed a bit of bread and cheese,

and what Dex guessed was every cake, candy and pastry he could lay hands on.

They wolfed it down, and continued on, enjoying the warm sun and green forest clad mountains. Dex occasionally picked up the lessons, both Rya and Rawn cantered a bit, and neither of them fell off. When they stopped to admire a view, he had them switch mounts, and get used to the different movement and personality of the beasts.

They bickered amiably over who got to ride Spot, and where Rya needed to go to find some real riding boots.

"How big are your feet?" Rawn asked, riding up beside her and sticking out his foot.

Rya was taller by half a foot, but Rawn's feet were a bit larger.

"Ha!" Rawn smirked. "I have hundreds of boots, to go with different clothes. Some of them are really horrible colors. The sorts of things only a girl should wear. I'll give them to you."

"Ha, yourself. If they are *your* boots they can't be girly. So there."

"Wait till you see them. My nannies think I'm *just precious* in them."

Rya tilted her hand slightly, finger up and stiff,

then tapped her chest. "That's sign language for 'be still my beating heart'. Well, you have to guess at a lot of it. Boys shouldn't have to wear girly things."

"Desert sign language? You know Toro Desert sign language?" Rawn lit up. "Will you teach me enough that I can insult my nannies?"

"Some times it's the only way the family can talk, with all the people around." Rya wrinkled her nose. "Yeah, I have these three duenas, and Fabrigel has two, plus two friends so stiff they might as well be... Nati and Fabrigel and I are getting together every evening to do some sewing, and we have to get them all gossiping with each other and ignoring us before we can bring out the riding clothes we're making. We're going to set a new fashion."

"Can you do that on purpose?" Dex wondered. "I thought fashion just... well, I suppose *someone* has to start it."

"I've never tried to start a trend before, so I don't know if it will work. But at least I'll have some actual trousers to ride in." She grinned at Rawn. "And boots, even if the color is horrible."

Fortunately Rawn was riding the chestnut when his flustered guards found them. Their officer shot Rawn some half worried, half irritated looks, but the troops seemed almost proud of the prinz as they fell in behind them for the last few miles to the barn, where the frowning Prinz Winstow could only look him over and suggest taking a jacket when riding. He frowned at Spot, but apparently with a lady aboard spotted ponies were not *too* scandalous. He waited, though, until Rawn had dismounted then ushered him off to the mansion.

The Guard Captain was tapping his foot in suppressed anger.

Dex shook his head sadly. "You've made yourself into someone to be avoided, Captain. Work your own way out of it, I take my orders from the prinz."

The captain glared. "He's not well."

Dex raised his eyebrows. "Really? He seems like a normal eight year old to me. If he was sickly when he was younger, he seems to have grown out of it."

Glare.

Dex let the grooms take the prinz's horses and he and Rya brushed Spot out and put her away. "I'm going to give Muddy a bit of exercise."

Rya smiled shyly, "I'll see you at dinner then."

The next day the Guard Captain had his troop

ready, and trailed Dex and Rya on a rather brief ride over the nearest hills. Rawn was nowhere to be seen. Until they returned to the barn and the captain stomped off angrily. Then he popped up and they saddled Muddy and two others of the prinz's horses and escaped before any guards noticed them.

***

"Dexter. Do come and talk to me."

Dex eyed Father Puli, then inclined his head.

"The archbishop thought I should be aware of several facts about you. Bishop Jurdis says that you over-stayed your schooling and owe the Church."

"I brought up the subject of my leaving school several times, but I was always persuaded that I was too young to leave yet. I'm sorry that the bishop feels it so keenly."

"I can get you an officer's commission in the army."

Dexter blinked in surprise. "Why? Oh, I see. You want me away from Rawn."

"You are interfering with our influence on the prinz, and the archbishop is not happy. If Rawn will take vows, we can try to heal him, and then, if it is for the best, release him from his vows to take his place as emperor. Or if the gods will that he is not strong enough, we can keep him, removing him alive and safe from Prinz Rondeze's advancement."

"Even in the Church he would be a threat— unless Prinz Rondeze had reason to consider the Church among his supporters."

"Leave the politics to your betters! Watch yourself, Dexter. And think very hard about taking my offer, because getting out of the way may be all than can save you from a very painful experience."

***

Dex settled himself comfortably and examined his neglected writing materials. The quill answered to a touch of Earth, and he had to add Water carefully to his ink and mix it. Then he penned a polite letter to the General, asking about Muddy's pedigree.

He looked pensively at the sheaf of paper. There wasn't anyone else he cared to write to. His childhood friends had outgrown him even before he'd been moved to Meadow Green Abby. He cleaned his quill with a shrug. He had friends now. And some deep responsibilities to his Crown Prinz.

**

"Hey Dex, what do you think of this?" Rya spun in place. Purple boots, loose black trousers, and a purple shirt so long it was nearly a dress, ending mid-thigh, with a black belt cinching in the waist.

"Is this your new fashion? Looks kind of like those fancy shirts the duelist wore in Imperial City."

"Yep, that's sort of what Fabrigel based the design on. And it's long enough to sort of cover up everything the duenas think we're unladylike about showing when mounted."

Dex frowned. "They don't think anyone should see the saddle?" Rya threw Spot's halter at him.

There were no saddled horses for them this morning. Had the Guards coerced the grooms?

"Do they really think we're spoiled little darlings?" Dex asked Muddy, as he groomed him.

Rya watched, and did to Spot everything he did to Muddy, and they headed out without an extra mount.

Muddy was perfectly happy to carry double, when Rawn popped out from behind a tree a bit further up the trail than usual. Dex made them trade off several times, promising a proper lesson when they got to the waterfall.

But Nati and Fabrigel were there, waiting for them. Also in the new fashion.

"What we want, Dex, is sword fighting lessons." Nati told him. "I can't think of anyone else I'd approach."

"We're tired of being helpless." Fabrigel added. "There used to be women soldiers. Generals even. I'm tired of being *useless*."

Dex glanced at Rawn, ready to use him for an excuse... but he was wide eyed and eager. "I've had lessons in how to *hold* a sword so I'll look like I know what to do with it. What a great idea. We can meet here every day."

Rya was bright eyed and eager too, he realized.

"Right. Well, what we need then, are some swords. Lacking that, some sticks." Tying up Muddy, he prowled into the woods, and sawed off and whittled down some straight sprouts.

He got a small stick of his own and demonstrated a simple thrust, and then a simple parry. Had them practice the moves, practice the moves against him, and then paired them up.

"Now. We are learning, not fighting. We are going to do this nice and slow, and practice the move until we get it right. Then we can speed it up, like it would be in a real sword fight. But we will start slow."

Fabrigel and Nati were cautious and awkward. Rawn and Rya were... interesting. Both fast and accurate, with a child's flexibility and enthusiasm.

He lined them all back up, and taught them some steps. Forward and back, "It's a dance, m'ladies. Thrust, advance thrust. Parry, retreat, parry. Tsk! You'd never be so awkward on the dance floor would you?" He paired them up again, and Nati and Fabrigel were much better, relaxed. Rawn and Rya were improvising at speed and giggling madly. He told them what a fine job they'd done and that they should rack their weapons.

Nati looked sideways at him. "So, how good of a dancer are you, Dex?"

"I was raised by the Church. Trust me, I have never danced."

The girls all swapped grins. "Oh, I don't think lessons are over yet," Fabrigel said.

After a week, he had to admit that they had potential. It took two weeks before they admitted he might not disgrace himself on the dance floor, and he showed them how to not injure their own horses while fighting from horseback as a reward.

The storm blew in that evening, and after raining off and on all evening, settled down to a steady drizzle by morning.

Dex loaded his plate and joined Stevan at their usual table. Stevan ignored him, his gaze riveted on the far end of the room. Dex looked over and spotted the three young women in their 'modern riding dresses' coming toward them.

"Dex, we talked it over. We think we should have our lessons in the salle today." Nati was the designated spokeswoman today.

An appreciative whistle from behind her pulled her attention away from Dex. "You like my riding dress, Pierre?' she asked icily.

"Oh yes. I like it very much," he said.

Nati looked unaccustomedly flustered, and Dex noticed that Pierre's attention was on her, not Fabrigel. She twitched away from his regard and faced Dex again. "As soon as we've eaten."

Dex nodded. "Might as well. How about Rawn?"

"Rya sent a note, we haven't gotten a reply."

"What's this?" Pierre demanded. "Making assignations with Dex instead of me? I'm wounded. And more to the point, I'll be in the salle as soon as I've finished eating."

The salle had a beautifully waxed wooden floor, benches along all sides for observers, and a supply of wooden practice swords. Dex chose two of the smallest for Rawn and Rya, longer ones for Fabrigel and Nati, and a longer, heavier one for himself.

The girls arrived altogether, with a sarcastic Pierre following them. Rawn walked in with the Guard captain on his heels, frowning again. *Poor man isn't good at adjusting his routine.*

Dex simply lined them up, handed out the weapons and started his lesson. They had the basic moves and the basic steps well down now, and he set them a combination of moves to warm up with. He paired them off and had them practice blocks and thrusts.

"Well, you seem to have the basics covered." The captain said, smiling rather unpleasantly. "But I'm not at all sure that you qualify as a sword master. Only the best should teach the crown prinz. Come spar with me... Dex."

Dex saw Rawn draw breath to protest, and shook his head. "Take a break, and watch. The basics that I've been drilling you on will get you through three-fourths of all sword fights. It's when you face someone with training that you need all the advanced techniques. I suspect the captain is planning on demonstrating some of them on me."

The armsman he'd gotten the swords from hustled up with padded jackets, and the padded stiff leather helmets they used for practice bouts.

"Captain, are we being purists, or are we brawling?"

"Oh, let's start out being purists." The captain showed his teeth, and they saluted each other.

The captain started with the traditional single edged slightly curved blade of the Imperial Style.

"Notice that the captain handles the blade like a saber, with a single curved cutting edge and thick point. Useful from horse back where sticking the point in someone means the horse's movements will either pull the sword out of your hand, or pull you off your horse." Dex skipped backwards. "The basic parries I've taught you work pretty well against this style. If you are quick enough, a straight blade with a narrow point can end the fight quickly with an accurate lunge." He demonstrated, getting solid hit to the captain's chest. "The main problem is that the heavier blade can break yours, and blocking the momentum will really tire your wrists."

"Can you attack with a saber, Dex or only defend with a longsword?" The captain looked pissed.

"Oh, sure. This is what you do, saber on saber." Aping the saber style, he started slicing the captain to bits.

After, so to speak, having had his arms and head hacked off the captain backed off and bowed. "Very nice saber work. How about the rapier and knife? Bortian Style."

They swapped to the long light sword and long knives and started again.

"I showed you just a bit of sword and shield fighting. This is similar, with the knife being used mostly to block strikes, but also available as a weapon if the opportunity presents itself." Dex lunged in and got a solid hit to the captain's abdomen. "Now in real life the captain would be out of the fight after that, but in practice he'll hit back, which is good to remember on the field too, as a mortally wounded man may ignore his spilled guts long enough to get in a last attempt to take you with him."

The captain was certainly trying, narrow eyed and focused. He managed to touch Dex twice while Dex "killed" him three more times. He stepped back and bowed. "I think I'll use my brains for once and not turn this into a brawl. Please do proceed with your lessons, you seem to be well qualified to teach the crown prinz."

Rawn chortled and they grabbed their wooden swords and lined up again.

Leonel frowned at the captain. "You should have tried broad swords and shields. Used your superior strength against the boy."

"I've sparred with swordmasters before, Vizduq. I was mistaken in my assessment."

Rawn glanced over in surprise, then turned back to pay attention to the new combination Dex was showing them.

Captain Linsk was more polite, and found himself being dodged less often, rather of a relief all around.

Chapter Eleven

Dex followed Rawn and Rya up a new trail. Bit by bit they were exploring the local mountains and the trails through it. They had nearly exhausted all the possibilities that didn't include them camping over night. That was going to be a bit difficult to carry off. He glanced back over his shoulder, "Captain Linsk? Do the nobles ever overnight anywhere around?"

Captain Linsk sighed. "Occasionally when they are out hunting, the gentlemen will camp. There are a few large farm houses, where we would be welcome. But not in this direction. There's nothing but lumber camps this direction. They cut the logs in the winter, and the floods of the thaw carry the logs down to inlets where they are assembled into rafts and towed south. This time of year the camps are empty. In fact the demand for lumber has dropped off the last few years, there were about half the usual number of camps last winter."

"Hmm, the blight, do you think? No new barns, no need for larger houses for children?"

"Could be. Hadn't thought about it."

Dex returned to his current problem, "But I take it the ladies don't stay out overnight?"

"No, sir, not even the married ones with their husbands."

"Well, that puts a damper on further exploration," Dex grinned back at him. "But don't celebrate, we may come up with something worse."

The captain shot a glance up at his Prinz. "I will look forward to it."

Quite a change in attitude. Welcome, however hard come by. Rawn wasn't even avoiding the troops any more, since they'd started running interference and keeping the bulk of the fawners away.

Rawn stood in his stirrups and whooped happily. "Father Hariban!"

"Younger gods! Here's your chance." The captain shook his head. "Ghastly old man."

Dex raised an eyebrow and sent Muddy forward.

Rawn had dismounted and was hugging a raggedly dressed old man. On second glance, the man's clothing was very good material that had been subjected to hard wear for long past the time it should have been sent to the rag bin. Rya slipped down from Spot, and Dex dropped down from Muddy as Rawn dragged the old man up to them.

"This is Father Hariban. Father, this is Rya and Dex. Or if you want to be formal, Vizmarquez Rya Amar of Karm March on Graf, and Dexter Fiz Ambalia."

Rya curtseyed a bit awkwardly in her riding outfit, and Dex bowed his head.

"Huh. Not very religious, boy?"

"I'm quite religious, Father. I am not, however, the property of the Church, however much they want me."

The old man cocked his head and snorted. "I see. Stupid of them." He turned his attention to Rya, today decked out in lime green and black. "You look like some silly dog all dressed up in something no sensible *human* would wear."

"But very practical for riding." Rya pointed out. "And *everything* is quite thoroughly covered."

"So it is. You look rather *competent*. Don't you think that is an insult to your husband?

"When I get one, I'll ask him."

Dex was fascinated by the exchange. He'd never heard Rya argue with anyone, let alone an older man, a Church man. He opened his mind to the elements and saw them swirling around the old man.

No. *Not* swirling, they were being pulled out straight. He was sensitive, not strongly, but perhaps enough to encourage automatic trust. Or honesty. Yes, those straight flows of the Elements would be hard to resist. Everyone probably spoke the truth around this man. Did he know it, use it consciously? Did the Church know? Almost certainly not.

Dex looked around the empty forested mountain. "Where are you assigned, Father?"

"Oh, I travel between all the little villages out here. Every once in awhile I get into the Residence and harass Father Puli. Sometimes I'm truly unfortunate and encounter the abbot."

Dex started grinning. "I'm sure he's completely honest in his appraisal of your ministry."

"Well, he certainly doesn't make a habit of softening it. Puli and I get along tolerably." He cocked an eye at Rawn. "And what is a Crown Prinz doing out here?"

"Riding." Rawn looked smug. "Dex has been teaching me and Rya. And sword fighting, and military tactics."

"Indeed? Experienced at all of these are you?" the churchman eyed Dex.

"I haven't got any practical experience with the

military tactics," Dex smothered a grin as he felt the influence of the Elements. "I have better credentials in riding and sword fighting—in practice, very little actual battle, a few bandits is all."

"Oh, that's all?" Hariban parroted dryly.

"Where are you headed now, Father?" Rawn bounced on his toes. "May we escort you? Would you like to borrow my horse?"

"You look very good Rawn, and I hate horses."

"I'm healed. Umm, Rya, do you think?"

"Of course. Here Father, Spot is an excellent pony and she'll take you anywhere."

After a bit of swapping around, Rawn and Rya ended up riding Muddy and Dex rode Rawn's horse.

"I need to find you a really good horse, Rawn." Dex teased. "And Rya. Then you two can stop borrowing mine."

"I think I own hundreds of horses." Rawn grinning down from his lofty perch. "Of course I've only ridden three of them."

"We ought to take a look at all of them."

Dex rode beside the Churchman, perched unhappily on the pony.

"I'm only doing this for Rawn," he grumbled. "Although the pony hasn't turned carnivorous yet."

Dex grinned. "She was fed raw mutton just this morning, so she'll be fine for a few more hours."

Hariban glowered up at him. "Not very respectful of the Church, are you?"

"No sir, the Church has turned into a grasping, controlling political machine. It owns too much property, too much treasure, and way too many people. It plays politics. The succession for instance. They've been treating Rawn like a pawn to be played when the time is right. Now that he's halfway out of their hands, what are they going to do? Who are they going to back?"

"The Church does not... " the old man gritted his teeth.

"It hurts to lie, doesn't it? If you are a friend of Rawn's, you can help him by finding out what the church has in mind for the future. Or not. After all, the Church owns you."

"Young man, you are amazingly rude."

"No, that's Pierre. I merely want to use you to help Rawn."

"I see. And do you think he needs help?"

"I am certain of it. Will you help him, or do you prefer a Winstow Regency be followed by Emperor Winstow? Or that Prinz Rondeze be the next Emperor?"

"That's all a bit beyond the scope of a wandering country preacher." The old man was scowling ferociously.

"Chatting with Father Puli? Possibly even going so far as to place yourself to encounter the abbot?"

The old man glared.

"Unless you'd prefer to write a eulogy for Rawn's funeral." Dex shrugged, "But then they wouldn't let you speak, would they?"

"Young man. Who are you?"

Yes, sensitive.

Dex reached into his pockets and pulled out a small pebble. Thought deeply about Earth, and shape. The rock flexed, squished, developed a hole in the middle. Then Wind. He handed the rock to the churchman.

Father Hariban felt the breeze through the hole. Turned the stone, blocked the hole, released it. Put in a pocket somewhere in his ragged layers.

"So. A demi-god. How did you escape the Church?"

"Made sure to never do anything where they could see it." Dex shrugged. "My father is Nevrille, my mother Saint Vythis. I suppose anything I did as a child was attributed to my mother. Dad always reminded me about how I'd find myself trapped if I gave myself away." He shrugged. "It worked well enough, but since I healed Rawn the suspicions are flying."

"So it's all coming out?"

"Most likely. It was pretty much inevitable once I took up with Rawn."

Hariban stared at the sky while Spot ambled a mile. "There will be a war, won't there?"

"Prinz Rondeze, Prinz Vasik and Conte Mongote all seem poised to make a grab for the throne. If we can get word of Rawn's good health around, their support may soften. If the Emperor lives long enough, we may avoid a succession crisis."

Hariban sighed. "Even so, Rawn is not quite nine. A year from now he will still be so young and vulnerable that Winstow's Regency will be seen as a step to his, or his son's, advancement."

"So far, in public, Winstow and the Church both back Rawn. In private, they seem to be playing tug of war, with control of Rawn the prize. *If* we can keep that *public* backing, and start adding nobles, we may be able to make the brothers decide the risk is too high. Then we just have to stick to Rawn and make sure he is guided, not controlled. That's my rosy scenario. My nightmare starts with an open repudiation of Rawn by Winstow and the Church."

"Any sign of that?"

"The abbot has hinted at having me declared a witch and a heretic. Nothing about Rawn, so hopefully he is still playing for the prinz's control."

"Hmm, that's how they'll wrest control of Rawn from you."

Dex grinned. "I don't control Rawn, although I am aware that I could certainly be a strong influence. My father may take a hand in the matter if they try to excommunicate me. It's hard to say, there's something *odd* going on with the Elder Siblings."

Hariban went back to studying the sky. Rawn glanced back uncertainly a time or two, and Dex signaled for quiet.

"All right. I'll poke about for Rawn. Elder Gods save me! And I know what you mean about the Elder Gods. There is a problem. I wish I knew what."

***

Dex watched from a distant table as Prinz

Rawn got fawned over by a bunch of Prinz Winstow's cronies, mainly the Duqs and relatives of the surrounding duchies. Second in line to plague the prinz on his ninth birthday were all the older group of guests. Dex was very glad they'd given Rawn a pre-birthday bash the previous day. They'd worked up a system of signals for rating presents and Rawn was signaling massive numbers of stupid, vapid, childish, insulting, and almost all with the accompanying 'very expensive' circular rub of forefinger and thumb.

He was all dolled up in full court garb and Dex had a feeling that only the silent hand language was keeping him from rebellion. Rya, one of the honored guests at a nearby table signaled a cumulative total. Eighteen toys, thirty-eight decorative and useless swords, twelve rings, five nightlights. The next gift that was paraded by was an enormous pale bearskin rug. Rawn sat up and blinked at it in astonishment.

"Someone actually has some grasp of what a boy of nine is interested in?" Pierre leaned forward and listened. "Who the hell? Clovil? Slow ville? Something like that."

Stevan blinked. "Aeje Clovil? Isn't that the general that the Emperor nova'd and sent to Iceland?" He craned his head as the bear skin was unrolled and the prinz paced its length. "No wonder no one else wants to colonize down there."

"That's a big fuckin' bear." Pierre sat back down. "Might be fun to hunt."

That started speculation on a local hunt. Prinz Winstow had, so far, been reluctant to allow his guests to risk their necks in this terrain. The number and unruliness of the assembled Bloods probably had a great deal to do with it as well.

Prinz Rawn was reluctantly persuaded back to his seat, and the parade of more ordinary gifts restarted.

When every Duq, Marq, Conte, and even the three kings had had a present delivered by their resident relative the music started. The little Prinz led Lady Pomfreit out for the first half of the first dance, then was allowed to escape.

"Usually I'm wheezing so bad that's the only dancing I have to do." He popped up behind them rather expeditiously, and Dex cast a beady eye on the paneling.

Rawn grinned. "Yeah, I know, Crown Prinzes are not supposed to use the servants passages to avoid the old fogies up there."

Fabrigel raised an eyebrow. "Surely you're

going to dance with *us,* your Highness?"

"Nope. If I do, every woman here will demand a dance as well. Not that I wouldn't dance with you three. But I suspect you'll all have more fun dancing with each other."

"Good thinking." Pierre grinned, "This way I won't be overcome with jealousy and end up challenging you to a duel."

The guards who had sidled quietly up into proper guard positions twitched, and Pierre's grin widened.

"I think you take after your appalling Grandfather." Nati said.

"Why, thank you, Vizconteza. May I have the pleasure of this dance? It's the only possible way to erase the horror of that comparison from my shuddering brain."

"Brains can't shudder." She led the way to the dance floor.

"They're so cute," Fabrigel said. "If I hadn't seen it with my own eyes I'd never, ever, have considered Pierre the answer to a girl's dreams."

Rya giggled. "C'mon Dex, it's time to find out if you remember your lessons."

Dex hesitated and Stevan and Fabrigel shoved

him.

"Go on Dex. We want to see if there is anything you don't do well." Stevan turned to Fabrigel. "Vizduquez, may I have the honor of the next dance?"

Dex managed credibly through three dances with his charitable friends, and Rawn finally danced with them as well and looked like he was enjoying himself.

Unfortunately his predicted results looked to be happening as the rest of the female guests closed in on him.

Rawn did not look like he was enjoying the overly suggestive and intimate grasps of the next two women, and the gang swapped glances and ran interference for him. Rawn ducked behind them and disappeared into another servant's entrance.

"Five or six years from now, and he'll not only not be able to beat them off with a stick, he won't want to anymore." Pierre offered his arm to Nati, again, and led her out for a dance.

Fabrigel attracted her own circle of admirers, and had to periodically hide within their group. Dex noticed that she didn't seem to mind dancing with Stevan, and that they seemed to both enjoy talking about politics in between.

Little Rya seemed relieved to be ignored, but did drag Dex out twice more.

"Relax Dex, it's just like sword fighting." She giggled, as he stuck strictly to the forms. "We're definitely going to have to drill you on this a whole lot. Regularly. *Relax*."

Chapter Twelve

"What do you think? Vito next?" Stevan danced Fabrigel across the floor, shifting their position relative to the other dancers slowly.

"Yes, he's chattier than Orser. They're the only men from Graf that I'm certain are backing Marq Inacig." Fabrigel was all business, and absolutely gorgeous.

As the dance ended, they stepped off the dance floor a few steps ahead of their next target.

"Why, Fabrigel, you look spectacular tonight." Vizmarq Vito obliged them by charging straight in. Orser joined them.

"Thank you Vito. Hello Orser. You two are always together, you must be neighbors."

"Oh no, Hufer is on the West coast, and Fenie in the north-east. Really, just across the straights from Roma. You should visit... actually you should dance with me and I'll tell you all about it."

As she danced away with Vito, Stevan turned to Orser. "You know he's going to make Fenie sound a hundred times better than Hufer. You going to do the same?"

"Of course, and easily. The West Coast is the best part of Graf, far enough south of the Equator to be cool, without being all the way down in the snowy area. Just enough rain for agriculture without humidity."

"Rain and snow aren't terms most of us associate with Graf." Stevan remembered Rya's descriptions of sand dunes and desolate rock wildernesses, interspersed with mining towns.

"Well, most of the continent is desert." Orser shrugged. "And rich in minerals, so there are trade offs."

"I guess there always are. Merd County has the richest soil imaginable, but brutally cold winters."

Orser curled a lip in disdain for a county so young. "We've got the tip of the southern ice cap on Graf, so we know about cold as well."

"Nah, C'mon. Sand and mines, that's what Graf is all about, isn't it?"

"Listen you little punk, Graf could be independent. We could be an economic powerhouse, without the Imperial taxes."

"Do you really think 'King Inacig' wouldn't tax you just as much? And then you'd have to import food. And then there's the Straight. Not wide enough for reasonable security."

"Bah. We give a lot more in taxes than we receive in Imperial services."

"Except, as a rebellious continent you'd need a navy all your own," Stevan shrugged. "We get the same sorts of arguments on Easterly. Without any sort of outside threat, how do you justify the taxes."

Orser nodded reluctantly. "And if you get rid of the navy, you're inviting the Island Pirates to start raiding again, and we never did quite figure out if there was some larger force behind it." He eyed Stevan. "You're pretty sharp for a baby Nova."

Stevan snorted, "It's sink or swim here in the shark pool."

Orser laughed out loud at that. Fabrigel and Vito returned, and Orser begged a dance from her.

Vito turned away, ignoring Stevan's opening comment. Stevan strolled over to the bar and got a glass of red wine. He sipped it, and scanned the area for another faction. Durant and Raulf were chatting with Syvinda and a young woman he hadn't met. He drifted that way and nodded to his fellow Easterlians.

"Stevan, this is Lady Nui Lionier from Crystal Bay Duchy"

"Lady Nui, a pleasure. I hope my neighbors

have been extolling the resources and promise of Easterly?"

She wrinkled her nose prettily. "Oh no, they've been telling me how beautiful it is."

"Er, quite. A pleasure to have met you." Stevan retreated hastily. He turned back to the dance floor and found himself beside one of Golezan's cronies. "Carlo, good party, eh?"

Carlo curled a lip, "Do you think so? Well, you're young. We'll party properly later."

"Oh?"

But Carlo walked away, and snagged a dance with Fabrigel.

Stevan worked his way around the room, but couldn't find either of the two men he'd identified as proponents of Prinz Vasik.

The older Guests had retired, and the music was getting more energetic. Stevan noticed more young women he wasn't familiar with. He worked his way over toward where Fabrigel's current dance partner's clique was concentrating, in case she needed succor.

She did indeed step back from Vizduq Golezan, and latch herself firmly onto his arm. "Oh yes, I owe you a dance, Stevan." He could feel the faint trembling of her hand, and steered her back onto the dance floor.

"Problem?" he murmured.

"I'm having trouble deciding which instrument I'm going to use to geld him."

"Hmm. Carlo hinted that they'd be partying 'properly' later." He flicked a glance at a woman wearing a very low cut gown. "I think they've expanded the guest list a bit."

Fabrigel scanned the room with narrowed eyes. "Indeed, and they aren't staff either. Surely they didn't manage to smuggle *prostitutes* into the Winter Residence?"

Stevan choked faintly, studied the women again. "Is this standard for parties among the nobles?"

Now it was Fabrigel's turn to blush. "Actually, this is the first soiree I've been to since my sixteenth birthday party, which I assure you did not include, umm."

"Quite." Stevan looked around and located Rawn's guard captain and danced Fabrigel over to him.

"Excuse me Captain. I'm sure you are on top of the situation, and these women who, umm, may not have been officially invited, and I'm sure you have Prinz Rawn very well guarded tonight?"

The captain switched a glance between the dance floor and Stevan. "There is always a guard on that hallway, however I will check again, since I was personally unaware of outside guests being cleared."

"Thank you, Captain."

Stevan and Fabrigel wandered back to the Unmannered. "I think we've found out all I'm willing to fish for tonight." Fabrigel wrinkled her nose.

"Yeah." Stevan jerked his head at the nearest door. "Is there any place, umm, suitably public, but distant enough to talk?"

"Suitably public?" Nati snorted.

"I think a number of reputations are going to be tarnished tonight, so we need to protect ours." Stevan zeroed in on a side table in the main hall.

"Mainly male," Fabrigel said, "But possibly not exclusively. Yes, this will do." She popped her elbows on the table and got down to business.

"Rawn is facing some seriously entrenched and prepared opposition. Prinz Rondeze seems to have the largest number of followers, but Vasik, Inacig, and Mongote have loyalists as well."

Stevan frowned, "Judging by Orser's

comments, the Graf nobles may be more interested in independence than actually trying for the throne."

Rya blinked at him in surprise. "Everyone is always complaining about Imperial taxes. But without the Navy we wouldn't be able to ship ore or refined metals, and we already have too many pirates and harbor raids."

"I mentioned that an independent Graf would need a Navy, and Orser seemed to agree. I'm tending to think that they are the smallest risk."

Dex nodded. "What about Easterly? Conte Mongote may back his wife and son's claims on the throne. He's new to Easterly, though. Ten years isn't going to get him much backing, will it?" He looked at Pierre.

"Oh hell, Grandfather is practically taking bids for his backing. Mongote and Vasik, as far as I know. I think my uncles are talking to them both, behind Grandfather's back. Rumor has it that they just might join forces."

"So it could come down to Rondeze against Vasik and Mongote, with Rawn ground up and forgotten between them." Fabrigel leaned back and crossed her arms.

Dex tapped his fingers restlessly. "All the local

Duqs tonight saw that Rawn was looking healthy. Would it help if we paraded him around to more of them, so the previous belief that he wasn't going to inherit will die?"

Nati nodded, "It probably would help, but what about Prinz Winstow?"

"Winstow's route to the throne involved Rawn being crowned and Winstow being his regent until the poor sickly prinz died." Fabrigel leaned forward again. "I wonder if he's changing his plans?"

"And the last player," Stevan eyed Dex. "The Church. Who are they backing?"

Dex scowled. "They'd apparently been counting on Rawn taking vows to get healed, so he was in their hands to either elevate or to clear the path for someone else. Prinz Rondeze was the name mentioned."

Stevan spotted Fabrigel's and Rya's duenas sitting in a loose cluster between them and the ballroom.

Fabrigel snickered, "Yes some other people are as concerned as you are for my reputation."

"What do they think about your riding?"

"They complain endlessly. I suspect their reports to my brother have been interesting."

"They report?" Nati looked appalled.

"Oh yes. I suspect my poor brother would prefer platitudes to the truth, or worse, their nattering about my reputation."

Rya nodded. "Every letter I get from my parents is full of 'Have you met any really nice, rich young nobles, and have you been careful to never, ever be alone with them?' I replied that if they weren't safe to be alone with, they weren't marriage material."

Fabrigel snickered. "All my older brothers and sisters are married, and they are all saying the same thing, as if I didn't grow up watching them trying to dodge *their* keepers long enough for a kiss."

Nati shook her head. "I think I'm not going to regret the lack of entourage. My father... isn't very political. He says any sort of government upheaval is bad for everyone except the very top of the winning group. He knows Conte Mongote, thinks well of him in a vague fashion, but I got the impression that he'd be happy if it all just went away."

"Has anyone visited him?" Stevan asked.

"Umm, regularly. I don't know... it's usually merchants... but a lot of old cronies have been showing up lately."

Stevan squirmed a bit, "I did wonder if your lack of entourage was an indication of poverty or a signal of non-support for Rawn."

"Oh, part poverty—the genteel type where you have everything you want—and not a stitch more. But, with me being out riding nearly every day, usually alone, it seemed odd to spend money on some silly woman for appearances sake." She shrugged ruefully. "But mostly it's lack of funds. If Daddy had had to buy a ticket, I wouldn't be here."

Fabrigel nodded comprehension. "Everyone is complaining about taxes. Responsible Contes are getting squashed between what they have to pass on, and how much they can take without reducing their economies." *Something I should look into. Where is the money going?*

"The blight has cut Daddy's income drastically." Nati said. "We used to raise horses. Now it's cattle. Thank goodness the blight doesn't effect cattle or sheep. Our income will recover eventually."

"Too f'ing late for you to get a bit a pomp, though." Pierre snorted.

"You're one to talk, Pierre," his cousin poked him. "Did Uncle Gressom cough up any funds?"

"Yep. Nothing like an appeal to snobbery. Can't

have an Ambalia looking destitute in front of all the other Families. You, of course, don't count, Dex."

Far from being bothered, Dex looked amused. "Never have, never wanted to, in the way the family does their counting."

"Wise beyond your f'ing years, cuz."

After kicking gossip around for a bit more, they all dispersed for the night, The girl's duenas trailing them discretely, but closing in quickly as they climbed the stairs, and the girls split off to their wing.

"Geeze, what do they think we're going to do?" Pierre grumbled. "Have an orgy, the six of us?"

In the men's quarters, the party seemed to have relocated and intensified. The revealingly dressed women were everywhere, as was wine, and a selection of the musicians were playing songs of a distinctly rowdy nature.

"So much for a good night' sleep." Stevan said.

Pierre scratched his chin thoughtfully. "When, not if, Nati hears about this, my reputation will be mud."

"Umm, do any of us qualify as duenas?" Dex dodged a laughing woman, who appeared to be down to her underwear. The man pursuing her was wearing nothing at all.

"Nope. We're toast. The only question is are we going to deserve it?"

Stevan took a good look at the nearest women, and made up his mind. "I'm too young to be contracting nasty diseases." He looked around at rapid footsteps.

The guard captain shot a tight lipped glare at the party. "The prinz is not in his quarters."

Dex turned quickly and opened first his door, then Stevan's. "Not here."

"The barn?" Stevan suggested.

"Was there any indication that anyone had gone to Rawn's rooms?" Dex strode toward the side entrance.

"Other than the three scantily clad noblewomen in a hair pulling contest in his bedroom?" The captain sounded *pissed*.

"Rawn knows where all the servants' hidden doors are. I expect he left as soon as they showed up." Dex said.

"All right, that's what I call avoiding the fucking temptation." Pierre frowned at their snickers. "Oh Hell, I didn't mean it like that. I was just swearing."

"It was still funny." Stevan glanced at the

closed door of the first barn, and led them onward.

"Where are you going?" Rawn popped up at their elbow. "I know, Crown Prinzes are not supposed to wander the grounds at night."

"Damn straight. And there's a disaster in the making back in the men's quarters. So we're going somewhere else." Pierre didn't seem inclined to mention the prinz's visitors.

"I heard the stars are really bright, and pretty from the flat top." Rawn told them. "I've always wanted to go up there and see them."

They split up to saddle their horses, and with Rawn on Spot, rode up to the mountain.

The stars were brilliant, and they argued amiably over the constellations until nearly dawn. The relieved Captain had settled down at a distance to keep his eye on them, and didn't seem to be in any hurry to return to the Residence.

The Residence was in an uproar over the party in the men's wing.

That some noblewomen had invaded Rawn's quarters was completely hushed.

Stevan made note of how many women were missing from breakfast. Obviously he wasn't going to find out who they'd been this way. Hmm, had the captain said hair pulling? He'd talk to Fabrigel about it.

"Was it actually an orgy, as reported?" Rya squeaked.

"We didn't stay long enough to check if the line between rowdy party and orgy had been crossed." Dex told her. "We went star gazing, with Rawn and we even have guards who can swear to the entirely proper, and totally male nature of our outing."

"So," Stevan said, "We're only smudged by the guilt of our fellow males, not guilty ourselves."

The girls seemed more inclined to be amused than indignant.

Rawn joined them for a late breakfast. "I still haven't slept." He announced proudly. "We should have gotten you three up too, it was really beautiful out last night."

"Maybe tonight if it stays clear." Fabrigel glanced at the fluffies, and sighed.

"Whatever you do, don't trust Pierre about the constellations." Rawn grinned, "I think he might have regretted missing the orgy." He eyed Pierre. "I don't know anything about orgies, do you? I ask you because you're the oldest and act more experienced."

Pierre was red and Nati's eyes were twinkling

with suppressed laughter.

"Orgies," Pierre said. "Are highly over rated. And that is *all* I am going to say on the matter."

That brought giggles and skeptical looks, but by and large the three young women seemed inclined to forgive them their maleness.

Chapter Thirteen

"Hey, Dex, you got a letter." Stevan handed it over, and settled down with his own. His mother wrote every week, and the uncertainties of the mail were such that this week he'd gotten two at the same time.

His two younger brothers had put in a brief comment each—"Thanks so much for sending Bartli back, so we can learn our manners. Parti" "Yeah. Thanks. Farlo" Stevan snickered. Served them right for being such ghastly brats. He glanced at Dex, surprised to see him scowling.

"Problem?"

"I wrote the General to ask about Mudball's pedigree. It seems that he's in the middle of a bunch of lawsuits. The mayor's son only paid half his price on the spot, and is now refusing to pay the rest. But that's just to the trainer, who hadn't actually paid the farmer Muddy's whole value, either. They've all gone to court, and the General has had to tell the Mayor to back off any threats against the judge. What a mess." He glared at the letter.

"Dex, a horse like Muddy is worth three or four

times what any of us paid for our horses. Can you pay for him?"

"Not immediately." He looked off into space, thinking. "I know how to get the money, though." he pulled out his neat little wooden secretary box. "First I'll write to the farmer and let him know Muddy's all right, and ask what he'd charge me."

"Deeex! Maybe you should just shut up and keep Muddy. After all, you saved him." Stevan pointed out.

"Yeah, but I probably don't *legally* own him."

Stevan sighed. "Yeah, well, but don't tell the farmer you healed him."

"I'll just say I'm trying to heal him. Ask him how much he wants for him."

Stevan groaned. "Why don't you just ask him to raise the price while you are at it."

"Oh, it's not that bad."

"Or he could sue you, after all you have his horse. He probably wouldn't have you arrested, I mean, you didn't steal the horse. You just bought a horse from someone who bought the horse from someone who didn't own him."

Dex sighed. "Go away Stevan. I'll write the farmer, tell him the horse appears to be recovering and does he want me to send him back to him, slowly and carefully. I'm sure he'll recover enough for breeding, and wouldn't mind keeping him myself, in case the blight ever passes off. Then I'll ask him how much he wants."

"All right, that's not too bad. But say 'if the price isn't too steep' as you can't afford much for an animal that's probably not sound, and with the blight, breeding isn't profitable right now. Just, at a minimum, try to not get yourself sued. If you can't afford Muddy, you can't afford a lawyer."

"That's true. And I'll be sure and put in something about if the court decides he's the legal owner."

***

"Dex, what the fuck are you doing?"

"Oh, hey Pierre, what are you doing riding all the way up here?" Dex straightened, a rock in each hand.

Rawn peeked over a boulder upstream. "We're looking for rocks."

"I was looking for some village called Masen's Gap." Pierre frowned down at them. "Those are just plain old pebbles. Utterly useless."

"They're flat cobbles." Dex said, "And Masen's Gap is about five miles further on."

"Right. Thanks." Pierre shook his head frowning. "Bloody rocks. What next." He clicked his tongue at Suzy and trotted off.

Rawn snickered. "Do you think this'll work?"

"Oh sure. I just have to find the right merchant." Dex placed a rock on a flat boulder. Two fingers thick, better than a hand across, didn't tip or rock. "Perfect."

"Why didn't you want limestone?" Rawn put two more flat stones on the boulder.

"Limestone doesn't have much Fire in it. Granite is cooled lava, each of these held a lot of heat, once, so they can more easily change energy into heat. I can channel that, turn the Fire all in the same direction, so the heat flows like water going downhill. Which makes cookstones."

"But cookstones are cheap. You'll have to make hundreds of them." Rawn protested.

"Yeah, it'll be tough on Spot, having to haul all these stones." Dex grinned at Rawn's expression. "Depending on the merchants that come up for the festival, I may be able to make some other things.

Things that are expensive."

"What I want to know is, why is Pierre going to Masen's Gap? All they have there is sheep."

"And people who make thing out of sheep, while they're snowed in half the year." Dex pointed out. "I'll bet it's something for Nati."

"Oh, yuck. At least you're not that bad. Even about Rya."

"Rya's too young to be 'that bad' about. Anyhow, I hardly know her." Dex retorted.

"Ha. Can she heal? Or make things? Which god helps you make things?"

"I don't know what Rya can do. I've never actually asked her. And I'm not a saint, I'm a demi-god. That means I can do it all myself, without any god at all."

Rawn sat up and stared at him. "Demi-gods are powerful. Master Mongo says they're more powerful than gods."

"Ha! Something else your tutor is wrong about. I'm really good with Earth; gods have the most trouble with that, and they need saints to do a lot of stuff, but believe me, even the younger siblings are better at a whole lot of stuff than I'll ever be. Stronger, too." Dex frowned. "And the Elder gods are flat out scary. I hide from them. I'll be really careful when I do these rocks."

"Master Mongo says that energy is always conserved. So how come cookstones work?"

"There are all kinds of energy. I make the stone turn all the energy it gets into heat, all going one way."

"So that's why you thump and bang a cookstone until it turns on?"

"Right. Movement—and stopping movement—is one form of energy. Static is another, and the energy that turns magnets to the north is another. And gravity, always pulling down. That's a very strong Earth force, I can only change part of it. Heft a cookstone, before and after it's started working. They're lighter when they're working."

"How come they aren't sorta hot all the time?"

"They have to be made that way, because we don't want to start fires, because you couldn't stick one in a saddle bag. Although that can be a problem, bumping around all day. Anyhow, they store energy until they pass a threshold of energy, then they start releasing it, according to how they are made."

"What about glowstones? You don't thump them."

"No, they are made to either soak up light or give off light. They only do nothing after they've used up all the light they stored."

"But they're pretty bright. Shouldn't they run out faster?"

Dex grinned. "I'm going to stop insulting your tutor. He's taught you how to think like a scientist. Did Master Mongo teach you about the spectrum?"

"Yes, like a rainbow."

"There's light that people can't see, that's bluer than purple or redder than red. A good glowstone collects it all and smushes it all together so it's all visible."

"So it's brighter than just the visible light that hit it, or it can last longer?"

"Right, one or the other, depending on how it was made."

***

Gaspif was trying. But this was going to be the only bazaar this year. If he was going to make any extra coin, it would have to be here. He wouldn't do anything big. He'd just, he'd just... Sit down and clutch his head and pull out his hair. Oh Gods great and small. He was an honest man now. He had to resist...

"Are you all right?"

Dex, of course. Gaspif looked up thankfully. "Is there anything I can do for you? Anything that will take me away from temptation?" He rubbed the thief brand on his right hand.

"Actually, I was wondering how to sell some things." Dex stared at him a long moment. "Cookstones. You sell them, I'll split the money with you. Three quarters for me, a quarter for you."

"All the servants know me." Gaspif ran his fingers through his neatly pulled-back hair. "Or maybe... "

"A disguise?" Dex laughed. "There's nothing illegal about cookstones. I just don't want to explain where I got them, who made them. My friend has problems with the Church."

Gaspif hesitated, but not very long. What did he care if a saint escaped from the Church? As long as he or she wasn't making hexes, of course. "Could I borrow that red shirt of yours? I can find a scarf. And a basket for the stones. How many do you have?"

"Four hundred. I think. I sort of lost count."

Gaspif stared at him. "Four hundred rocks?"

"Yeah. I was thinking about where to put them so I could go back and refill the basket. But if you're selling them, I can come and go, bringing you more."

An hour later his skin was reddened by a bit of Fabrigel's rouge, his hair was in greasy strings, hanging down from the purple cloth scrap from Rya's suite, clashing wonderfully with the bright red shirt and yellow sash. The basket that had formerly held puppies was fully of river cobbles.

"Cookstones! Get your cookstones! Only twenty pence! Cheap at half the price! Cookstones!" It was too much fun to be legal.

"Cookstones! Top notch cookstones!" Gaspif shuddered suddenly. What if they weren't? He grabbed the one on top and started swinging it about, thumped it on a convenient shelf until the merchant owning it glared at him, then he walked off, tossing the stone into the air and catching it. "Cookstones! Twenty penYow!" He dropped the stone and waved his burned fingers. "Ow, ow. Damn." That drew snickers from the onlookers, that turned into laughter as he carefully flipped the stone over with his boot and tried to figure out how to pick it up without burning his fingers worse.

"Doubt it's that hot," one youngblood sneered,

and made a grab for it himself. He barely touched it before snatching his hand back. His friends laughed even harder, and he switched his glare to them.

"Trust a man to not know how to handle a cookstone." Gaspif froze at the sight of Mistress Reaso. But with barely a glance at him, she slipped her hand under the stone and hefted it. "Now, that's quite a nice stone, young man."

"Only twenty pence, Mistress. Keep a Lady's teapot hot, that would." Gaspif kept his eyes downcast.

"Indeed. I'll take this one and nine more." She turned to the little scrub girl who was following at her heels. "Dit, you take these right up to the kitchen, and tell Marli to test them all." She fished two gold marks out of one of her pouches, and handed them over as Gaspif finished loading the scrub girl with nine more stones. The cook caught his eye briefly, "They had better all be properly charmed."

Indeed. The pouch she'd used was embroidered with the Imperial Crest. His first sale had been to the Empire, not Mistress Reaso herself.

The transaction complete, he turned away, and found himself being eyed by several other women. "Cookstones, my goodwives?" He pulled out another and started juggling. It had worked once...

Three basket loads of stones later, a giggling group of young Ladies stopped to watch himself singe his fingers, and started a new round of buying. He glanced up to see the little Vizmarqez Rya Amar staring at him in wide-eyed horror. She clearly recognized him, and turned away quickly. He dropped the suddenly hot stone on his foot and hopped and cursed a bit.

Of course.

Everyone knew her mother was a demi-god. She must have inherited her mother's talents. She'd trusted Dex to help her stay hidden from the Church, and here she probably thought Dex had given her away. By the time he managed to pick up the hot stone, she was gone.

Why was she making so many cookstones? What did she need the money for? Charming cookstones was a slow way to get enough money to run away on. Gaspif shook his head, baffled. Unless she and Dex were planning to elope. Now wouldn't *that* be a scandal!

He held the cookstone out for a pair of local farmers.

"Now isn't that a nice one! You'd save ever so

much work chopping wood for the kitchen stove if we had one of these." The wife held her hand over the top of the stone.

Despite the awkwardness of carrying a working stone, they wouldn't be talked into paying for what looked like a flat river cobble, and carried off the hot stone.

He turned away, checking the number of stones he had left. It was about time for him to find Dex for a refill of stones.

"What's this? Who let a tinker in?"

Gaspif looked up at Father Puli.

An ancient old man in worn clothing that had once been magnificent, staggered up beside the preacher. "Oh, Tinkers just show up. Mind your purse and enjoy the show. You juggle boy?"

"Yes, sir." Whoever the oldster was, he was important. Gaspif pulled three cold stones from the basket and set it down so he could juggle properly. This was going to be disastrous unless they lost interest quickly. He tossed the stones and quickly caught the rhythm, but when he tried a fancy toss, he dropped the stone, and then the others as he tried to pick that one up. The last one hit his head and the old man cackled.

"Call that juggling? Pathetic."

He started again. Then a stone flared up. He dropped the one in his hand, dodged the next one and caught the third, and hastily dropped it as it flared. "Ow, ow." He blew on his fingers and danced around a bit. It helped the pain, and was apparently *very* amusing to the old man.

"Who charmed these stones, you buffoon?" Father Puli wasn't amused. He obviously wasn't sympathetic, either.

"Don't rightly know, sar, we traded for 'em an' I got sent to sell 'em." Gaspif had a nasty feeling he had the accent all wrong. Tinkers probably didn't talk like Imperial City dock workers.

"Witches." Father Puli spat at his feet. "We should burn them all. Begone."

Gaspif collected his hot stones and went. But not very far.

Keeping a careful eye out for the Churchman, he made four more circuits around the fair grounds. He had exchanged the weight of quite a few stones for rather a lot of coppers. His arms were limp, and he folded up in a patch of shade at the side of a wagon. The merchant frowned at him.

"Those are pretty strong cookstones. No one is

buying mine—not that I have many."

Gaspif nodded. "I expect they sell better around towns." He cocked his head thoughtfully. "Could I interest you in about three hundred stones at fifteen pence? There's no way I'll be able to sell many more."

"Could be, although I could only pay eight pence apiece. Now, if whoever you've got charming them could make cold boxes, now that would bring in some money."

"I'm not sure." Gaspif waffled. "I'll ask. I might be able to take ten pence each."

"You do that. How many stones do you have right now?"

Gaspif counted them out. "Eighteen. I'll see about getting some help moving the remainder."

"I'll be here. Remember what I said about cold boxes."

Gaspif pried himself off the ground. Dex was with a mixed group of Bloods, but spotted him immediately and slipped away.

"I found a merchant who'll take all the rest for ten pence each." he told him.

Dex brightened. "Excellent. I figured we'd be stuck with the rest. I'll start bringing them down."

"He said the real money was in cold boxes."

Dex wavered. "But how could we sell them?"

Dex was frowning as if *making* the boxes was the easy part. Large and small gods! Was Rya that powerful?

"This merchant'll take 'em. Look at those nice little storage crates." Gaspif pointed. "We could buy one for pence, and sell it for marks."

"Maybe." Dex chewed his knuckles, and glanced around. "All right. One."

Sometime between taking the box away and bringing down stones from his room, Dex managed to get the box charmed. Gaspif held his hand inside and marveled at the chill. He'd never actually seen one before. The merchant handed over a hundred marks and begged for more. Gaspif conned Dex into three more.

At the end of the day, after washing the grease out of his hair in a stream with soap Dex brought him and putting on his usual clothing, Gaspif was faced with the fact that he was now rich. By his own standards, mind you. Over a hundred marks in one day! For money like this, Rya could elope with whomever she pleased. He just hoped he didn't end up flogged.

Chapter Fourteen

The Great South Abbey was as far north-west of Shingay as the Winter residence was south-east. So the abbot's visit was notable.

Perhaps, Dex thought, he wanted to study all the young bloods gathered together here, a representative from every governing family in the world.

In any case the tenthday sermon was well attended, all the fine young ladies herded by their duenas into the front right side, behind the Imperial family, and all the young bloods in their finery filling up most of the rest of the seats. Some of the staff crowded into the rear pews, or stood at the back, most no doubt were laboring away in the kitchens, readying a feast for the august visitor.

Stevan, to Dex's surprise, seemed quite serious about the sermon. Listening, while most of the bloods fidgeted, preened, yawned and whispered. The abbot enjoined their prayers for the Emperor's health, for the local leaders, for the people of the world and all the expected routine. His sermon was heavy on duty to the Church and light on one's other duties, and then focused down to a lecture on 'special talents' and how they were cherished by the Church and used for the good of all. He wound back to his starting point of duty and especially the duty of the talented to serve the Church.

Dex sighed quietly, hoping his indiscretions weren't catching up to him. This might be a good day to skip the formal lunch and take a ride all by himself.

"Dexter Fiz Ambalia?"

He looked up in surprise at the Church robed acolyte. "Yes?"

"The abbot wishes you to join him at the head table."

Not good. "Certainly," Dex said. "I'm honored." *Unfortunately.*

Better than poor Rawn, who was trapped between his uncle and the abbot. But with the abbot on one side and Father Puli on the other, Dex felt intentionally hemmed in. Rya was on the other side of Father Puli, looking a bit baffled and uncertain. She wasn't used to being the Lady who attracted all the attention. Fabrigel was sitting lower down, with their group for a change.

"So Dex." The abbot turned to him. "What did

you think of today's sermon?"

"It was very interesting, sir." Dex answered politely.

"Don't you think you should give your talents to the Church?"

"We are all called to serve the Gods, the World, the people, the Imperium, the Church, our home counties and our families in unique ways, sir. I am not called to the Church."

"You are mistaken. You throw talent away, and the people are the poorer for it."

"No, sir, the Church is the poorer for it." Dex looked the abbot in the eye. "The Church looks too much to its own power, and too little to the good of the world."

"Do you claim to be a Saint, to speak for the Gods?"

"Saints speak *to* the Gods, and sometimes relay their speech to others. A Saint who speaks *for* a god is most likely speaking *for* himself. I am not a Saint." *Literal truth, but probably not something I want the Church to start thinking about.*

The abbot leaned back, frowning. "You are a very ill mannered child."

"So am I. He deserves rudeness." The voice

echoed oddly; only Dex looked around. A faint shadow, like a young man stood there, a bit behind the abbot and making crude gestures behind the abbot's head.

"He didn't do anything for my little Prinz." the Younger God continued. "They were going to shape him into an obedient tool, then release him from his vows so he could take the throne. Just a bunch of power mad sexually frustrated dictators."

Dex nodded. "Yes."

The abbot frowned. "You agree that you are ill mannered?"

"I'm too honest to ever be perfectly polite," Dex told him.

The god snickered. "Good catch. I'm Cruiz. Glad you're here to watch over the boy. He'll be a good Emperor." He faded before Dex could figure out how to answer without being misunderstood by everyone else.

The abbot turned to Rawn on his other side. "And how are you doing, your majesty?"

"Very well, your Grace." Rawn looked to be tamping down a smile. "The air here seems to agree with me. I have a lot more energy than I do in the city."

"You look well." The abbot looked back at Dex in frowning speculation. "Very well." He applied himself to his food then, looking like he was thinking.

Father Puli had been listening, with a frown. Now he turned to Rya. "Vizmarquez Rya, you have your father's looks."

She nodded. "All of Father's family are redheads."

"What have you inherited from your mother?" He was watching her like a hawk.

Rya looked puzzled. "Mother doesn't have any titles of her own, nor property."

"But she has talent."

Rya's brow crinkled. "As Abbot Merisk said, we all have talents, and need to make the best of them. I'm afraid I haven't really seen much in myself."

The servants removed plates and brought tiny cups of fruit ices to clear the diners' palates for the next course.

Dex spooned up the ice, wondering if Rya had done something to bring the Church's attention to her. Or had the cookstones drawn the Church's attention to the area, with the two of them the main suspects?

Plates came and went, with one Churchman or the other poking and prodding Dex and Rya.

"A healing talent, nurtured by the Church might even find a cure for womb blight." Father Puli pointed out to Rya at one point.

"Does the Church have any indication of the cause of the womb blight, sir?" Dex pulled his attention away from the abbot. "In as much as it happens to some species of animal, it cannot be punishment for sin, as some people have suggested."

"And since when have you become an expert on sin, young man?" The abbot joined the conversation.

"I had an excellent education, sir. Both theological and scientific. The pattern of illness doesn't seem to fit most plagues. Isolation, looking for contacts and even large area quarantines haven't worked. All the healers I've talked to are quite worried about the possibility of a wild carrier species."

"Science." The abbot scowled. "Yes, we spent a great deal of time and money educating you, for all the thanks we've gotten. Now you presume to put it above the Gods."

"Above the Gods? Studying the creation of the

Ancients could not possibly be... " Dex shrugged. "The Gods created everything, including this blight. We just have to stop being dull and stupid, and figure out why, and what to do about it."

"If anything." Father Puli inserted. "The gods have reasons, even if we can't see them."

"Indeed. You wouldn't want to be a heretic, would you, Dexter?"

"Certainly not. But the Creators of all gave me a brain and the power of reason. I expect they expect me to use it."

The final sweet demolished, people were beginning to leave. Prinz Winstow suggested that the abbot join him in his private rooms. The abbot reluctantly released Dex, who stood respectfully and bowed to the prinz and Abbot as they left. Father Puli excused himself and withdrew as well.

Dex sank back into his seat. "Ouch."

"He's after you." Rawn said, sitting down in the abbot's seat.

Rya sat down again too. "I thought he was after me. The Church is always like that, because of Mother."

Dex nodded. "Can you do anything? Or your mother?"

Rya stiffened defensively, and he continued. "My mother was St. Vythis of Nevrille. Even though I've been pretty careful to not show any of that sort of talent, they still didn't want to let me go."

One of the older servants appeared with three more plates of cake and deposited them in front of them.

"I think they're trying to feed you up, Rawn." Dex said, happily digging in.

Rya poked at her wedge unhappily. "Nobody ever taught me anything. Sometimes I see thing or hear things. Mother always says it's my imagination. Do you know how to do things? Did your mother teach you in secret?"

Dex nodded. "Lots. Want lessons in that, too? It's almost more fun than sword fighting."

Rawn snickered, then sobered as one of Prinz Winstow's men approached him. "Prinz Winstow requests that you join him in his office, sire."

Rawn sighed and rose. "I'll talk to you later."

Dex nodded, and polished off his cake. He eyed Rya. "Think about it. I don't want to do anything until the abbot's gone."

She nodded and rose, as her duenas marched up to the head table. Seen in public talking to the crown prinz was all right. A penniless bastard? Unacceptable! Dex rose with her, but turned the other way. No use giving those women an excuse to pick on her.

***

Stevan looked up from carving something that ought to look more like a rose than a blob, and blinked in surprise.

Rawn grinned. "I know, Imperial Crown Prinzes are not supposed to just pop around to visit. But Dex, the abbot really is after you."

Dex nodded glumly, "I just got a note. He has requested my presence in his rooms tonight, for a private interview. If I disappear, please don't let him leave with a large rolled up rug."

Stevan snickered. "I take it your magic healing powers have been noticed?" he studied the prinz, "And perhaps this rather healthy looking Prinz really was sickly, up till a couple of months ago?"

Rawn nodded. "The abbot is really ticked about it. In fact, I'm ticked about it. It took Dex about three minutes a day for three days to fix my heart."

Dex shrugged. "It was just a hole. Infections

and cancer are the hard ones. The Church is deadly serious about politics and power. People don't seem matter to them, so long as they do what they're told. Oh, I was wondering who Cruiz was?"

"You mean Prinz Cruiz? He was my father's older brother, he died fighting pirates in the Smoking Islands about a year before my Grandfather died and my father became Emperor."

Dex frowned, "Only about fifty years ago, then? He's going to be strong, if he can do a spirit form and talk just fifty years after his last death."

Rawn sat up. "He's a God? You *saw* him?" At Dex's nod he jumped up, "Come here."

They followed him through a maze of back corridors, and back into a long gallery full of pictures. "Here." Rawn planted himself in front of a portrait.

"Yes, that's him." Dex was impressed. *In another forty years will I be able to see my mother again? Speak to her?* "Who is the traditional God of this duchy?" he asked.

"Gammot." Rawn frowned. "Do Gods move around?"

"If they want to. Gammot may have really liked Cruiz, and made him welcome, given him room in a familiar place. Or Gammot may have moved away from the whole duchy."

Cruiz popped in again. "Saint Portersburg. He was worried about Prinza Lamirand." He faded, his voice trailing off, "She married a demi-god, and not a nice…"

Dex blinked, then noticed Rawn's and Stevan's wide-eyed looks. "What?"

Stevan cleared his throat, "You were looking at thin air and nodding. Did Cruiz come back?"

"Yeah. He said Gammot went to Saint Portersburg with Prinza Lamirand." Dex left the rest off.

"I guess that makes sense." Stevan said. "Merd was like a soldier-saint, the general of the 1st lancers, killed in the Fornath rebellion. She stayed with the regiment until my great great grandfather retired, then she followed him to the allotment the Emperor gave him."

Dex nodded. "Nevrille says that there's a lot of Easterly that doesn't have a local god, and no one has ever taken over the whole continent. Not enough Elder Gods to go around, or something." *Thank gods, so to speak.*

***

"I have read a letter from Bishop Jurdis to the archbishop. The archbishop thought I should be aware of several facts about you. Bishop Jurdis says that you over stayed your schooling and owe the Church. And he says there have been reports of you healing people." The abbot leaned forward and stared at Dex.

"I brought up the subject of my leaving school several times, but I was always persuaded that I was too young to leave yet. I'm sorry that the bishop feels it so keenly."

"That doesn't explain the healing."

"I worked with the brothers in the hospital regularly. I am quite familiar with the care of wounds."

"He spoke of magical healing. If you have the ear of a god, and can open yourself to their healing through you, you have a rare gift, one which should be treasured."

"Any gifts I have I will use unstinting. But not at the behest of the Church."

"The Church has the good of the world in its hands.

"Indeed it does, your worship. But to further it or twist it to its own advantage? Take, for instance, the Church withholding healing from the Crown Prinz unless he took vows. Now we have this tangled mess of ambitious brothers and son-in-laws. How can a war over the succession possibly be in the world's best interest? Why doesn't the Church acknowledge the superior claim of Rawn, and the Church's support, unconditionally. The Church could still stop this madness, if the archbishop gave up his own ambitions."

The abbot showed his teeth. "Don't lecture us. If you are not a Saint of the Church, you are a witch. Don't think for a moment we won't burn you at the stake. You've cost us dearly, healing the prinz."

"Do you see how corrupt you have become? Shouldn't you be looking at helping the people? Perhaps the government? Certainly helping to maintain the peace. Instead you only count the cost to your own power."

The abbot's eyes narrowed angrily. "Glorifying the gods is quite different than hoarding power for ourselves. You are mistaken about our motives."

"Then why doesn't the Church support Rawn, under a Winstow Regency, as the best way to prevent a brutal civil war?" Dex tried to sense the currents swirling about the man. Was he venial, or merely mistaken? Was he looking to boost his own power in the Church, or was he playing a part in a dangerous political game?

"We do not trust any of the prinzes to do what is right. If Rawn were our ward, we could ensure the best for the world, for the people." The abbot leaned forward. "Are you going to be a problem, Dexter?"

***

"Stevan? Is Dex around?"

Stevan looked up from his diary in surprise.

Rawn grinned, "I know, Crown Prinzes are not supposed to sneak around through all the servant's ways." He glanced at the diary, then leaned in as something caught his eye. "You're writing about Uncle Vasik?"

Stevan squirmed. "I'm trying to figure out from how everyone talks who their fathers or grandfathers are backing." He shrugged, embarrassed to have to say it. "Everyone sort of figured you'd die and then there'd be a bit of a mess until someone took over and made everyone else accept it. They all want to be on the winning side." He suddenly thought of the gray old man who'd hosted a dinner he couldn't hardly eat. "Eventually they'll figure out you're the best bet, but for now... "

Rawn nodded. "I grew up knowing that Uncle Winstow figured he'd be regent, I'd die, and either he or Choa would be Emperor." He kicked the corner of Stevan's desk. "That's what I figured, too. It seemed the best thing for the Imperium. Now?" he shrugged, "I don't think there's going to be enough time to change people alliances, for all my uncles to, to, oh, stifle their ambitions, and decide to be loyal to me."

Stevan nodded. "The Emperor didn't look very healthy."

"Father's dying." Rawn whispered, "Cancer. Dex says there's not a lot that can be done with cancers unless they catch them early. He said he looked at Father, and there's nothing he can do."

"Oh." Stevan shivered at the thought of his father dying. "But Dex has fixed you." Stevan stated, "And now we have to figure out how to make *you* emperor."

"The one thing I need, to be Emperor, is a god backing me." Rawn said. "And Dex is the only way to talk to a god that I know of. Besides, he's my friend. He's, he's *good*." he took a deep breath and held out an envelope. It had the seal of the church on it, opened.

Stevan took it, opened it.

"'Your Eminence,'" he put the letter down and stared at Rawn. "You stole a letter from the abbot to the archbishop?"

"Damn. Even I'd think twice before doing that."

Stevan and Rawn both jumped as Pierre's overloud voice rang out behind them.

"Get in here, close the door." Stevan hissed. To his surprise, Nati and Fabrigel followed Pierre.

"Your duenas would have palpitations." Stevan shook himself and turned back to the letter.

"They're onto Dex, going to take him to court over his extensive education, claim him as a debtor." Rawn wrapped his arms around himself. "We've got to stop them."

They gathered in a knot and read the brief message.

Fabrigel, fingered the letter. "The abbot's secretary has a well drilled court hand. If I had the paper," she tilted the paper to the light and examined it. "And ink, I could forge a letter, and say that Dex *doesn't* seem to be any sort of Saint."

"You could mention that I seem to have spent time with a country preacher named Hariban, and that you'll examine him next." Rawn suggested.

"Is that a nice thing to do to a country preacher?"

"No, but they'd have to find him first, and the abbot won't know about him." Rawn pointed out. "So they won't even look for him until the archbishop writes back."

"And maybe not then." Fabrigel said. "Depending on exactly how discreetly the archbishop words his missives."

Stevan gulped. "The abbot has been using Prinz Winstow's library as his office. I could go in there, get some paper, borrow the ink well…"

"No, we'd better do it right then and there." Fabrigel said. "Prinz, could you escort the abbot to dinner? If he leaves before one of us give you a nod, try and slow him down, distract him."

Rawn gulped and nodded. "All right. I'll do it."

"Pierre, Nati, We're going to need a lookout and a distraction."

Stevan grabbed his littlest carving knife and pulled a chip of soft wood out of his collection. "Let me see that broken seal."

Chapter Fifteen

"Now remember, keep everyone out of here, and hold their attention if they peek in." Fabrigel glanced nervously from the door to the desk the abbot had been using.

"Just be your usual loud-mouth self, Pierre. Argue with Nati, or something." Stevan followed Fabrigel to the desk, and Pierre stepped out to where he'd be in plain sight of anyone walking into the prinz's library.

"So, Nati, how does it feel to be one of about fifty eligible maidens being courted by a couple of hundred young Bloods?"

Nati rolled her eyes. "That is a pathetic but sure fire way to start an argument, Pierre, and in any case, no one is courting *me*, they're all after Fabrigel."

Fabrigel sat down at the far corner of the desk, out of sight of the door and centered a piece of the abbot's personal stationary before her. Uncapped the well of expensive blue-black ink.

Pierre snickered, "Damn. All of us? How did I miss noticing that?"

"All right, maybe Dex isn't pursuing her, he

acts a bit younger than his age... how old is he, any way? Sixteen?"

Fabrigel wrote carefully, copying the opening of the abbot's letter.

"Bloody hell he is. He's older than I am."

"Pierre, please, don't be silly, you don't do it well."

"I do too," he protested. "Really, he's just a naturally tall skinny sort, well, medium tall, muscular skinny sort."

"Oh, ho. Jealous of your little cousin?" Nati smirked. "I can see why. Everyone trusts him, and nobody wants to be seen in public with you."

Fabrigel changed the phrasing just a bit '... seems a bit simple, which some take for Holy, but there is no sign that he is a Saint.' How odd, it had never occurred to her that Dex might be gifted. It would explain a lot though, wouldn't it? 'I am seeking a traveling country preacher named' What had Rawn said? Well, it didn't matter, did it? 'Heribete that the crown prinz is said to have spent time in the company of.' Oh dear. The abbot would not have ended a sentence... well, so what if the archbishop thought the abbot used poor grammar?

"Oh, you wound me! You trust Dex because he

looks young and innocent... ask *him* how old he is and see if he tells the fu..." He choked back a curse. "Truth. Oh, to hell with *him*. Wouldn't *you* be seen in public with me?"

"You called me a sheep."

Fabrigel glanced up at that. She could see Nati's face, but only Pierre's back. Nati appeared to be enjoying herself.

"Nah, when did I do that?" Pierre sounded baffled for a moment. "Oh, wait, wait a bit. Damn it, you looked so frail and pretty, I called you, what the hell did I say? Prime lamb?" He shot her a nervous look. "You'd been sea sick, see? But I could tell quick enough that you weren't one of the Do-nothings."

"Do-nothings?"

Fabrigel signed the letter with as good a copy of the abbot's hand as she could, and blew to dry the ink.

"Yeah, you know, those Laaaadies who lay around and maybe do a bit of stitchery now and then. You were," he gestured inarticulately. "You had energy, you get up and go places like you intend to get there and get to work, no lollygagging about."

Nati looked taken aback, "Well, I never had the luxury of laying about, and in any case, I can do stitchery quite well, thank you. Lots of it. You probably have no idea how much labor goes into a lady's wardrobe."

Pierre sounded dubious, "Yeah I suppose those huge fro fro things are hell to make, but you've got better sense than to make a spectacle of yourself in ridiculous clothes like that. Not to mention lace. How can it possibly be worth the effort?"

"So you like my clothes? You'll be seen with me in public? Hmm, does that count for or against my sense of style?" Nati speculated, her eyes on the top shelf of books, arms crossed.

Fabrigel wiped the quill carefully, and replaced it in exactly the position she'd found it.

"For." Pierre was firm. "There are plenty of women I won't be seen with... Although that has nothing to do with their clothing."

"Indeed." Nati raised an eyebrow. "Or no doubt their lack of clothing."

"Oh, low blow, Vizconteza. We aren't speaking of that sort of, of... "

Nati raised both eyebrows, looking a bit smug. Yeah, the boys were going to have a hard time getting over that little incident. Of course, as far as she knew Pierre hadn't had a part in it, but none-the-less the soot had rubbed off on everything male in the palace.

Fabrigel folded the paper carefully, and slipped it into the envelope.

"Take Syvinda, no way in hell would I want my name linked with hers in gossip. *Utterly* useless woman."

"Have you considered it from the other side?" Nati smiled sweetly. "Perhaps she wouldn't want your name associated with hers."

"I doubt she's that perceptive." Pierre turned suddenly in the direction of the door to the hall. Glared. Then turned back. If someone had planned on using the library, they had evidently changed their mind quickly.

"Very funny." Nati sniffed. "Why do you suppose any woman would want to be around you?"

Pierre stared at her indignantly. "How can you ask that, with my good looks?"

Stevan's hand wavered as he lit the stick of sealing wax. Fabrigel quickly took it and puddled the right amount on the flap, being careful to cover all traces of the first seal, and handed it back. She pressed the stick into the wax and lifted it.

There was a faint snicker from the direction of

the doorway.

"And, damn it," Pierre glared at the doorway, "despite being the second son of the third son of a conte, I do have a fair amount of money, and some small inheritance of land through my mother."

"And that is enough to overcome the handicap of your foul mouth?"

"Hell with the ones it doesn't." Pierre levitated his nose. "I prefer practical women. Women who could sew their own entire wardrobe in the morning, and break a green colt in the afternoon."

Nati eyed him warily. "Oh, so now sewing is an advantage?"

"I never said it wasn't, I just used the damn stitchery thing to," Pierre waved his arms. "To illustrate the sort of work some women pretend to do as cover for their doing nothing."

"I see." Nati eyed him cautiously. "Do you know, I really have no idea of what to make of you."

Pierre stepped in close and took her hand, then knelt. "What you should make of me is your husband. I love you. Will you marry me?"

Dead silence from Nati.

Dead silence from the doorway.

"Damn it, Nati, say something." Pierre looked

up at her, imploringly. "Please?"

Loud, authoritative footsteps from the hallway. Fabrigel sank down beneath the desk. Stevan carefully shifted the chair to exactly the right angle and joined her.

"Yes." Nati choked.

From beneath the desk, Fabrigel could see Pierre's feet and knee where he knelt, and could tell when he rose to his feet, and those feet closed in on Nati's.

"You know," Stevan whispered. "If they don't both mean it—or both not mean it—there's going to be a problem."

Fabrigel blew carefully on the wax seal. "I'm afraid to look."

"What do you two think you are doing?" Lady Pomfreit's icy tones sounded from out of sight.

"I am kissing my fiancée." Pierre sounded smug.

"The two of you will accompany me to see Prinz Winstow. Right. Now."

Apparently they left, as the Lady's voice faded with distance. "It is our responsibility to return our young guests in … How shall I put this delicately? In an unencumbered state. Engagements are encumbrances, Vizconte, Vizconteza." Her voice faded down the hallway.

Stevan wrapped his arms around his chest and bit his lip, not looking at her.

Fabrigel rose and stepped back to eye the desk.

"It looks perfect." Her shoulders shook, and she darted a glance at Stevan, who snorted and slapped a hand across his mouth.

"Let's get out of here," she hissed. "Don't you dare laugh until we're at least two corridors away." She dare not put too much breath into her words, too much air would be available for laughing.

The corridor was empty, and they strode quickly away.

Fabrigel popped into her rooms and emerged again with a bundle of letters. Their glances passed and they both dropped their eyes. Merci Bronth stalked out of the door and eyed them suspiciously. The two older Fluffies followed on her heels.

"I'll just take these letters down to the castelain's office." Fabrigel got her breath back fast enough when the older woman was the one she was looking at.

"Of course, Vizduquez." She dropped a faint curtsy, "But perhaps I should take care of this menial task. And the gentleman can see me there, so there won't be any talk about you and him running about the back corridors together."

Fabrigel straightened and glared. The, the, *damned* woman smirked, and grabbed Stevan's arm in what was probably a very tight grip as she took the letters.

Poor Stevan. "Goodnight then, Vizconte Stevan."

She turned back into her rooms. Just as well she didn't have the opportunity to be alone with Stevan. Someone might catch them … laughing. Yes. Laughing. Together.

Chapter Sixteen

Dex set the last pebble in place and stood back to watch.

"I'm sending out scouts." Rawn announced, shifting a few of the quartz pebbles forward.

"Ha! Me too." Rya advanced black stones.

Stevan and Pierre stood back and looked superior. Fabrigel and Nati paid close attention, and Dex offered occasional suggestions, as the Black Rocks defended their side of the little sandy strip from the brutal assault of the Quartz troops.

Nati and Pierre were keeping the required ten feet apart, and not speaking to each other, as Prinz Winstow had 'requested' of them. But they kept sneaking looks, and they both looked insufferably smug.

Rawn looked irritated. "It's not fair that defenders always win. I think I need more rocks."

"Attackers generally need a three to one advantage against a fortified position." Dex said. "The next time you besiege a town, remember that."

Rawn grinned, "I'm looking for plans of the Grand Temple in Imperial City. Do they really have their own troops?"

"Treaty of 3587, Rawn." Fabrigel said, "I suspect your tutors covered it."

"Ugg. I had to memorize it. The church was certainly different back then. Siding with the people against the Emperor."

"And they've had troops ever since." Fabrigel started collecting pebbles. "Nati? You want offense or defense?"

They'd taken to bringing lunch with them and staying out nearly all day.

Rawn's guards had joined forces with Stevan's, Rya's and Fabrigel's armsmen, and lounged about 'watching the perimeter'. Dex occasionally roped them in for mounted exercises. Rawn was quite partial to forest ambushes. The captain had started out angry, but wound up looking proud after the third time he'd been "killed" by the young Prinz. He'd dropped quite a few hints, since then.

***

"My brother says the Emperor looks very frail." Fabrigel bit her lip and looked over at the other two women. She sighed. "Nati! Get your mind out of the clouds!" She couldn't help but smile, though. *Who would have thought the first of us to make a conquest would be Nati?* Fabrigel was thoroughly enjoying the outraged jealousy of the other women. Not that they wanted Pierre, but they positively lusted after his obvious devotion. His ability to stay at least ten feet away from Nati, by remaining exactly ten feet away for quite remarkable lengths of time had rehabilitated his reputation remarkably. The long gazes, both of them confident and smug, radiant even, had all the girls sighing wistfully. The Young Bloods, for their part, were completely baffled by what Dex called Pierre's shield of total indifference to their opinions.

Nati blushed and hustled over to take the letter. "If the Emperor is not expected to live much longer, we should expect an attempt to take control of Rawn. Possibly several attempts. Prinz Winstow will want to limit outside influences. We know the Church wants him, so they can play kingmaker. And some of the other factions might try an out-and-out kidnapping, if they thought they could get away with it. If they could get Rawn to Imperial City and themselves installed as Regent, Prinz Winstow wouldn't have enough backing to go up against him. But would the Church sanctify the Regency?"

Fabrigel nodded. "We need to watch the church. I don't know if we dare another forgery, but could we sneak a peek at any letters that come?"

"If he leaves." Rya put down the little knife she was sharpening. "If the death is coming soon, I expect he'll stay. He's trusted by the archbishop, a personal friend. I expect he knows more than the Bishop does."

Fabrigel nodded. "The Bishop is old. Everyone expects the abbot to ascend to his place when he either dies or retires."

Nati was suddenly leaning way out the window. "There a large party approaching. Let's walk out and see who's come for a visit."

They walked quickly down the hall, then slowed to a ladylike stroll as they approached the grand staircase. Prinz Winstow hustled out, looking alarmed. From the balcony they viewed the party disembarking from the heavy carriage.

Fabrigel felt her knees go weak. "It's the archbishop. He's come in person."

Chapter Seventeen

"Well, Dexter," The archbishop smiled coldly. "It seems that you have lied to the Church, and taken advantage of our desperate need for saints to abuse the agreement we had with your mother."

"Indeed? I thought the contract admirably clear. Surely your Eminence didn't come to discuss a minor matter of tuition?" Dex didn't like the oozing shadows behind the archbishop, the feeling that *something* was looking over the man's shoulder. He softened his mind just a hair and saw the black weight of some sick and oozing soul stuff. He closed his mind quickly. It was alarming enough that the archbishop had come to the Winter Residence. Dex wasn't sure he really wanted to know what the man had brought with him.

"You remained in our schools and we supported you without payment for eleven years after the death of St. Vythis. *That* was not in the contract."

"I don't recall that there was a time limit, nor that the obligations of the Church ended with her death."

"I think we will let the court decide." The archbishop showed his teeth. "They will no doubt determine the amount you owe us for your advanced education, and if you cannot pay it, you will be declared a debtor, and we can take your person."

"So now the Church has come down to slavery, has it?" Dex shook his head. "Do you really expect to hold me?"

"Or we can just look into the matter of interference with official church mail. Oh, don't look so innocent. We know who had the motive. Do you prefer prison to helping the Church help people?" The archbishop snorted. "We know how to deal with saints. Let me give you a small sample of our power." He reached out and rang the little silver bell on the desk. The armored men outside the door answered to it.

"Take Dexter, here, to the room I had you prepare." He turned back to Dex. "We'll talk in the morning, when I have this succession issue in hand."

Dex stood and walked between the two guards, going where they nudged him. Either they couldn't talk, or their silence was supposed to un-nerve him. Or maybe it was just a tradition of the Church troops. They directed him down the back servants' stair, one preceding him and one following. In the lowest basement, they led him to a room, probably a food store originally. But it had a thick door and a new hasp and lock. He walked in and surveyed the bare stone until the closing door left him in the dark.

He snorted in contempt, and sat cross legged on the floor.

The archbishop's last comment, about settling the succession bothered him. It did not sound supportive of Rawn. He decided he'd better not dawdle. "Well Dad, I guess we'll find out if I've been paying enough attention to my lessons." He let his mind empty, and slowed his breathing. He could feel the Elements. Earth was strong down here. Water a bit scarce—it was a nice dry basement. Air stirred sluggishly, not much circulation either here or in the main basement. Fire was present in himself and more quietly in small amounts inside the stone, wood and metal around him. He let his senses feel carefully around the new hasp. It was screwed into the old wood. He reached for Water. The wood was old and dry; the water oozed reluctantly out of the wood and pressed against the metal intrusions, formed a layer around them. Dex reached into the metal of a screw for the Fire of refining and forging and pulled it to the edges. The water exploded into steam, and even through the thick door Dex heard the screw hit the far wall. He went on to the next screw, then the next, until the hasp dropped and hung from the padlocked tongue and the door swung open.

First, he needed his sword, then he needed to find Rawn. He crossed the dark basement, not even aware of using his mental senses instead of his eyes, as he found the door to the stairs and turned to cut through the kitchen to the other wing. Should he involve Stevan and Pierre? Or the girls?

He wound up the servants stairs and emerged into an empty, silent corridor. Down a cross corridor, two of the Bloods' servants talked in whispers.

He slowed a bit, scanning for any problems, but aside from being devoid of the horde of Bloods, nothing seemed amiss. Gaspif jumped up quickly when he poked his head into Stevan's room.

"Where's Stevan?"

"The archbishop wanted them all in attendance. He ordered all of us, and the armsmen, to stay in quarters. There's a rumor that Emperor Ranold has died."

"I think there's going to be a fight to control Rawn." Dex bit his lip, "If you can, check on the armsmen, make sure they aren't locked in. I'll go find Stevan and the others. It may be time to run like hell."

Well, if the archbishop was collecting all the hostages, there was only one place they'd be.

Both puppies were locked in his room. They picked up on his worry and whined. Dex belted on his sword, then slung the wrapped bundle of his father's sword over his shoulder. *Because this is starting to look like it could end with me running away really fast.* He headed for the audience chamber. The puppies galloped along with him, but he didn't have the time to deal with them. As he approached the main stairs, he could hear a muffled uproar and spotted the guards posted at the head of the stairs. They were looking the other way, so he backpedaled and dodged through one of the servants' doors and down the steep stairs to the passage between the kitchen and the audience chamber. No guards down here, at least on this side of the servants' door. He edged up cautiously and opened the door a crack.

The chamber was packed, all the young Bloods in mandatory attendance, all apparently talking at once. The guards were drawn up in a loose group behind Prinz Winstow, and with a foursome in front of every door the young "guests" might have used.

The Bloods sounded angry, but started falling quiet as the conversation on the dais heated up.

Dex spotted Stevan, Pierre, Nati, Fabrigel and Rya toward the front, then turned his attention to Prinz Winstow.

"...said he was sickly and unfit to rule." The elderly prinz was glaring at the archbishop.

"He may have been healed by a rogue witch." the pontiff replied, that bloated dark shadow looming over the boy. "Thus rendering him doubly unfit to become Emperor."

The abbot nodded, "Who knows what promises he may have made."

"None." Rawn spoke for the first time. "Unlike the church, this healer simply did what was needed, without trying to obligate me in any way."

"So you think, nephew, but what geas has he placed on your soul, unbeknownst to any?" Winstow snapped. "You had a responsibility to the Empire that transcended your desire to be healed."

Rawn was surrounded by the three men, his only followers thirty feet away with guards in between.

Dex bit his lip but decided to not move as long as they were only talking.

"I'm afraid that my regency will have to be extended until such a time as the Church declares you free from malign influences." Prinz Winstow glanced from the boy to the crowd. "It would be best if you would voluntarily sign this petition to the Council. It would demonstrate your responsible recognition of the situation."

Oh no. No signatures to haunt him all his life.

"Better that the boy be given entirely into the hands of the Church, that we may examine him and if needed remove any malign influences."

Not quite allies...

"So *you* can control him. I think not." Prinz Winstow glared at the archbishop.

The abbot stiffened. The various guards were suddenly eyeing each other.

Dex slipped through the door in the long pregnant pause. With everyone's attention on Winstow and the archbishop, Dex walked right up to them before the church troops noticed the interloper from an unexpected direction. They started forward to stop him, the prinz's guards stepped toward them.

"Prinz Winstow, Archbishop Harding. Prinz Rawn has friends who will oppose your attempt to usurp his rightful place as Emperor Ranold's heir."

Chapter Eighteen

Rawn slipped between the abbot and the archbishop as they leaned to grab him and leaped to Dex's side. Stevan led the rush obliquely forward to block the troops as Dex backed Rawn toward the door. The Imperial Guards leapt into action from the rear, cutting off Winstow's men.

"Blasphemer!" The archbishop shouldered through the tense guards, and Dex could see the Fire flowing down the shadow, down the archbishop's arms to the floor. It dripped to the floor and Nati gasped as it burst into visible flames. Even the church troopers recoiled.

"Door's open and clear," Rya announced.

"Go. Rawn, it's time to disengage, get somewhere safe, and make plans."

"Right."

Dex kept backing, keeping an eye on the guards, staying warily back of the fire as it licked along the stones. He had to leap over a finger of flame as it tried to cut him off. He paused long enough to bolt the narrow door, but the guards were now a secondary worry. The fire leaped up from the stones below the door, growing taller and hotter.

"Run," he shouted. "Stay together and let's see if we can outdistance this."

Rawn led the way down the passage and into the kitchen. The main room was empty, and Rawn headed for the buttery.

"There's an old tunnel back here... " he flinched back as unnatural flame flared in front of him.

The flames were roaring up behind them as well.

Dex skidded to a halt and yelled, "Dad! Dad! I need help! Emergency! Right now!" He reached out frantically, without regard for the looming blackness.

The flames whipped in a unfelt wind and retreated to form a circle around them.

"I should say so." Nevrille frowned at the youngsters in the circle.

"Rawn, where's the entrance to that tunnel?" Dex asked.

Rawn quit searching thin air and pointed, flinching back as the fires roared higher, then suddenly subsided between him and the wall he'd pointed at. He quickly opened the door, dancing on the hot floor.

Dex scooped up Blackie, and when Rya

attempted to do the same to Fang, Pierre grabbed the dog and they all followed the prinz down the dark tunnel.

The fire didn't follow them, but Dex could feel it surging beneath his feet.

"You know, Dex?" Pierre put the puppy down and brushed hair off his shirt. "Perhaps I should mention that anything I said about your Mother was just to try and rile you, and that in actuality I have nothing but the greatest respect for St. Vythis."

Dex snickered. "I'm sure of that, Cuz."

The tunnel let out through a hole in the bank behind the first barn. They ducked through the drooping branches of a flowering willow. They split up to grab horses. Rawn and Rya following Dex to Muddy's stall.

"Should we take Spot?" Rya looked nervously around at the other horses.

"We may need something faster," Dex looked around as well. "Those two you've both ridden." He ran a hasty brush over Muddy's back and around the girth. Dropped the saddle on and cinched it up. His nerves were crawling, he could feel the pressures on the elements. Fire being summoned and suppressed, an unseen wrestling match between his father and the dark shadow. He slipped the bit in Muddy's mouth, and the bridle over his ears. Led him out of the stall. The horses were feeling the energy crackling around them, nervous and shifting. He looped Muddy's reins over his head and left him standing in the passage, with just a quieting stroke, to help Rawn and then Rya.

The pressure slipped suddenly, flames rising then extinguishing. Grooms tumbled out of their loft beds, instantly alert at the smell of smoke. Muddy pawed with one fore hoof, but stood steady, sweating.

"Out." Dex told them, "it's too flammable in here." He threw Rawn up on his horse and led the way out. Out of the corner of his eye he saw Rya throw Spot's door open, then she led her saddled horse after them.

The grooms were moving horses as well. Two of them wrestled with the pale stallion. He reared and shrieked as Muddy trotted past, and dragged his grooms after them.

Outside, Air and Water were being thrown about, swirling spouts gathering up dust, then a flurry of rain to damp them down.

Stevan, Pierre, Nati and Fabrigel rushed out of the second barn, mounted, the horses prancing and eager to get away. *Good thing they don't realize it's going to follow Rawn.*

The whirlwinds were stronger now, muddy and thick. And suddenly one was human. No. Not human. A gross monstrosity, lumpy with souls, writhing with energy. The face was familiar, the basic clean lines now interrupted with bumps and swellings. The face of Roma, from the bas relief in the old Temple in Imperial City. Armored, it pulled a sword out of thin air and advanced on the other whirlwind. Dex shucked off the Nevrille sword and hastily unwrapped it, as he crabbed out onto the battlefield.

The whirlwind danced away from the monstrosity, toward the barn, and spun into a man. Armored like his opponent, and reaching for the sword Dex handed him. He advanced to meet the other god.

"Are you the source of our problems? What do you plan to do with those captured souls?"

"You dare question *me*?"

"I don't know why I bother. Your crime lies open to the world's sight. How many souls do you hold, prevented from their return to a new life?" He circled the lumpy creature. "You can't even form a normal body, if you want to keep hold of your perverted hoard. Do they give you more power? I don't feel it."

"That is because you are weak. You can't control Earth, so it holds you and keeps you from seeing the power that waits us when we reach the heavens. I will create worlds, entire worlds, larger and finer than this paltry trap we must now content ourselves with."

"Ah, not content to be an elder brother, are you? No, you want more, you want to equal the ancient ones. But how can you hope to reach so high when you make yourself so much less?"

"Get out of my way, puppy." Roma lunged then, his sword clanging against the Nevrille sword, as the younger god twisted away, and lunged in turn. The sword skidded along the lumpy arm, and sparks stripped off and fled.

Roma roared in fury, lengthening his sword and swinging with both hands. Nevrille deflected it and stepped in to kick the elder god. More sparks flew, souls, Dex realized, fleeing their captor.

Panicked horses galloped between them, and they both stepped back. Smoke was coming out the door of the first barn. People were emerging from the mansion, and not much less panicked, fleeing back into the barns and mansion. All the Bloods and servants, and then the armsmen, in their various colors. And the Church Troops in their pale blue. The Church troops were gesturing, not quite pursuing the armsmen, but they all ground to a halt as the fight before them registered.

Roma was becoming more human, more agile, as he lost his grip on his horde, or perhaps he was adjusting, remembering being human better. But Nevrille still pushed him, evaded the larger figure's powerful swings and slipping in and out to stab and slash.

Roma backed away, then turned suddenly and snatched the lead lines of the pale stallion. The grooms fled. Saddle and bridle appeared from thin air and dust as the god mounted and rode at Nevrille.

Nevrille dodged and slashed the horse's shoulder, making the beast flinch away, but the stallion pinned his ears and returned to the attack, as much on his own as infected by the god that rode him.

But Dex had used the moment to run in with Muddy. Nevrille vaulted aboard and turned the dark stallion to face the elder sibling. Dex stepped back, edging Rawn and Rya out of the battlefield as the gods created lances and charged.

Nevrille's lance slipped under Roma's, pushing it away but missing with his own point as well. He visibly braced as it hit Roma sideways, nearly unseating the elder god in an explosion of sparks. Nevrille's more recent experience as a warrior—a mere five centuries past—was giving him the edge. But Roma fought from the experience of over a thousand years of godhood. He twisted back up and spun, sword in hand, growing in size.

Nevrille turned Muddy, and they were growing as well. Hoof beats thundered and the clash of their swords flashed like lightning.

"Time to get some distance between us and them." Dex said, boosting Rya up on her shivering horse, and vaulting onboard Spot, sans tack of any sort. The pony took the hint of shifted weight and turned for the hills.

Fabrigel led off, heading for the flat topped mountain. "We should be able to see everything from there."

Glancing back over his shoulder, Dex decided that the distance would be a good thing. The slugfest was turning into one of the legendary battles, with twenty foot gods on horses to match, and lightning, rain and wind as spare weapons.

People were still pouring out of the Residence, and then sensibly fleeing back inside or up the mountain behind the residence, as Roma knocked Nevrille and Muddy off the training ground and down the hill. The lumpy god on the pale horse pounced after them and received a kick from two hind hooves, followed by a spin and swing of sword that shrieked off Roma's helmet.

Dex spotted the archbishop, and unfortunately the prelate saw them as well. He waved his troops toward the barn.

Then the trees closed in around the path and Dex could only follow the fight by ear. The deep rumbling worried him, as Spot scrambled valiantly to keep up with the longer legged horses. Earthquake or merely a landslide?

Was that a column of water from the ocean or a column of water dropping from the clouds? The clouds were getting thicker, not thinning, so he guessed the former. The water burst into steam with a scream from a god's teapot, and a bank of hot fog rolled up the mountains. Dex followed Rya's horse blindly until they climbed above it and burst into sunshine reflecting brilliantly off the fog below. Two mounted warriors spurred their horses over the fog as if it was snow, white lances of glittering ice in their hands, aimed at each other's hearts. They crashed together and eye-searing splinters flew. On foot, with swords, they circled warily. Roma was nearly human now, divested of his hoarded souls. Their blades crossed with blinding speed, ringing off the mountains with pure metallic echoes. Two giant hounds burst up out of the fog and threw themselves at the Elder God, holding him, dragging on his legs as he kicked, desperately keeping his sword between himself and Nevrille, his eyes on the other god. The black hound released his grip and circled, fangs bared, looking for a better target. Roma swung at him, stumbled as the other hound held on tight. The Nevrille sword slashed in, and a flare of light flew from the battle. No longer the sparks of souls, but pure Fire, the essence of God-stuff. The sword swung back and took off another piece, and another. Suddenly Roma was no longer a man-like god, but rather a chunk of creation that needed hewing. The streams of Fire flowed bountifully, brilliantly away. No gore on this battle field, just scintillating flashes until only one god stood on the clouds. A last ringing clash echoed off the mountains and silence fell.

Chapter Nineteen

Dex could hear more hooves on the trail up from the Winter Residence. The archbishop was driving a wild-eye bay well ahead of the disorganized string of troops. He hadn't waited for a formation.

"Prinz Rawn. You will come with me." The archbishop's voice was thin and weak. Perhaps it was the distance, or perhaps being outdoors. Dex rather thought it was the absence of that black shadow.

"I will not." Rawn raised his voice, clear and carrying as he reined his horse around to face the archbishop.

The archbishop charged toward the boy.

Dex eyed the approaching troops, measuring their competence, and their mounts. The archbishop really ought to have waited for them. He slipped off Spot and walked out to meet the charging horse.

"The Cold Valley." Dex said. "Fabrigel, Nati and Rya, get Rawn there. Pierre, Stevan, let's slow them down."

"Dex, what are you going to do on foot? What are you doing?" Pierre wheeled his horse to face the church troops.

"Loaned my horse out, guess I'll have to borrow another." Dex flashed a grin at Pierre over his shoulder, as he kept walking. "The archbishop's will do." The archbishop aimed his horse straight at Dex. He waited until the last moment, slipping into his center, and the charging horse seemed to slow. He stepped sideways to the horse's charge, and reached out for a foreleg. He grabbed the horse's lower leg and pulled as the horse's weight should have fallen on it, then jumped out of the way as the horse went down hard. The archbishop flew over the horse's head, rolled, stopped face down in the dirt and grass.

Dex followed the flip-and-skid, collected the horse's reins and gave the shaken animal room to stand.

"Get away from me, Hellspawn!"

Dex turned to find the archbishop climbing to his feet, ignoring Dex and his injuries to stare out over the thinning fog and the figure walking across it toward them, shrinking as it neared.

Dex dropped the horse's reins and walked out to meet Nevrille. Rawn swung off his horse and joined him. "Archbishop Harding, may I introduce the newest Elder God, Nevrille."

Nevrille frowned at that. "I suppose that is the

case, isn't it?"

"What happened to Roma?" Dex asked. "I didn't think even a god could kill a god."

"Nothing lives forever. Not even gods. When we die, our Fire becomes a part of the Fire of the world, part of all the new souls that come into being. Roma refused to die, and began collecting souls, trying to increase his power enough to avoid the inevitable. He has now returned his Fire to the world." Nevrille was man-sized now, although large. He turned the sword in his hands and glanced apologetically at Dex.

Dex grinned and nodded his understanding.

Nevrille nodded in return and turned to Rawn.

"Emperor Rawn, my sword, at your disposal, for the good of the people of the Empire."

The boy reached out wide-eyed and accepted it, his wrist trembling at the weight. He held it correctly at low guard and nodded solemnly.

Nevrille switched his attention back to the archbishop. "Your church has lost sight of its purpose. You are the conduit through which the gods serve the people, not an establishment that owns and rules people. You will sell three-fourths of all property, excepting only church grounds. You will heal as needed, not according to payment or political gain. You will not pressure people to take vows. You will release all unwilling priests from their vows. You will free all slaves. You will not over-charge for artifacts. Disobey me at your peril." He had faded all through the speech, and disappeared without waiting for a reply.

The last of the fog was torn apart by a fresh breeze from the ocean.

Rawn turned his back on the sight of downed trees, the rubble of avalanches, and the saltwater only now pouring back into the ocean. He looked up at the prelate. "Archbishop Harding, do you acknowledge me as Heir to the Empire, pending official notice of my father's death?"

The strong old man straightened, mopping the blood on his face. He faltered then, glancing about, but with no deity in sight he crossed his arms imperiously. "I must consult with Prinz Winstow, and of course, we must await news of the Emperor. Come with me, it's time you recall that as a child you are subject to your uncle's control."

Rawn shook his head slowly. "Not any more. Go back and inform my uncle that I forgive him his actions to date, but henceforth he is either my

Liegeman or my enemy."

For a moment, Dex thought the man might actually try to strike the boy. The archbishop's hands clenched, and his eyes kept jerking back to the place Nevrille had stood.

The Church troops had stopped a few lengths away from the archbishop, and half their attention was on the growing collection of armsmen behind them.

Dex looked back over the devastated landscape. "Good thing not many people live around here." There was smoke coming from the direction of the Residence, but it appeared to be thinning.

"Yeah. I'll send out search parties to check on the few who do." Rawn straightened his shoulders and switched hands on the sword. "And get a scabbard."

Dex chuckled, "Or hang it on the wall over your throne. Pity there weren't more people here to see that." He ran his eye over the small crowd of people who had fled this direction. "Well, no matter, you've got some of the world's worst gossips as witnesses and that's nearly as good. Shall we head back down and see what support the Bishop has raised?"

"Yes."

Rya handed Rawn the reins of his horse, and offered her own to Dex. "I think I'll walk. Or maybe ride double with someone going really slow. Spot seems to have wandered off." She blushed.

Pierre laughed, looking down the slope. "Hey Dex, your pony appears to have eloped with your Mudball."

Dex refused to dignify that with an answer, and boosted Rya up behind Fabrigel.

The puppies galloped out of the brush and pranced proudly around him.

"Good dogs!" He watched what might have been a swatch of cloth eroding away into the air as Lady Fang shook it. "Mighty hounds, dogs of the gods. You are definitely getting some nice treats tonight."

The archbishop had backed into the safety of his troops and was conferring with his Captain.

Captain Reddeer circled around them, followed by about half the armsmen staying at the Winter Residence. "The Bloods are choosing up sides, down below. Vizduq Golezan has raised a faction for Prinz Rondeze. They wish to capture the prinz and make Rondeze the Regent. Another group has formed up around Prinz Winstow, and some of the Graf contingent were pulling together and standing aloof from the rest."

Rawn sighed. "What was that about Cold Valley?"

"That was before the armsmen showed up." Pierre said.

"None-the-less," Fabrigel was watching the movement of all the groups on the mountain top, "whoever captures you wins the prize, so I expect the prize needs to stay at large." She looked at Rawn. "Your majesty, I recommend we make our way overland to Imperial City as quickly as possible."

Rawn paled a bit, then his lips firmed. "Good advice, Councilor. Let's go."

Chapter Twenty

The only other trail off the flat top was steep and winding. It had the advantage of being near, with no troops between them and it, and it also made fast pursuit impossible.

Fabrigel led, and Dex brought up the rear. Half the armsmen they sent back to the Residence to find their lords and gather provisions. They'd set up a tentative rendezvous point a week's ride to the north.

"Looking for an excuse to do something else weird?" Pierre grinned at him, "That trick with the horse was nasty. Could of hurt the horse."

Dex winced guiltily. "For a minute there, I thought I might have killed the archbishop."

Three men in pale blue came down after them. "Just a scouting team." Dex commented. At a particularly steep spot, he reached out and leaned a hand on the rock wall for a long moment. It collapsed behind him.

"Really, nothing but the greatest respect..."

"Shut up, Pierre."

***

Stevan watched curiously as Rya approached Dex. Dex had been sitting cross-legged and relaxed looking for several minutes. The full moon shone down through the trees, where they'd camped well off the trail in, not really a clearing, more of a thin spot.

"What are you doing, and will you teach me?"

Dex grinned without opening his eyes. "I'm trying to get Muddy to come this way. Just sit down and relax and listen to everything around you."

Then they just sat there.

"You'd think a demi god could conjure up dinner, wouldn't you?" Pierre muttered.

Pine needles crunched under hooves and Stevan stood up and fingered his sword.

"Damn it horse, the trail is over there!"

"Gaspif?" Stevan yelled, "We're over here." He trotted in the direction of the horse, and stopped dead at the sight of Gaspif on Muddy, who was decked out in full battle gear. Carter Ostlie, Fabrigel's groom, was riding a spectacular black mare in parade gear. A string of horses followed, all loaded with a miscellany of bundles. Spot was bringing up the rear, bags hanging on her saddle.

"There you go, Pierre," Dex sounded a bit smug, "Dinner."

Gaspif had apparently turned the panicked flight from the fire into a major looting expedition. He had all of Stevan and Dex's goods, a fair selection of Pierre's, Nati's, Fabrigel's and Rya's. And food. And grain for the horses. He even had a dripping sack that turned out to be eight roasted chickens, still warm from the oven and wrapped in Lady Pomfreit's fancy embroidered napkins.

They all helped unload the horses then settled down to devour the chicken.

"Muddy brought his harem home just as I was looking for a way to get all this stuff to you." Gaspif shrugged casually, but a great deal of smugness seeped through. "So I just saddled them all and headed out the least noticeable way. Damned horse kept trying to go in strange directions, and it finally occurred to me maybe there was a reason, so I stopped trying to steer."

"I was just trying to save the horses from the fire." Carter claimed. "And after all, most of them probably belong to the prinz." He bowed awkwardly.

"Grand Larceny and Horse Theft." Rawn grinned around a chicken bone. "Remind me to write you two out some pardons."

"Thank you, your majesty. We may need it."

Gaspif shook his head at the spread. "I should have thought of dishes."

"We'll buy anything else we need." Fabrigel said, digging through the two bags he'd handed her and pulling out a hefty bag. "I can't believe you thought to get all our money. Or maybe I can't believe you also packed clothes." She pulled out a leather folder. "You got *everything*."

Dex grabbed another piece of chicken. "You know, maybe you should write out some pardons, and then some appointments."

Rawn grinned. "As in appointing my cabinet? Do Prinzes have cabinets?"

"Emperors do." Gaspif nodded at Rawn. "That's what they were saying, that the emperor had died."

"I'm not actually sure," Rawn's mouth quivered for a second, then firmed. "The first messenger was just saying that Father wasn't expected to last more than a few days and that I should return immediately. Then a second messenger came, just a couple of hours later, but Uncle Winstow met him alone. He *said* father was still alive, but then why that meeting in the hall? They wanted me to, I dunno."

"Give them absolute control, forever." Dex split his chicken skin between the two dogs. "I don't suppose you have any nice meaty bones, do you?"

Gaspif shook his head.

"Anyway," Dex licked his fingers tidily. "I was thinking more along the lines of declaring us Defenders of the Realm. What do you need in the way of ministers? War, Finance?"

"Most of those positions need to be left in the hands of experts. They're practically all paperwork, anyway." Fabrigel said. "You need us to be your personal guard, councilors and hatchet men."

"Oh! Can I be a hatchet man?" Rya begged.

"Maybe after Dex has taught you a few things." Rawn grinned. "Until then, hmm, can you and Dex talk to each other? From way far apart?"

Dex scratched his chin thoughtfully. "Maybe. Probably not more than a couple of hundred miles, though." He glanced to the side suddenly, and nodded. "Good idea."

Rya was staring at thin air. "Was that a god?"

"Cruiz, a real young one." Dex glanced over at Rawn. "He said he'd carry messages and that a bunch of younger gods would probably be coming back now that Roma wasn't trying to eat them."

Rya gulped. "I thought everyone saw Nevrille."

"We did." Rawn looked around, "or at any rate,

I did." He glanced around, everyone was nodding. He raised an eyebrow at Dex.

"People are sensitive to soul stuff, some more than others. Anybody with a pulse could probably have seen Nevrille just then, and with all the Fire running around just now, all the younger gods will be easier to see." He glanced at the horses. "The Blight should be over now, or at least a lot less... See, I think at least one more of the Elder gods, probably Formia, may also be collecting souls. I'll umm, take a look when the road swings us closer to the bay."

Stevan poked at one of the cookstones Dex had made to reheat dinner on. "So, lots of babies, and baby animals and so forth, probably. Unless your Nevrille needs to beat up another of the Elder Gods?"

Rawn frowned, "Aren't there are still two Elder Gods? Well, apart from Nevrille? Formia and Graf. Are they both old and wobbly now too?"

"I don't know." Dex went all absentminded looking for a long minute. "There's no one around here, right now. If we get into the next younger god's territory tomorrow, I'll ask."

Rawn leaned forward and tapped Dex's box. "I think you are all now the Emperor's Own, Knights, and Defenders of the Realm. Let me get a list of everyone, and make that official."

Fabrigel got the all the armsmen's names and added Gaspif and Carter at Rawn's suggestion. "Quartermaster and Horsemaster," he pointed out. "But I'm not figuring out any other organization stuff until I figure out what I need."

Captain Garitch, Rya's man, cleared his throat, "We need to have a clear chain of command."

"Ah. Dex is in charge."

The three captains nodded appreciatively. Dex scratched his chin. "All right. You three captains will remain in charge of your current men, and we'll add people as we can. Pierre, you've got the most experience, so you are in charge of the irregulars. Nati, that means you can't hit him if he gets fresh."

"Can I hit him if he doesn't get fresh?"

"No. Commanders aren't supposed to get fresh with the troops. So, sire, you have four small troops. We'll trade off scouting, rearguard, night watch and caring for the extra horses. For now, everyone will take care of their own mount.

"Right now it is well past midnight, and we should sleep. Captain Reddeer, you have the watch."

Stevan settled down in the somewhat scant bedding they'd shared around. Dex had been the first of them to befriend the prinz, the first person to not write him off as a contender for the throne. No surprise he was Rawn's choice to lead. Even if he hadn't been a demi-god. Battles between gods. He'd gotten himself into a very strange place.

Chapter Twenty-one

Dex left off most of the fancy barding when he saddled Muddy in the morning.

Gaspif shrugged, "It was just sitting there. I couldn't resist."

"The first thing we need," Dex tightened the cinch, "is an immediate goal—someplace to head for. Rawn, who is the nearest noble that you trust? That you feel will be loyal to you?"

"Nearest?" Rawn wrinkled his nose. "Most of the Lords around here are old friends of Uncle Winstow's... but when it come to loyalty... Duq Fostell Tierald. It's kind of far though."

Stevan nodded. "His grandson Hoad seemed to be a quiet, responsible sort, didn't run with any of the obvious cliques."

"Better far than unsafe." Dex rubbed Muddy's forehead, and shook his head. "Idjit. Forget about the mares for awhile. Be a big mean warhorse. Mount of the gods."

Rya claimed Spot for her mount, and Dex wandered among the new horses and finally put Rawn on the black mare. The rest of them swapped horses around until they were all on sound mounts and spread their scanty goods among the other horses. Carter and Gaspif took charge of the pack string and Captain Whipp sent his men out as scouts. They stuck to the back trails, but were still able to make nearly fifty miles that day.

The riders were as tired as the horses, and Dex rubbed down the horses, smoothing their flows. The humans he helped slightly from a distance. They'd already been treating him too carefully, he didn't want to reinforce his appearance of being uncanny. Except...

"Rya?" She looked up cautiously from the remains of dinner. "Do you want to try some more meditations?"

She gulped, but nodded, putting her improvised wooden plate down for Lady Fang to finish off.

"I didn't *see* anything, last time."

"Hmm, I've been doing this so long I barely remember learning." Dex admitted. "Listen to the wind in the trees. Can you tell when it's whipping the high branches, and when it's rustling the low brush?"

"Sure, but, but that's just the wind."

"Yeah. Now try to picture those winds in your mind, as if they were a slightly foggy, a bit white, or even sparkly." He looked at her, so tiny and vulnerable looking "Mostly just relax. You have to relax to see and feel and taste the Elements."

***

The duchies of Roma continent were smaller than counties in sparsely populated Easterly, but as they stuck to the mountain trails, it took them six days to get to the border of Tierald. Dex led them to the other half of the armsmen, and so they were well supplied when they stopped at a tavern in a small village on the border, taking a private room for the girls and the rest of them sleeping in the common room.

Fabrigel chatted with the cook and the owner's daughter who served them ham and fresh greens for dinner.

"So the duq passed through?"

"Oh yes, he has this lovely, well I've never seen it, but everyone says, country place, but The Ridge is so steep that the best way to get to it is to go around, so he came through last week."

"Coming or going?" Fabrigel took a deep breath as the girl sliced into a hot pie. "That smells wonderful. Peaches?"

"Peaches. We grows 'em ourselves." The cook announced proudly. "The duquez, they was on the way up to t'country house, she had a piece and then had her man buy a bushel of fruit straight off the tree to take with them."

The girl scurried around with plates and silence fell as they gave it proper attention.

"I can see why. That was excellent, and only half because of the fruit. What do you... " They discussed pie crust and spices at some length, and in the morning they turned and followed the duq's trail.

They took the steep path slowly, and slept at the top of the ridge. The next day they found the Duq's country house midafternoon.

A bell's peal heralded their being sighted, and they were met by a force twice their size, the elderly Duq fuming at the head of it.

"I'll not be bothered by these disgraceful matters. You go back and tell Winstow that Ranold was quite clear, and he'll have to be content with being Regent for a few years. I'll not be a party to putting him on the throne in his own right, not even for the pleasure of squashing that... " the irate Duq's mouth dropped open as Rawn kneed his horse forward.

"My lord Duq, I, umm... " Rawn broke off as a huge smile spread over the Duq's face.

"Your Majesty." He swung off his horse with the agility of lifetime on horseback, and knelt. Looked up. "Hoad's letters have been full of how healthy you looked. I feared he exaggerated, but clearly not." He cleared his throat, "How may I serve you?"

"Get up, m'lord Duq, umm," Rawn looked around at Dex.

"For now we need to rest a bit, and catch up with news. What we do then will depend a lot on what other people are doing." Dex dropped to the ground. "Dexter Fiz Ambalia, sir, of his majesty's own. You seemed to assume that we were from Prinz Winstow? Has he communicated with you?"

"He has demanded that I join him on his march to Imperial City to prevent Prinz Rondeze from crowning himself." The duq spat on the ground.

"Did you send him your refusal?"

The duq's scowl deepened. "I decided to be absent, and give him no cause to attack my people." His eyes glowed. "Now. Now, knowing that you are safe, I can make some sort of coherent plans. You need to get to Imperial City before one of your Uncles gets himself crowned."

Dex nodded, abstractly. "How many troops are on the road, how dangerous will it be?"

"Hideously. Rondeze's people pulled out of the Winter residence quickly, and have been ambushing Winstow's people, who have been returning the favor. I've even heard rumors that none of them dare take to ship because of the number of ships lost. Some say Formia backs Vasik, and none others are safe on the water."

"But you didn't *actually* turn down Prinz Winstow?"

"What do you mean, young man?" the Duq sounded forbidding.

"That traveling along with the prinz's troops might be the safest thing to do." Dex eyed Rawn. Medium brown hair, getting a bit long and ragged. "Dye or bleach your hair. In fact, we'd all have to change our appearances... What do you think Duq? Are you willing to lie for your young Emperor."

The Duq was looking over the group and nodding thoughtfully. At Dex's question, his lips split into a predatory smile. "I'll take the greatest of pleasure in diddling the man."

Demi God

***

They settled in, in relief and started planning their next move. Which was mostly a matter of outfitting everyone in the duq's livery and hair cutting and dying.

"All we need is a huge dose of audacity." Pierre studied himself in his shaving mirror. "Nati won't tell me what she think I look like with a shaved head."

"Like someone no sensible person would want to meet in a dark alley, Pierre." Dex ran his hand over his own bristles. "Duq, it occurs to me that that wagon over there looks not unlike a Tinker's wagon. Could we borrow it?"

"I thought you wanted to be taken for ordinary armsmen?"

"We do, sir, but Fabrigel, Rya and Nati can't. It occurs to me to wonder, Duquez, if you might have some wigs?"

They made *marvelous* Tinkers.

Gaspif and Carter were naturals.

Spot was teamed up with another pony, a black gelding about her size, to pull the small wagon. Nati drove the wagon, Fabrigel, in a wispy grey wig and egg whites smeared on her skin to wrinkle it occasionally sat beside her. Rya demonstrated her flexibility by looping one leg up and hobbling on a crutch and begging.

Nati borrowed a lute from the Duquez, and practiced. Her attempt at a parody of chime dancing was actually *quite* voluptuous. Pierre loved it and threatened to carry her off physically if she tried to do it in public. Nati smiled. "Promise?"

"Damn right I promise. I *might* stop long enough to beat the crap out of anyone else who looks tempted to do the same."

On the men's side, they quickly gave up on Rawn looking like a soldier, and bleached his hair and made him one of the Duq's pages.

"You can be a squire as soon as you grow a bit." Dex assured the boy emperor.

"Thanks, Dex, appreciate it." Rawn grinned suddenly. "I never actually thought I'd have this much fun in my entire life."

***

The inland road passed through the Duq's seat. They found an envoy of Prinz Winstow's on the Duq's doorstep, waiting for their return.

"I got his message." Duq Fostell pinned the messenger with a glare. "I don't like it, but better Winstow than Rondeze. I've gathered up some people still owing me service, and I'll get the troops here on the road inside a week. Where's Winstow now?"

The envoy blinked. "He's had to leave the coast road—the fishing villages are barring their gates to him, for fear of their fleets being sunk. They are planning on reaching the inland road at Barioc."

"When?"

"They should be reaching it about now."

"Humph, well then, I'd best hustle my people. Tell Winstow I'll catch up with him by Cheero, or if he's resting and resupplying in Barioc, sooner."

It took the Duq only four days to organize his troops. He sent a quarter of his total levy ahead to scout for problems, two days ahead of his own departure. The supply wagons left the next day with another quarter, and the remainder followed on the fourth day.

"That was impressive." Dex muttered. "I can't believe he got a hundred horse and two hundred foot on the road so quickly."

"With supplies." Stevan pointed out.

Dex had assigned himself to the Duq's personal

guard, so as to be near the Duq's new page, and split the rest of them between the front and the rear file, nearest the various camp followers, and specifically the Tinker's wagon.

Chapter Twenty-two

Lieutenant Pierre "ed'Morn" was in command of a section of the second hundred foot. The worst of the bunch, they said. The criminals working off their sentences, and debtors working off their taxes. Whatever their other woes, relief from financial troubles revitalized them a bit. By and large it was a willing enough mob.

Captain Jennic, in command of the entire hundred, hadn't even tried for sword proficiency. After two days of drill, they were able to march with pikes without hurting themselves. They'd been shown how to set up a line and brace for a charge. How to form a turtle, locking shields to shed an arrow volley. He'd even gotten *longer* pikes for his center's front line.

Pierre's contingent was mostly native Tieraldians. Men in debt, or young men serving to pay their father's debts. Petty criminals. They were merchants, farmers, craftsmen, and a few retired sailors returned to home, or 'foreigners' living here now.

Their condition was poor, but they did not drag

too badly. Being fed regularly helped. They were, however, mostly ignorant of soldiering. But they were learning.

They would need to learn faster, Pierre grimly realized, looking at the sloppy formation.

"Ready for inspection, sir." The grizzed old Tieraldian Sergeant he'd been given looked more hopeful than confident.

Captain Jennic strode along, eyeing all the foot soldiers. "Lieutenant ed'Morn, turn and inspect your men. Do you see a problem?" It took a bit of doing, but Pierre finally got his men lined up in a useful pattern from which they could maneuver to either form a line and lock shields to brace against a charge, or form a turtle to protect against plunging arrow flights. Two days ago, he had started with great hopes of being able to rotate his flanks in or pivot. He sighed. Right now, marching with their newly supplied pikes and shields was challenge enough.

The other two platoons had addressed their problems as he worked with his. Captain Jennic rotated which platoon got inspected first, sharing out the criticism and, even occasionally, praise.

Pierre mounted his horse, a perk of office, and led his platoon out on the road.

The Tinkers were quite popular, in the evenings. Carter did trick riding, and taught Spot and the puppies tricks. Gaspif ran a poker game all night, the ancient crone Fabrigel told fortunes, and the little beggar girl didn't much bother people. The soft lute music in the background was rather pleasant. Speculation as to either the extreme beauty or extreme ugliness of the lute player was rampant.

The rest of the camp followers were mainly the families of the soldiers. Along the way they somehow added landless men with no place to live but on the road. And women.

With the addition of a few prostitutes, the advances the Tinker women had to fend off pretty much disappeared. Pierre hadn't actually had to kill anyone—having fortuitously been absent when Nati had to pull a knife on one drunken sot.

"Why did I *ever* want to be admired and pursued?" She had polished away the bit of blood on the knife tip as Carter steered the only slightly punctured drunk away.

"Because you hadn't met Pierre yet, nor realized how unattractive drunks are?" Fabrigel suggested.

"Humph. Men. Sometimes I think we've got the only decent young ones—and sometimes I wonder about Pierre."

***

Colonel Burkdoll rotated the cavalry units regularly, so that the dangers of the lead position were shared among all his mounted troops.

Dex and Stevan had been out with the forward position a bare hour when an arrow rattled across the pommel of his saddle, slapping his left wrist in passing. His instinctive jerk backwards brought Muddy to a halt.

Captain Zegar screamed as one hand went to his shoulder and the arrow imbedded in it. An experienced fighter, he also immediately put spur to mount. "Charge!" He led them straight ahead, getting up some speed, and then wheeled to the left, where the arrows had flown with the wind behind them to increase their range, but fortunately also decrease their accuracy. Either poor training, the gusty wind or a combination of both had minimized their initial injuries, and the captain's command had jarred the stunned column into action to make targeting harder.

Dex kicked Muddy into a gallop, and stirred up the wind. The next volley of arrows scattered and tumbled. Ahead, the captain turned left, and Dex reined Muddy off the track and charged up the brushy slope.

He drew his sword, and as men in blue jackets started coming out from behind the thicker clumps of brush, bows in hand, he leaned down to make a smaller target of himself and started twitching and mixing the flows locally.

The wind whipped up; he heard a curse and crash from his right, and then he was chopping down at a pale man who dodged too late. Two men came at him at once, with long spears. To his left a chestnut horse surged up and rammed one soldier. Dex had a brief glimpse of Stevan swinging at the man as his horse veered, then he had to concentrate on the spearman to his right. He knocked the point away, and heeled Muddy to swing his quarters away from the man's desperate lunge. Muddy jumped forward and Dex's sword scrapped along the spear shaft then snapped up and into the spearman's throat.

He reined Muddy back uphill, spotting Stevan as he ran Muddy over another spearman. Stevan's horse wasn't battle trained, and was frantically trying to escape the blood and screams. This was making the sword-wielding armored officer cautious in his attack, and he backed away altogether as he saw Dex coming.

The officer prepared rather obviously to deal with the horse first. He drew back to take a swing at Muddy's front leg, and Dex grabbed his pommel and leaned over and down to block it awkwardly. Both swords rapped the stallion's shin, and the battle trained horse pinned his ears and struck out with both front hooves in a pounce that nearly unseated Dex. He hauled himself back into the saddle, and, seeing no one else to fight, turned and headed for the sounds of battle. Stevan spurred his gelding after him, the panicked animal still white eyed and trying to bolt.

They came up on another pair of spearmen from the back, Dex chopped at the one on the left and Stevan attempted to do the same on the right, spooking his horse into a bucking fit that tumbled the spearman and then trampled him. There were bodies scattered about, most of them in blue jackets, and a few fleeing blue backs with mounted men in pursuit. Whoever had set up this ambush wasn't going to live long enough to regret it.

He scanned back down the hill. A few horses

were loose, but sticking with the herd. Captain Zegar was hunched over his saddle. Dex turned to Stevan, who had his horse turning in tight circles. "Stevan, if you can, get back to the road. Warn the main column that we've had an ambush, and to keep their eyes open."

As Stevan left, Dex trotted over to the captain. "I've sent back to the Duq that we've been ambushed. What else should I do before I take that arrow out of you?"

"Get us into a defensible situation." the captain spoke through gritted teeth. "Recall all pursuit."

"Yes sir." Dex backed Muddy off and surveyed the area for a quick head count. A group of four was returning from the pursuit, two men down... everyone was accounted for. He raised his voice, "Bring the wounded up to that hill." He pointed at a tiny knob that would have a slightly improved line of sight. "Sentries out."

One of the downed men was dead, the other had a bad head wound. Dex reached gently in to smooth the flow, and then deeper to stop bleeding and repair blood vessels. Then the arrow in the captain's shoulder. He moved the flesh gently out of the way of the barbs, numbing nerves and sealing leaking blood vessels behind, meshing the muscle fibers behind as he gently pulled the arrow out.

"Damn, boy, what are you doing with a sword in your hands?" The captain was still pale, and Dex bandaged his shoulder.

"Until this political mess is wrapped up, His Majesty need swords more than healers." Dex stepped back to recheck the other man. He was breathing better, and his color had improved. Dex combed the flows out straight again, then turned to watch the faster approach of the main column, all alert and ready for battle.

He busied himself; checked the downed enemies. For the most part they'd been archers, not well trained in sword work, nor well armored. Against mounted troops they hadn't fared well. He patched the survivors up well enough for questioning, but not enough to be dangerous. After ascertaining Prinz Rondeze's location two weeks ago when this group had last been in contact with the prinz's main Army, Duq Fostell released them on their personal oaths to return to their homes. Dex circulated among them again, fixing their injuries enough to get them home. Dex leaned in close to the officer Muddy had trampled. "Yes, I am a demi-god. Yes, Roma was slain in combat with one of the younger gods. Nevrille has become the newest of the Elder Gods. Tell Prinz Rondeze that it is time for him to make peace with his family."

The next day they reached Barioc and found Prinz Winstow still camped there.

Chapter Twenty-three

Stevan and Fowlie Petrove accompanied the Duq to dinner with the prinz.

"Damn it, Fostell, took you long enough to make up your mind." Prinz Winstow was in a foul mood.

The Duq snorted. "Tell me what happened to Crown Prinz Rawn."

Winstow narrowed his eyes. "Is that your problem? After his father holding out from indebting the boy to the Church all these years, the boy found himself a witch and got healed. Elder Gods know what sort of spells and charms the witch put on him. At any rate, the Church got nasty about it, there was a very confused battle over half the duchy and Rawn hasn't been seen since. I think the Church has him, the Church says the witch has him. Unless we find a body, we must conclude that he's alive, and under malign influence."

"Malign influence." The Duq crossed his arms. "What does this witch look like? Pretty girl, perhaps? Rawn's a bit young to run off with a woman, but... "

"No." Winstow made a chopping motion with

his hand. "A young man by the name of Dexter Fiz Ambalia. A heretic who fled the Church that educated him and raised him. He concealed his arcane skills, but now the Church realizes what power he has and has excommunicated him."

"Ah, couldn't force him to take vows, so they attacked him? The Church isn't to be trusted on these matters, and we both know it. Who is the archbishop backing in this mess? Rondeze?"

"Of course. The archbishop claims that Roma has chosen him." Winstow leaned his elbow on the table and fixed the Duq with a steady stare. "Do not believe the crazy rumors about an actual battle between gods. Roma is not dead."

The Duq jerked back at that. "Dead? There are rumors that Roma is dead? You should be shouting them from the rooftops. That would seriously undermine Rondeze."

"I'm having enough trouble with Formia and the sea side villages." Winstow's lips thinned with anger. "I don't need Roma pissed at me for spreading stupid rumors."

"Well, gods are not something any of us can control." The Duq made a throwing away gesture. "What are you planning? Who's backing whom?"

They got down to particulars, and as Stevan poured wine and fetched and carried, he made mental notes. As soon as they were done he wrote everything he could recall down in his diary, then joined the Duq, Rawn and the inner circle.

"I've got ten Duqs backing Rondeze, eight for Winstow, four for Vasik and two unknowns. You, of course, I've got in Rawn's column. Fabrigel? Your brother? And do you know Duq Larue of Leckman?"

"My brother will be for Rawn as soon as he knows he's alive, if he isn't already, and Larue is our neighbor and staunch friend. They'll be together."

"Three." Rawn looked grim. "That doesn't look good."

The Duq of Tierald leaned forward. "No, but the whole game hinges on how solid those allegiances are. Once you are known to be alive, healthy and with some backing, how many will abandon the other claimants. What else do you have there, boy?"

"Of the twenty-nine Marches on Graf Continent, I've got practically nothing. Little hints from how the sons and nephews seemed to lean. For better or worse, rather a lot of them were pushing Marque Inacig."

"Aunt Gualged's husband." Rawn nodded. "I suppose he may make a claim in his wife's and son's names."

"Is he on Roma?" Dex asked. "If not, he may not be able to get here to make a claim. Formia... who is Formia backing."

"Conte Mongote."

Dex looked up, relieved, as Nevrille formed up.

"She became material for an entire two years to bear a son with an admiral she'd taken a fancy to, and the admiral saw to it that he got preferment and a county on Easterly. Prinza Lamirand was a surprise bonus. The conte and the prinza are on their way to Imperial City, should dock within a week, with a small but very well armed fleet. Prinz Vasik is with them. I don't know who will prevail in that matchup."

Dex nodded. "All right."

"Umm, Dex, who are you talking too?" Stevan asked.

Rya elbowed him. "Nevrille, hush."

Nevrille smiled at her. "The archbishop is denying that Roma has died, and is still backing Rondeze. The Church is in an uproar, and is probably his weakest point." He faded.

"Formia and Graf?" Dex asked.

"Collecting souls."

The Duq was eyeing Dex uncertainly. Dex raised an enquiring eyebrow.

Stevan snickered. "They're referring to you as a witch and said you've been excommunicated."

"Oh, horrors!" Dex smiled at the Duq. "A Church without a God is rather lacking in authority. My mother was Saint Vythis, my father Nevrille, one of the oldest of the Younger Siblings. Roma was capturing and keeping souls, to stave off his own death. They fought, Roma lost. I'm not sure 'died' is quite the right word. The Fire of his life returned to the world as a whole, and will form new souls. He, and the other elder gods, were the cause of the womb blight. Are. Formia and Graf are both still collecting."

Firm fast footfalls preceded Hoad Tierald into the firelight. "Grandfather? You can't be actually supporting Winstow. I told you... Oh. My. Younger. Gods." He stood there staring at Rawn, then twitched his gaze around the group.

His grandfather chuckled. "Prinz Winstow is escorting us into Imperial City."

"... "

Rawn grinned at his expression. "It's too dangerous to try and sneak in, by ourselves, so we figured we'd sneak in by hiding inside Uncle Winstow's Army. Mind you, we haven't figured out how to separate ourselves later."

"I see." Hoad's eyes were brightening. "This is either insane or brilliant."

"The main problem will be staying far enough away from people who know us, as from your recognizing us, we're clearly not disguised enough." Dex looked around at the Unmannered Children. They really did look like themselves.

Hoad considered them. "I think it's the light. In broad daylight, with colors showing and all, I think it'd work."

"Who's with Prinz Winstow, from the residence?" Dex asked.

"Mostly the older set, his local friends. He grabbed most of the hostages, but a bunch had already taken off for their parents. His supporters' relatives he sent some off with messages, and kept the rest of us close." Hoad glanced at his grandfather. "He was uncertain of whether you'd join him, without Rawn, so he kept me and sent a message. The supporters of the other factions, the ones that he managed to grab, he's keeping tight hold of, in the Winter Residence."

"Did Golezan get away?" Stevan flipped through his diary, check alliances.

"Yes, that whole faction left early." Hoad narrowed his eyes in thought. "You know, your main problem is going to be the women recognizing you. Winstow's got a lot of them along, ones whose parents might be swayed. Then he's got Vizconte Durant, and Vizmarqs Orser and Vito from Graf."

"Do they go out on patrols, or is he keeping them close?" Dex asked.

"He's keeping us close," Hoad said.

The Duq looked up at that.

"Yes, he expects me back. There's just so little trust in his coalition. For that reason if no other I couldn't support him."

Dex nodded. "We should get you in the habit of coming and going, good old reliable Hoad. So you will have less trouble leaving when you *aren't* going to return."

***

Dex smiled to see Rawn enjoying himself, running errands to back up his page outfit. There were boys about his size and larger doing the same all over camp. No one gave him a second glance.

Except a bully from one of the other Duq's trains.

Some of the pages were getting tired of the early risings and long days and were taking it out on younger and smaller targets. Like Rawn. The boy hadn't started any sort of growth spurt, and the page in green and orange was just drawing back a fist to paste him when Dex spotted them. Rawn ducked the blow neatly, and nearly tripped the older boy with a nicely extended foot while he was off balance. Rawn turn to walk away and the older boy lunged and grabbed his shoulder.

"Coward! Don't you turn your back on me."

Rawn turned back shrugging off the hand, but before he could reply, Lord Lissle stepped in.

"Cease." He frowned at them. "Loui, the charge of cowardice is serious, and not to be thrown lightly." He switched his frown to Rawn. "None-the-less it had been thrown. Cowardice is something we don't want to see in a page. An older lord so accused would demand satisfaction at sword point. We do not allow pages to duel. However, a bout with practice swords should settle the matter." He shot a glance at his own men. One man turned away, and returned quickly with two wooden swords.

Dex gritted his teeth, wishing he'd had more time to teach the boy.

At least with his bleached hair hanging over his forehead, he wasn't very recognizable.

Duq Fostel pushed through the crowd, looking a little pale. "Just face him bravely, he can't really hurt you. Show them you can take it."

Rawn nodded, "Yes, m'lord."

Fostel hesitated, but the prinz reached out and took the sword in a competent grip.

Loui swung at Rawn, hitting him across the knuckles and knocking the sword from his grip.

"Hold!" Duq Fostel snapped. "Has your master taught you no manners?"

Lord Lissle flushed. "Clear a space."

Rawn's face was blank and unreadable as he flexed his hand then picked up the sword and stepped out to face the older boy.

Lissle glared between them. "When I say begin, you will begin. When I say stop you will stop. You will fight to three touches."

He stepped back. "Salute." Rawn snapped his sword up, Loui wagged his. "Begin."

Loui lunged from nearly out of reach—

definitely from out of Rawn's reach. Rawn intersected it neatly, deflecting it to his left as he stepped in, disengaged and cut across Loui's belly. He stepped back out, smooth and fast. Louis jumped back, then swung furiously but with no control. Rawn dodged and lunged, hitting Loui under the ribs and driving the air out of him with a whoop. He followed Loui's backward scuttle and tapped him on the throat with his rounded point.

"Stop." Lissle stared at the boy, then frowned at Fostel. "A relative of yours? Some one has taught him well."

"An orphan, sir." Fostel looked torn between boggling and pride. "His father was a friend, and asked me to take him."

"Indeed." Lissle frowned at the red faced Loui. "We'll soon have time for regular practice. Teach these youngsters some manners." He turned away and the crowd broke up, heading for the picket lines.

Dex gave Rawn a thumbs up and Fostel beamed at him. "Taking after your father. I wish he could have seen that."

Dex kept a closer eye on Rawn, after that, and Fostel's errands all seemed to keep him in camp for the last two days to the Imperial City.

Chapter Twenty-four

The Imperial Palace was surrounded.

Occupied by Prinz Rondeze and guarded against all comers.

And they were indeed coming.

Prinz Winstow's men in the City met them with maps, showing where Rondeze's Army had built strong points on the major roads, and where Mongote had landed and raised the flag for his wife and eldest son, with Vasik's co-operation and assistance in the form of ships, crews, troops and a Goddess.

Rondeze's move had caught the Imperial Guard in mourning, and mostly in their barracks. The prinz had wisely given them a route they could retreat through, and they had retreated with furious reluctance, and not at all as far as Prinz Rondeze had probably hoped. The Imperial Guards now occupied a significant wedge of the City and still held one gate in the outer wall of the Imperial complex.

Stevan had again accompanied the Duq, and on their return, they marked up maps of their own from memory.

"It's no wonder Rondeze couldn't spare more

men to keep us out of the City altogether." The Duq smoothed his hand over the southwest to western areas of the City. "And he's left most of these areas lightly manned. Prinz Winstow will be moving his main troops in tonight, so as to not give his brother time to shift troops and make us fight for every inch. Winstow hasn't yet decided how much of this arc to occupy."

Dex studied the run of the streets. "He probably doesn't want to make contact with either Mongote or the Imperial Guards. But the more he spreads out, the more troops Rondeze will have to commit. These streets here, and again over here look like they have obstructed lines of sight. Is that correct?"

Fabrigel and Rawn put their heads together, and agreed.

"Then, Duq perhaps you could suggest that a light screen of troops could put on a show of being many more troops in sight of Rondeze's men, and draw him to man those spots more heavily, while Prinz Winstow's main forces are better placed for an assault."

"And if we can get ourselves placed on the west, we'll be able to contact the Imperial Guard." The duq nodded. "I'll see if I can stage manage that."

"Vizduquez, Vizmarquez, Vizconteza may I recommend that you stay well back, until we see how much opposition we will be meeting tonight? I hate to send you out into this countryside or city with so little protection, but it may become necessary for you to contact the Imperial Guards and let them know that Emperor Rawn is here."

The young women nodded their understanding, and the Duq rose to return to Winstow with 'his Captain's' suggestions.

Dex studied the maps for a long moment. "In case of utter disaster, withdraw to the west, any of these three roads, at this town, turn north. We'll all try to meet there, tentatively to retreat to Fabrigel's duchy."

***

Prinz Rondeze's spies must have reported that Winstow was settling down for the night. Their late move was only lightly opposed. Archers retreated before them, trying to slow them, and in two places vastly outnumbered foot troops tried to delay them long enough for a heavy force to be brought against them. They were not delayed enough, and dawn found Prinz Winstow's troops occupying the crests of hills outward of Rondeze's strong points in an arc covering the west and southwest.

And the Tierald forces were on the left flank, west and a bit north of due west from the Imperial Palace.

Chapter Twenty-five

Stevan rode out alone to contact the Imperial Guard.

He felt both horribly vulnerable and hideously embarrassed. The people of the City were, by and large, trying to get on with life. Produce was still coming into the city, but everyone but Winstow had control of substantial grain stores. The citizens were a bit nervy about that, and a swordsman riding down the middle of the street with pink ribbons tied around his sword was drawing an awful lot of looks.

"All right, stop right there." The spokesman had men flanking him and spreading out to cover Stevan from all angles. He was large, ugly and very confident, in a very predatory way.

Stevan drew rein and displayed empty hands.

"Are you Rondeze's men or Imperial Guards?" Stevan managed a polite, neutral tone, eyeing the crossbows aimed at his midsection.

"Imperial Guards, and who might you be?"

"Vizconte Stevan Longbow of Merd County in Easterly. I need to speak to an officer of the Imperial Guard."

"You are Winstow's faction?"

"No sir, and anything further needs to be discussed in private, and with a high ranking officer."

"All right, hand over your sword, nicely."

Stevan unbuckled his sword belt and let the whole thing drop.

Two more Guards appeared with horses for the trio, and Stevan followed them.

The Guards had taken over a walled estate for their head quarters. Stevan dismounted when told to, and followed the officer inside. Into a large office, where the officer circled the desk and sat down.

"You caught me out making a surprise inspection. Now talk to me."

"I have a letter in my vest for a General Ren Ringaugh of the Imperial Guard."

"You've found him, hand it over."

Stevan pulled it out and handed it over.

The General frowned at the seal, broke it and glanced at the signature. His hands tightened. He read the whole thing over twice. Then he looked at the two crossbowmen. "Put those things down. Al, go get Dee and Fred." His attention switched back to Stevan. "In just a moment, I'll have you tell me all about it. Right now all I want to know is, is he all right?"

Stevan blinked a bit at the genuine concern in the General's eye, and possibly even a hint of moisture. "Sir, he appears to be having a great deal of fun."

'Dee and Fred' turned out to be two of the scariest looking men Stevan had ever seen. The man that accompanied them... looked a lot like Fabrigel.

"All right, as concisely as possible, tell us everything."

"I was the hostage for my father and Merd County. On the way I met a young man just leaving a church school, against the wishes of the abbot, and later the Bishop, both of whom felt Dex, Dexter Fiz Ambalia, should take vows. I invited Dex to join me, as I was rather thin on entourage. Dex was hiding that he is a demi-god. When he met Rawn, he healed him. Period. No controlling spells, no vows, no promises.

"The abbot talked to the archbishop who came to the Winter Residence. Believing him to be a saint, they again pressured Dex to take vows, and then threatened to denounce him as a witch and excommunicate him. Then the news of Emperor Ranold's extremely dire condition arrived, and shortly there-after another message which no one but Prinz

Winstow saw.

"The prinz, the archbishop and the abbot all combined to attempt to force Rawn into signing something about his possibly being under the influence of a witch or heretic, and extending the length of Winstow's Regency."

All four men didn't so much as twitch. Didn't change position or expression. But frozen in place, anger radiated from them.

"He did not sign. Dex led us all in cutting Rawn out of the middle of the group and retreating. That's when things got really eerie."

Stevan hunched. "This fire ran down the archbishop's arms and even the stone burned, it chased us, and Dex yelled for help from Nevrille, his father, one of the older of the younger siblings. The fire... withdrew a bit and we got to the stables and grabbed horses. That's when the gods both evinced? Is that the word? Anyhow they fought all up and down the mountains and we all rode off, trying to get out from under foot, and stay away from the Church troops.

"Nevrille slew Roma. The archbishop went all queer... and we decided that if Rawn was going to be free, we'd best start right then, and took off from there. We headed for Tierald Duchy, and after talking about the various possibilities with the Duq, we all disguised ourselves, and hid in Duq Fostell's troops." He touched his hair, "I'm a red head, naturally. Rawn bleached his hair, and played page."

"Page!" There was an edge of outrage there.

"He's too small to be a squire, and we really didn't want him out where he could get killed, anyway." Stevan failed to stop a grin. "Any how, he thinks it's a great adventure." He snuck a look at the fourth man. "Almost as much fun as Vizduquez Fabrigel is having dressed up as a Tinker."

"What!"

"I noticed a resemblance sir. She is quite safe, with female companions of good repute and her armsmen nearby."

The man sighed. "Yes, I'm her brother. Dare I ask about the women of good repute?"

"Vizconteza Nati ed'Treliff of Hastur and Vizmarquez Rya Amar of Karm March."

"Oh good. I was afraid it would be real Tinkers."

"No sir, no real Tinkers with us at all." Stevan cleared his throat. "In any case, sir, Duq Fostell is holding Winstow's left flank, and is nearest to you.

He would appreciate some co-ordination as his loyalties become clear to Winstow. He needs to get his son away from Winstow, and we need to shift that Tinker's wagon this direction as well.

He straightened self consciously. "Emperor Rawn and Duq Fostell invite your presence and however many representatives and experts you wish, at your convenience and, as I said, quietly, for some mutual strategizing."

General and Duq accompanied him on his return. The General practically fell off his horse, and actually hugged the Emperor, tears in his eyes. The Duq did fall off his horse laughing when the old hag Tinker asked him if he wanted his fortune told.

"Hoad isn't back, and the Duq is shifting his people this way." Pierre joined them. "He thinks he can disengage entirely before Winstow catches on."

"That would be best." The General said. "Now, I want to meet this Dex person."

"He is my friend, you will not take action against him. You may verbally argue about my associating with him." Rawn stared at the General, who looked a bit taken aback.

"Err, I've heard, in rumors and from Longbow here... "

"He's a demi-god. He healed me without demands, or even requests. He taught me how to ride and how to fight. He is currently attempting to get Vizduq Hoad away from Uncle Winstow, on my orders. I certainly owe Duq Fostell that much at a minimum."

The general nodded. "I beg your pardon, sire."

Rawn glanced at him quickly, and nodded. "I wish Dad could have seen me, one more time."

"He got plenty of reports. One of his last actions was to appoint Dexter Fiz Ambalia, Stevan Longbow and Pierre ed'Ambalia to the Emperor's Own. Based mainly on Captain Linsk's reports, which started out requesting permission to at a minimum evict your Dex, changed to cautious approval, then riotous endorsement, about the third time you ambushed him, if I recall correctly. His last report contained his witness of that confrontation with the archbishop and your Dex. Haven't heard from him since."

Rawn winced. "Me neither. Now I'm sorry I was so bad to him."

Stevan blinked in surprise. "I think I just figured out why you told me to tell the truth to the Guards."

Rawn nodded. "They've got the best spies in the business. Really, I had trouble getting away with *anything*." He grinned at the General. "How many eye witness accounts of the gods fighting do you have?"

"Several hundred, sire. Compiled by my people who have gotten away from Winstow."

A clatter of hooves and Duq Fostell rode up, trailed by Hoad and Dex. And a collection of other youngsters, male and female.

"You got all the hostages?" Rawn said.

"As many as wanted to come." Dex slid off Muddy awkwardly and Hoad looked like he couldn't decide whether or not to laugh.

Pierre spotted the stiff limp and started laughing. "Oh, don't tell me you've got an arrow up your arse?"

"In, Pierre, *not* up," Dex said firmly. "And barely at that, but we didn't have time to stop and take it out, and, well, I can't pull it myself. Volunteers?"

Pierre laughed even harder. "Mine! This pleasure is all mine!"

"Sadist."

"Bend over, don't look ladies, it not a sight for

the weak of stomach, and that was *before* he got stuck."

"Owww!"

"Here, souvenir."

"Thank you, Cuz. I will cherish it." Dex looked apologetically then at Rawn. "Err, sorry sire."

"Well, you got Hoad out, and didn't get killed, so I'll forgive you for not following the royal command to not do anything silly," Rawn grinned. "I give you my royal permission to eat standing up. Was there much trouble? Hoad, are you all right?"

"Fine. These wild winds blew the arrows all over the place." He slid a look at Dex. "Can't imagine why."

"Yeah, I warned you about those beans, Cuz."

Fabrigel's brother leaned over and whispered something to her. She giggled and shook her head. "Don't worry, his heart belongs to Nati."

The general cleared his throat. "Dexter Fiz Ambalia, I presume."

"Yes, sir. General Ringaugh?"

"Yes." The general studied the demi-god carefully. Tall, with the just-starting-the-teenage-growth-spurt lankiness that even a shaved head and eyebrows couldn't make look older. "How old are you?"

"Twenty-seven. Demi-gods are hideously slow growing."

Nati leaned forward, "Really? You are older than Pierre?"

"Yep."

Pierre smirked. "Told you."

"I apologize for doubting you."

"If you two could stop that, we need to maneuver the Duq's people rather soon," Dex said. "He's well aware that about three-fourths of his hostages have escaped, hence our introduction to the wrong end of an archery barrage."

Fostell nodded. "I assumed Vizconte Stevan would find you, so we're retreating in your direction. Where is a good place to face him?"

They bent over the map, Dex a bit cautiously, but Stevan noticed the paucity of blood about his nether regions, and suspected he was nearly healed.

Hills and intersections and buildings were discussed, and the size and makeup of the Duq's forces, and repositioning of the Imperial Guards.

Pierre took a sheaf of orders and mounted up. He'd deliver the orders and stay with his own foot soldiers while they backed away from Winstow's troops.

Fabrigel's brother had taken physical possession of some City property he owned, "Remember Leton Place? I evicted Cousin Baso and his hideous family on the pretext that they needed to be somewhere safe. Mother and Jesia will probably kill me. It backs up on the estate the Imperial Guards are using as their headquarters. Why don't you move all of your young friends there, and these youngsters as well."

***

Pierre halted his retreating platoon at the high point of the narrow street. They'd caught up with the wagons, and this was the best place to avoid being flanked, if pursuit was close.

"All right, perfect time for a bit of practice. Let's set up for battle. Mind, we're hoping they are far enough behind that we can retreat to the next hill, and then the next." He explained himself to his sergeant, keeping his voice loud enough that all the men could hear. He might as well let them all in on the Great Secrets of Warcraft.

Ha! What a joke.

"Any attacking force will have to charge up the long grade. This will tire them out and slow them. If I had some damned archers, they'd be losing men all the fucking way up the slope, tripping them, messing up their formation. But the main reason I'd pick this spot is that shit ass deep creek to the east and the wool warehouses to the west. Those two barriers mean that to go around us will take them at least a mile out of their way, either direction. With ordinary square city blocks, a quarter mile detour and they'd be running up our fucking backs. Hopefully Prinz Winstow will realize that expending troops in our direction doesn't further his goals and he won't pursue once he sees a fucking organized retreat that is ready to fight back.

"But, being prepared for the worst is more fucking fun than all this damned marching, so let's stop here and set up while we wait to see if they are going to pursue.

"If the fuckers tried a mounted charge, I'd meet it with the long pikes." He turned to the troops. "Men, lay out the pikes!"

They shuffled a bit and a few of them dropped their points forward and laid the pikes down. He dismounted, handed to reins to young Denny, and stepped in among the men. He drilled the whole first rank, having them brace the butts of the pikes and lift the points on command. Then he made the second and third ranks practice thrusting. "Any horse that gets past the front line will be slow, aim for the rider. Any riders that are down and still fighting, make them keep their distance with a pike. Work in pairs Or three or four, this is war not some fucking fair duel with a bunch of damned rules."

He let the center rest and maybe even think about their pike work, while he worked on his flankers showing them how to stab down at attackers, and how to move in and out of position. "You and your mates will get injured. You will need to retire to bind a wound, to stop bleeding, to replace a lost or broken weapon. The reserves need to be able to step right in. You will get cross-eyed fucking *tired*, and the fucking reserves need to rotate smoothly in to replace you, so you can rest your precious bodies. Drink. Eat. A battle doesn't fucking stop for regular meals, and damn few are short enough that it doesn't matter."

One bright one called out, "Sir, does that mean we take breaks to piss?"

"Piss on them. You have my permission.

Consider it a fucking order."

That cheered them up.

But when the laughing died down, he could hear the ring of horseshoes on stone. Lots of them.

"Damn. Listen up troops! We've got some visitors from Prinz Winstow come calling." He eyed the ranks and picked out a youngster.

"Denny, isn't it? You've just been promoted to messenger. I have an urgent message for Duq Fostell. Repeat that."

"I have an urgent message for Duq Fostell."

"There are mounted troops approaching on the Cockscomb road."

The boy swallowed as his eye widened. "There are mounted troops approaching on the Cockscomb road?"

"We will hold them at the ridge before Kestle street."

The faint choking noise was Corporal Hanski, his right flank man.

Pierre kept his attention on the boy. "Private, repeat the whole thing."

"I have an urgent massage for Duq Fostell. There are mounted troops approaching on the Cockscomb road. We will hold them at the ridge before Kestle street."

"Good. Now, mount up. Any one tries to stop you, ride over them. The important thing is to get reinforcements out here as soon as possible.

Pierre boosted the boy aboard his horse himself, and was relieved that he gathered up the reins competently and left promptly.

He turned to his corporals. "Now, are the men ready?"

"Yes, sir, but knights? We'll be slaughtered!"

"No. We won't. Prinz Winstow only has light cav, he doesn't have those fucking big heavy horses and plate mail."

He looked over the situation and nodded in satisfaction. "Do it just like we practiced, Corporal Micio, get your men into position and lay out the pikes. Demia, get your men into position, but pull back your reserves a bit. Hanski likewise."

He quickly put the reserves to work levering a couple of large barrels that could be rolled up the slope into position and wedged.

Then Winstow's knights topped the next little hill. The double line of horses was already at the gallop, lances high. Six wide they filled the street. He judged the length of those lances and nodded in satisfaction.

He stepped confidently in among the center troops. "Take a couple of deep breaths. Relax. Now. Brace the butt of your pikes. C'mon, look down and check. Good. Now put your hands where you always do, and lift the points. Other hand on your shield, tilt it to push the lances up... "

He had the timing just right.

Six horses hit eight pikes. Horses screamed, men shouted. One horse shoved between pike men. A man in the second line lunged forward, his pike not hitting hard, but interfering with the swing of the rider's sword. Pierre stepped close and stabbed up under the ribs of the rider. He jerked his sword free. "Second line pikes, thrust!" It was ragged as all hell, but it was aimed in the right direction, and the second line of horses retreated, taking their wounded with them.

The man Pierre had killed was the only one that had made it through. The men of his front line were looking shaken, but a bit of astonished pride was starting to show through. The injuries looked to be limited to bruises.

"Damn fine job."

The failure of the first charge to run over them

seemed to have heartened the men and slowed the enemy. *They have no idea how few of us are up here.* He tried to look confident and cool.

He had his center inspect their pikes, and in some cases swap to abandoned cavalry lances. They laid them out, and as time dragged on, he rotated them out for water and stretch breaks. He sent scouts back to watch for any flanking movement.

"Sir, movement behind. Reinforcements."

He turned and looked. It was a damned thin column of horse coming.

"Sir! Archers!"

"Shields up, lads, get ready to turtle!" Thank the younger siblings he had drilled them on that one.

The ranks of archers were moving across the road, and getting deep. It was going to rain arrows, but by the way the archers were blocking the road, there wouldn't be an immediate charge behind it. He trotted forward, to be with the center.

"Front, keep your shield tilted and on the ground, second rank, scoot up and get cozy, cover the front line over head, third rank, cover anything they leave hanging out, you lads don't want to have to explain anything to their wives." Not much of a laugh, but a hair of relaxation. He joined Corporal

Misio behind them all, shields raised and the whisper of arrows filled the air. They hit the shields hard, rattling and crashing. There were several screams, but the turtle held.

"Stay all tucked up lads. Let me get shot sticking my nose out." He took a very quick look. Then looked longer. "All right, the archers are retreating. What are they going to try next?"

Next was a white parley flag.

"Prinz Winstow would like to speak to Duq Fostell." The flag bearer bellowed.

"We will so inform him." Pierre yelled back.

Hoad was leading the knights, and sent a messenger. The messenger returned, handing Hoad a note.

He stepped out to where he could be seen. "My father will come and speak to the prinz. Where is he?"

"I'm here," the prinz stepped around a corner. "Where is that traitorous father of yours?"

Hoad looked back to where five horses pushed through the knights.

Duq Fostell, Prinz Rawn and General Ringaugh pulled up beside him.

"Uncle Winstow, did you receive my message

that from henceforth you were either my liegeman, or my enemy? It is time for you to choose."

"Rawn, I am your regent, and I need to remove you from the influence of malign... "

"No, Uncle Winstow. You will never be my regent. Choose, Prinz."

Winstow stood silent for a long moment. Then he bowed his head, and bent his knee.

"Thank you Uncle. You and your men are pardoned of all treasonous actions taken against me. You and your troops will remain where they are, until further notice."

"Yes, Sire."

Chapter Twenty-six

Fabrigel looked around the big house and shook her head. *All of us ladies and gentlemen, and perhaps half the women managed to cling to a maid or companion.* "Maybe two women old enough to count as chaperones. Mother would have fits."

Nati snickered. "Pierre and I discussed the matter. We decided we'd get married as soon as we could find a priest. That will save you one bed, right there."

Fabrigel nodded. "Then you and I will share the master's quarters for now. I'll move in with Rya later. Everyone's going to have to double up, and do for themselves."

Nati smirked. "Can I watch when you ask if one of them can take over the cooking?"

Fabrigel grinned. "So you can imagine what Pierre would say? I'm glad he's going to be here, not staying with his soldiers. He can be a civilizing influence on the fellows. I'm shoving all of them up in the third floor. The women will have the first and second. Thank goodness the Imperials have drafted all the armsmen."

"Gaspif and Carter have taken over the stable. The Imperials took most of the horses, just as well since you've just got six stalls. Carter grabbed Muddy, Dancer, Pierre's two horses, and two others. Spot is out in the Garden."

Fabrigel nodded. "They managed to lose Stevan's horse. Dex said he was a liability in a fight, and I think he suggested which ones to keep."

"A demi-god. He looks so young... "

"Yeah, all the stories have them about eight feet tall and bulging with muscle."

Nati nodded. "You never think about how they grew up, or the possibility of them having trouble with the Church."

Fabrigel paused for a second. "We're all going to wind up in the history books, aren't we?"

"With battles between gods? We're going to be in history books, tales, ballads and myths."

***

General Ringaugh was cautious about admitting potential traitors into his elite troops. So it was mainly the Unmannered Children and their armsmen who were added to the Imperial Guard's patrols of 'their' territory.

Dex was a bit alarmed to find himself a lieutenant, running one of the patrols deployed under the watchful eyes of Captain Dee. The equally alarmed patrol seemed rather grateful for his admission of limited experience, especially involving coordinated horse maneuvers, and their patrols quickly turned into mobile training sessions. They were doing a fancy advance, the horses facing diagonally across the street, and trotting half sideways to advance straight down the street with swords out and forward when the little man rounded the corner and jolted to a stop at the sight of them.

Dex recognized him immediately. A couple thousand miles of walking hadn't made Father Hariban's clothes noticeably more ragged.

"Halt!" He straightened Muddy and dismounted. "Father Hariban! Following your chick home?"

"Ha! More like I was dragged along with most of the churchmen when the archbishop decided to head for Imperial City. Where's Prinz Rawn? I see you've found the Imperial Guard."

"And Rawn is not so much under their wing as having taken command. May I offer you a ride... "

"Certainly not on that brute. That nice little pony was almost more than I could deal with. I'll walk, thank you."

"The Guards hold the northwest gate to the Imperial grounds. If you are familiar with the city? Yes? Head for it, I suspect you'll be intercepted before you get there. I'll ask after you when I'm off patrol, in case they've tossed you in jail."

Hariban snorted. "Unfortunately, I think I appreciate that. No doubt I will see you later, Dex." He walked with a wary and untrusting eye between horses and kept going.

Dex's sergeant gave him a questioning look. "Father Hariban is a long time friend of the prinz. Rawn will be very pleased to see him. And you never know, it may come in handy to have a churchman of our own around to do the coronation ceremony."

The sergeant muttered something about that being the job of the archbishop.

Dex nodded. "The last time I saw the archbishop... he appeared to be quite deranged. I think we'll find ourselves with a new one real soon."

More than one dubious look was cast after the scarecrow figure, but Dex didn't explain further. "Now, what was that you were saying about two ways to do this diagonal advance?"

"Yes sir. It's a bit subtle, but if the horses are bent slightly toward the front, they're balanced and ready to turn forward and charge. If they're bent slightly to the side, they're balanced to turn back and retreat."

"Bent?'

"Their spines, from crown to tail, just every so slightly. That's why fighting from horseback is called an Art, not just riding."

Muddy didn't have any trouble with it, once Dex figured out how to tell him properly. He figured in a few years it would all become automatic. But he suspected that right now he'd forget it all as soon as the fight started.

When they got back to Imperial Headquarters, Dex found Hariban sitting stubbornly in the front hallway and refusing to leave.

Dex shook his head at the watchful guard, who looked about ready to lay hands on the Churchman. "You didn't tell the prinz he was here, did you?"

The man looked indignant. "The Church is backing Rondeze!"

"And Father Hariban is a long time supporter of Prinz Rawn." Dex nabbed a private and sent him off with a message. They heard the prinz's whoop from the hall, and the boy galloped in to hug the ragged priest and drag him away.

General Ringaugh shook his head. "And I thought I'd gotten used to irregular attendants."

Dex grinned. "A word of warning. Father Hariban is an odd sort of saint. It is very difficult to lie in his presence. You'll need to be a bit forgiving if diplomatic speech slips a bit when he's around."

"A saint?" Ringaugh shook his head and walked away.

Pierre found Father Hariban's effect particularly amusing. His own speech was unchanged, having always been brutally honest, but he might have been quieter than usual, listening to others sputtering indignantly as they found themselves saying not quite what they'd intended.

Stevan and Fabrigel appeared to be taking mental notes. Dex had warned them, but they seemed to consider the Father's effect a useful tool, rather than something they needed to be wary of. *We're all honestly behind Rawn, and never did see any reason to be particularly diplomatic when speaking to him.*

He frowned a bit, thinking about it. Somehow he'd slipped from escaping from the Church School and seeing the world, to a highly placed backer of the heir to the Imperium. And he hadn't even noticed himself changing. *Just like I never seemed to need to think about backing Rawn. It just sort of felt right.*

***

Fabrigel led Father Hariban around the central area where most of Rawn's backers were beginning to gather. It was an excellent opportunity to rate their degree of waffling.

Father Hariban eyed her disapprovingly. "I'm beginning to think you inherited your father's political sense."

"I certainly hope so. Rawn and General Ringaugh need to know how dependable their allies are."

"I'm afraid I tend to think in smaller terms. What does this very unlady-like behavior do to your soul?"

"I doubt that using my brains in support of the best candidate for the throne will harm my soul. It may damage my marriage prospects, but that a whole different problem, and not one that concerns me— since any man who considers either stupidity, timidity or a lack of loyalty and patriotism desirable in a wife is no one I wish to marry."

"Humph. Women. I fail entirely to understand them."

She eyed him thoughtfully. "Do you understand that Pierre, for instance, is harming his position with his family by backing the prinz? Do you understand his loyalty?"

He eyed her. "Are you saying it's the same thing?"

"It's certainly close. If you stopped thinking of women as some strange species, and judged us as you would men who weren't terribly useful in battle, nor trained for it, and raised to be well mannered and prissy about their clothing, but otherwise normal, I think you'd understand us quite well."

"Prissy about their clothing?" He snorted. "All right, I suppose I must make that effort. I swear half my training in seminary was how to scold girl students for being forward, and praise boy students for being forward."

Fabrigel took a deep breath and plunged in. "I expect you learned a great deal more."

"Yes. Odd, how exaggerating is so difficult. Do you know I never thought about everyone always telling the truth around me. Or why I couldn't seem to control my tongue. Your Dex took one look at me and said I was a saint. Me! But Dex... Since you've been so happy to use me, perhaps I should return the favor. I was disturbed by the archbishop's accusation that Dex actually stole from the abbot, forged a letter... I see you know all about it."

Fabrigel bit her lip... honesty was going to be awkward. "That was a group effort. Dex was the only one of us who wasn't in on it. I, umm, I did the actual forgery."

"The seal?"

"Stevan carved one out of wood."

"And who performed the actual theft?"

"I would rather not say." And that was the literal truth.

Hariban stopped dead. "Rawn stole... *Rawn?*"

She met his eyes. "The Church, through their life long attempts to own him and control him, have seriously warped his perception of the Church. Or perhaps they have given him a starkly honest one. I suspect you are the only reason he isn't an out-and-out heretic." She cleared her throat. "Of course, Nevrille was enough to make anyone a believer. But not give them a better opinion of the Church."

Hariban sighed. "The archbishop has much to answer for. If you will excuse me, I think I need to back track to that little church we passed, and do some praying. And thinking."

"Are you reporting to the archbishop?"

"No. Although no doubt he'd think I should, had he even bothered to actually notice me." He turned to walk away.

"I think that you are trying hard to think about anything except Gods at war with each other. Killing each other. And an insane Archbishop."

Hariban stopped.

"Where were you, when the Gods fought?"

"I was walking up from the south... I didn't see all of it, but I made it to that mountain in time to see the end. To see what happens to a God's Fire when he dies. To see a newly elevated older God give his support to Rawn, and an Archbishop deny it all."

"You have to think about it. Your church has become corrupt, and no surprise if the Gods themselves are corrupt."

"They were human once... and in the face of the Final Death, they reacted as men, and women, do. They are not all corrupt. That I will not accept." He glanced at her once, then walked away.

Fabrigel turned a different way. She'd meet Stevan, write down all her observations... She stopped and watched clouds racing across the sky, and building into dark thunderheads to the east.

Too fast to be natural. Are the Gods up to something?

Movement caught her eye. A man down a side street. She spotted the short red hair and trotted down the alley to catch up. "Stevan?"

The red head turned and she jerked herself to a halt. "Umm, sorry, I mistook you for someone else."

Something about the man...

Oh. The lumpiness.

She backed up, and cast a glance behind her. The right redhead was down the street. She signaled a silent 'get Dex' and slowed her retreat.

"Who are you?" she asked.

"Shouldn't I be the one asking questions?" the god-or-whatever looked like a man. A bit oversized, lumpy, and there was something odd about how he moved. Fabrigel was reminded of gods' mounts charging over cloud tops as if on snow fields. Who ever this was simply walked, and minor irregularities, high or low... didn't exist for him.

"Graf, perhaps?" Fabrigel really, really, hoped

she was wrong. She stopped trying to back up as the god circled her, rather like a shark giving its next meal a good looking over.

"Why, yes. Not the god you worship, eh?"

"Well, with Roma dead things are a bit confused. Are you going to move up here? Have you had a chat with the archbishop?"

"I'm looking the situation over, and the archbishop seems to have lost touch with reality. And who are you backing for Emperor, and what god does he answer to?"

Quick footsteps from the rear. "Emperor Rawn does not 'answer to' a god, but he has the backing of Nevrille." Dex, thank... something.

The god looked over her head then, and she dared a quick look. Stevan and Dex, others, staying back, sensibly cautious.

Or not. Rya came at the run, stopping suddenly and looking around. Fabrigel wondered how many other gods were present.

"And my granddaughter. Are you also one of Rawn's advocates?"

Rya gulped. "Yes."

The god's eye shifted to Dex. "This Nevrille is quite strong. Does he think he can beat me?"

Dex studied the god. "Does he need to? You have collected some souls, but not the number Roma had accrued. Are you less corrupt as well?"

"I should certainly hope so!"

"And Formia?"

"She has... " The god broke off and paced. "I know it is wrong. But they were getting so powerful, I was beginning to fear them myself. I know I shouldn't have... " his hand went to a series of lumps running down his arm.

"Will you help us fight her?" Dex kept glancing at the sky in a way that made her very uneasy.

"You and all these *children*?" The god made dismissive wave at the empty looking street.

"And Nevrille. Yes."

The god stared at him, stared beyond him to the young prinz. Then he slowly nodded. "Yes." He faded from sight.

Chapter Twenty-seven

Fabrigel retreated all the way to Stevan and Dex. Dex was nodding at thin air.

Stevan hugged her. "Negotiating with gods? Now I'm *really* impressed."

Rya hugged her from the other side. "What's he doing calling himself my grandfather, anyway?"

"Guys, I think we need to get somewhere, where we can see what is happening." Dex threw another look eastward.

Stevan nodded. "If the gods are going to mix it up, is this a good or a bad time for us to attack?"

Fabrigel shrugged. "They are still saying that they crowned Prinz Rondeze. If we could take the Imperial Palace, our claim that their god—who didn't show up for the fight—is dead, will invalidate their coronation, and we'll be in position to crown Rawn."

"And," Rawn added, "they've still got all of Father's old cabinet locked up, and all the city dignitaries on hand for a new coronation."

General Ringaugh nodded. "I'll detail a substantial guard for you sire, and we'll..." he broke off as the emperor shook his head.

"Did you know there's a tunnel between the Main Palace and the House of Arches?" Ran grinned, "Yeah, I know, Royal Prinzes aren't supposed to be poking about in basements looking for old secret passages he read about in his ancestor's diaries."

Dex grinned. "General? What do the maids wear in the Palace? We just happen to have three scouts who could never be mistaken for soldiers."

***

The black clouds to the east were forming up into a solid wall of darkness. It bulged and writhed, buffeted by a constant wind from the west.

Fabrigel gulped. Was it her imagination that made that part of the cloud wall look like a woman?

"Roma is dead. Your rites are without power." The strong soprano rolled over the city. "Mongote will be Emperor."

A flickering wavering fog rose from the ground. "Rawn will rule."

Stevan grabbed her and pulled her away from the vantage point. "We need to get to the House of Arches while everyone is watching the gods."

They rode through a maze of streets to the

north-west gate of the Imperial Palace grounds. The gate was closed, but in the hands of the Imperial Guards. Holes in the wall marked the new egress from the outside.

General Ringaugh didn't even dismount. Two officers jogged up to him and they spoke briefly. Then Ringaugh led them further around the grounds to a spot where the bare wall was still in sight of the north-west gate, but still out of sight of the next gate. They dismounted a block away, and ladders were brought out from several buildings.

"Looks like they've been planning this for some time." Fabrigel murmured.

Stevan nodded, chewing his fingernails as the ladders went up and the Imperial guards swarmed silently upwards.

Rawn bounced on his toes. "This is the only chance I'll ever get for real combat, and I can't make up my mind whether I want it to come to that or not."

Dex chuckled. "Not. I hope. All right. Our turn. Pierre, Stevan, Frabrigel, Nati, Rawn, Me, Rya."

Rawn didn't even complain about being stuck back with the girls. They were all fit enough to climb the thirty foot ladder, and then climb down another on the far side. They ghosted from shrubbery to shrubbery, behind the backs of the troops watching the north-west gate. The House of Arches was a graceful beauty, just full of shadows to hide them while they got a window open and crept across the dark house to the stairs down to the basement. Several of them had very dim glow stones, and Rawn led them quickly to the old wooden chest that, once emptied of musty blankets, had a false bottom that gave onto steep steps downward. The arched stone passage had obviously been built for the passage of people. It led in a gentle arc to a similar arrangement in the basement of the Palace.

Ringaugh growled. "Damned lecherous emperors. I wonder how long this has been here?"

"Great grandfather's diary said he found mention of it in Freck the Elder's writings."

"So four hundred years." Ringaugh handed down a box that jingled as its contents shifted.

"Some old harness bells and stuff. I looked."

Then more cloth and then they were all climbing up into another basement.

Chapter Twenty-eight

Dex tore his eyes away from the epic battles and down to the people watching from the lower level. He leaned toward Ringaugh. "How many of the important people are right here?"

The general pulled his gaze away from the battle outside and studied the crowd. A wicked smiled crossed his face. "All of them."

Dex taped Fabrigel's shoulder. "Do you know this pile well enough to find most of the servants? Go, tell them Rawn is here, and he wishes all the exits from the formal entry closed and blocked as quietly and quickly as possible."

The girls slipped back the way they'd come. In their pilfered servants' dresses, they probably wouldn't attract too much notice... Dex signaled four armsmen. "Keep back, but guard them. And watch for guards inside, try to keep any alarm from being raised."

Ringaugh cocked an eye over the balcony rail, then turned to Dex. "If we can capture or kill Rondeze, we've won. If he's smart and heads out the door to rally the troops he's got all over, he can turn this into a civil war that lasts for decades."

Dex looked back out the windows, where sheet lightning lit the cloud forms of gods.

"Hard to say. I think everyone can see that Roma hasn't shown up for the fight." He winced as the lightning twisted and slashed. *Gods can be killed.*

***

Formia wasn't taking a chance with the vulnerabilities of a solid body. She was the ocean, and she battered at him as her people fled the waterfront for higher ground.

Nevrille used a mix of air and earth against her. Tornadoes danced across the ruins of the harbor, whipping water and a few hoarded souls away, but unable to inflict any real harm. Solids picked up by the tornadoes punched holes in the waves as they rose up and claimed another block of houses. The people had fled before the invaders arrived. Mostly. A few stubborn souls died as their homes collapsed under the pressure of the waves.

The younger gods were darting about, snatching those souls away from the Elder, occasionally turning the lightning back against her, then retreating hastily as she struck back. And every time she turned her attention away from Nevrille, his tornadoes advanced, pushing the sea back, tearing it apart. Her voice snarled on the wind.

"You are too young to harm me. Too inexperienced."

"What do you protect, so deep and carefully in the depths of your wave? A soul you value? Your Admiral, perhaps? Why do you deny him rebirth? You suck away his soul's fire and bring him to the brink of the true death. Will you kill him, mistaking possession for love? And what of your son? You risk him for misguided political ambition."

"Misguided? Our son should be Emperor, see how he glows!"

"All you taught him was ambition. A demi-god needs more. He needs to understand the elements, to be able to manipulate them. Your attempts to make him a ruler only made him weaker."

"He is not weak! Ah. That touch I felt. That was your son. I'll deal with him once I've dealt with you."

"You felt his touch. Can your child reach so far? I don't feel him, have you taught him to reach out with his mind? Can he manipulate Earth? Wind?

Water? Fire?"

"He is not a clever monkey, doing tricks for the Church. Show me your son's Fire."

***

Ringaugh waited with the patience and focus of a snake.

Dex tried to copy his immobility and failed. He withdrew several times to stand in the shadows at the back of the balcony. No one below could see him, but his view out the high windows was unobstructed. A standing wave of water stood above the lower city, wind holding it back, keeping it from crashing down. The fight between the human-like forms of Roma and Nevrille had been so much easier to understand...

Ringaugh moved as shouts rose from below. The Imperial troops formed up on him, charging down the stairs. Ringaugh had ordered the irregulars to remain on the balcony with the Emperor and his close guard. Dex hung over the rail, Rawn beside him, watching the Imperial's chew their way through the assembled officers and sycophants.

"There! That's Rondeze! He's going to get away!" Rawn jumped up and down with frustration.

"Dex? Is there anything you can do?"

Dex bit his lip. *I'm good with air. Really.* He turned and ran for the side of the balcony opposite the fight. Everyone was heading for the fight, leaving this end lightly populated by the civilians, especially the ladies. Dex climbed over the rail, and hung by his fingertips. Pulled up the wind and dropped. He hit the floor hard enough to doubt the efficacy of air as a deterrent to falling. He rolled to his feet, decided his feet and ankles were sound enough. He drew his sword and limped for the doors. Women shrank away. A pair of men ran at him, swords out. He sidestepped rapidly, knocked the right man's blade to the left and kicked, knocking him into the other. Ahead, Rondeze and a woman, surrounded by guards, pushed out a door. Dex ran out the closest one, and was nearly flattened by the gusting wind and stinging salt spray. A carriage lurched to a halt in the courtyard, the horses prancing and white eyed in the weather.

Dex was just a few steps behind the Pretender's escorts as they hurried down the steps.

The clink of a shod hoof was his only warning of the man in Rondeze's red and gold charging down on him. He threw himself left and rolled, as the trooper spurred around for another pass. Dex ran forward, snatched a hand full of Fire from the air and threw it left handed at the horse. The mare flinched and as the rider raised his arm for balance Dex lunged and slid his blade in between his ribs.

He grabbed the frantic mare's reins and hauled her around facing south before he released her. The four troopers galloping at him weren't in formation, and dodged wildly to avoid the bolting mare.

Dex lunged at the nearest guard. His sword was battered down, but slid between the saddle and leg to stab deep into the man's thigh. Blood spurted, and Dex threw himself backwards to avoid the man's return thrust. He dodged behind the horse and ran up behind a guard who was just turning to look, and slid his sword under his backplate and up. He withdrew the sword and was knocked spinning to the ground. A horse reared over him, and he slashed with his sword and dodged. The sword caught the cinch and the rider came off in a tangle of rear girth and breast straps and dangling saddle. The panicked horse bucked. Dex ran around the crazed animal and found himself facing the last guard. A snarling streak of black leapt at the horse's hind quarters. The horse spun and Dex jumped in and grabbed the guard's sword arm and dragged him off the horse as he slashed his sword across his neck.

More men poured down the steps. Imperial Guards. But the carriage was away, with a mounted escort between them and the Pretender.

Ringaugh looked at the four bodies, and shook his head. "Damn. Guess I should have believed some of those reports."

Dex grinned. "Nah. If I was that good I'd have managed to keep one of those horses." He watched the carriage as it turned away from the wild harbor and headed south.

"I think it's too late even for you. I just hope he keeps on running for a good long distance." Ringaugh huffed out his breath. "Lets see if we can get the abandoned troops to surrender. Secure the palace, and hold a coronation."

Dex backed up the steps, watching the water in the harbor subsiding. The wind was dropping, and the rain washed the taste of salt from his lips. Cruize's voice spoke briefly. "Formia has withdrawn, with her son and the prinza. I think you caught her attention with that handful of Fire. Vasik is dead."

Ringaugh's head jerked around, as he tried to see the speaker.

He could see other gods, Merd, Hastur, Lesto, Herm. Graf was nearly visible. Still lumpy. "I will release them. But they are mine. I will release them back on Graf, where they came from." He faded away.

***

"Archbishop? We need to talk." Father Hariban looked around the ornate cathedral. Paintings of the Ancient Gods graced the ceiling, the Elder gods held the walls. *I suppose the Younger Gods are stuck in the basement.*

The prelate was surrounded by the upper echelons of the church management. One in the back turned angrily and motioned him to silence.

"No. It's too late to hush anything up. The archbishop witnessed a battle between Gods, and it broke his mind. Some versions of the Histories of the Gods speak of wars between the Gods, they speak of the Ancients removing malign influences from the world, so they could not ... "

"Shut up!" The archbishop's voice was more scream than shout. "Roma is not dead. Roma is not dead!"

"His Fire has enriched the World. He is gone, forever." Hariban walked forward and they fell back from him. The hand he reached out to the archbishop was glowing. Perhaps that explained why they were kneeling. The archbishop clutched at his chest, and sank to the floor. "No... no... " He fell over, and when Father Hariban knelt, he could find no hint of breath, no pulse. He stood and looked around at the other Churchmen. "I have an Emperor to crown. We'll clean up this mess you've made of the Church after that's done."

***

A faint ray of sun shown through the clouds.

"Looks like a very good day for a coronation, to me." Dex followed the Guards inside.

It took hours to sweep through the Palace and find all of Rondeze's guards. And friends. And ambassadors.

Then they spread out over the grounds and found that Rondeze had gotten most of his troops away with him. Conte Fostel and Prinz Winstow moved their people onto the grounds, and took over all the outer guard posts.

Most of the members of the council, and a large selection of the nobility had been the "guests" of the Pretender. They were invited to witness Rawn's coronation, and most were delighted.

Roma's sword was missing.

One of the Councilors had seen it go. "It just disappeared in a flash. That bothered Rondeze, he got the Bishop up here, and cursed the archbishop for being in Winstow's hands."

That brought on a contemplative silence. Winstow broke it. "He left the camp and headed for the cathedral as soon as we got here. Haven't seen him since."

Another Councilor harumphed. "That's all well and good, but we need a god's sword for the coronation. We told Rondeze his crown was a sham without a sword. . . "

Dex nudged Rawn and whispered. "Hold out your hand."

Rawn grinned. A gleam of light coalesced into metal; steel and brass. His hand wrapped the hilt and took the weight. "I think this one will do."

A faint shift crossed the room, a faint physical sign of the shock of realization. *They* still *didn't believe the gods were taking a hand in this?*

"Well." Father Hariban stepped up. "It appears the necessary backing from the Gods is demonstrated, so let's get on with the crowning and swearing part."

Rawn handed the sword to Dex. "Will you be my Champion and stand at my side?"

"I will, sire."

Three other Churchmen hustled to take over, but it was Father Hariban who placed the crown on the new Emperor's head, and stood at Rawn's other shoulder while the nobles came forward to give their oaths of allegiance. There was a fair amount of stuttering and hesitation on the steps.

"Instant mental conversion, when they realize they can't lie. They all mean those oaths, at least right now." Dex barely breathed it. Rawn kept a straight face.

Chapter Twenty-nine

General Ringaugh organized the rounding up of the troops that hadn't followed Rondeze in his retreat. Most of the soldiers were disarmed and sent off to their homes. The few from Graf swore loyalty to Rawn and were accepted into the trains of various loyal nobles.

Dex rode out with scouts, trailing Rondeze and Inacig down the coast.

Then he returned to report to the young Emperor.

"Prinz Rondeze and Marque Inacig took ship at Matej." Dex resisted the impulse to scratch. He ought to have washed, found a clean uniform, but he'd been hustled straight in to the Emperor. "The prinz leaked troops all the way. Maybe a quarter of his men went with him. Vizduq Golezan was with him."

Stevan frowned. "His father publicly disinherited him, but rumor has it that he sent a great deal of gold off just before. I know some of the Marques will back Rondeze, but the majority preferred Marque Inacig, despite him staying away from the fight. I don't know what sort of reception

Rondeze will get."

Rawn nodded. "Well, no doubt we'll find out. Formia isn't interfering with shipping, so I've sent messages to all the rulers. Rya sent a letter to her parents, so with luck I'll at least have one neutral Marque. I pardoned Vasik's family, and deeded all his property to family members, in hopes that they'll stay loyal. Stevan and Fabrigel are analyzing everything to death. The worst case is looking like Graf declaring independence with Rondeze forming a government in exile. And Easterly declaring independence under Mongote and Prinza Lamirand and backing Rondeze in any attempt to put him on the throne of Roma."

Dex sighed. "I hope it doesn't come to that. Or if it does we could at least be peacefully separate. Sorry, I suppose that was treason, wasn't it?"

Rawn snorted. "No. It was common sense. If the World splits into three empires, the probability of war soars. It'll be like before the unification. Archbishop Hariban and Nevrille have tried to talk to the other Gods, but it's the men that are the problem. We'll just have to see if common sense wins out over ambition, and whether Inacig and Mongote will be satisfied with what they have.

"However, it's a good thing you got back now. I don't think Nati and Pierre would have waited much longer. I think it's time for a wedding, so go clean up. All the others are already dressing."

***

It was a beautiful wedding, and very well attended. The Unmannered Children all snickered to see the former "guests" of the Emperor bragging about how well they knew Vizconteza Nati ed'Treliff of Hastur. And somehow failing to mention how appalled they'd been by Pierre's mannerisms, while mentioning their long rides and political discussions with the groom.

Nati and Pierre's families were represented by their uncles. Both men had choked. But however appalling they considered each other's niece and nephew, they both had leapt at the potential for political advantage, both at home and here in the seat of a possibly still intact Imperium.

Nati was radiant in sweep of white silk with red roses.

With Fabrigel and Rya on one side, and Dex and Stevan beside Pierre, they put on a good show for the nobles.

Rawn had gleefully co-opted the father's place, saying that while it was more common for a conte to stand in for the emperor rather than the other way around, there weren't any rules about it.

Archbishop Hariban had officiated.

And then they had a grand party.

Chapter Thirty

"I think, instead of destroying a perfectly good secret tunnel, what we need to do is secure the far end. Therefore I designate the House of Arches to be the headquarters of the Defenders of the Realm." Rawn pointed at a building to the side. "It even has its own stable, so you're *seriously* independent."

"Do you still want us?" Nati looked hopeful. "I mean, you've got all of them now." Her chin pointed at the ranks of the Imperial Guard.

"Yeah, but they're different. You guys are personal friends and political commentators and, well, people I can send to do things. You and Pierre, neither of you are in line to inherit, so you can stay here. Stevan will eventually have to go back home. Fabrigel, has your brother said anything?"

She sniffed. "Just at the moment he doesn't quite dare. He hasn't figured out if my 'adventures' have increased or decreased my marriage market value."

Rya giggled. "Increased, trust me, the status of the men eyeing you has jumped considerably. They're even starting to look at me, and it's a bit scary to suddenly be the meat in the market."

"I'd like both of you to stay, as long as family and your own desires allow." Rawn said. "Stevan? Have you heard from your family?"

Stevan nodded. "I just got a letter. Father says I should stay as long as I can, learn the ropes over here, while he dances around any attempt of Mongote to continue his rebellion."

"Excellent. Dex, you will stay, won't you?"

"Certainly."

"Pierre?"

"I've got a General who's determined to turn me into a damned proper officer. Since you seem to be needing to rebuild an army, I was thinking about taking him up on the offer." His eyes slid uncertainly toward Nati.

Nati nodded. "An excellent idea. Rawn *needs* someone inside the regular army to bring things to his attention.

So they moved into the House of Arches.

Nati and Pierre grabbed the big fancy suite, Rya and Fabrigel took over the upstairs of the west wing, Stevan and Dex the east wing, and arranged a bedroom for an occasionally visiting emperor.

Dex waved an airy hand. "I know, I know, we

ought not encourage an emperor to run away from the palace. But it's our duty to keep him safe when he does."

***

"Dex, I owe you a humongous amount and I haven't a clue how to reward you." Rawn plopped down on the nearest mounting block and grinned at their expressions. "I know, I know, emperors are not supposed to run around horse barns."

Dex grinned and started to shake his head. "Oh, wait. I know, or at least I think I do. Muddy's ownership is all scrambled. I haven't a clue what's going on at the moment, but several months ago the farmer who bred him, the trainer who sort of bought him and sort of trained him, and the Mayor of Shingay's son who had sort of bought him were all in a lawsuit about who owed whom any money. I don't know whether the knacker I bought him from or my name has been brought into it, yet. Would it be unethical for you to interfere enough for the mayor's son who broke his coffin bone to have to pay the farmer the other half of what he agreed to pay the trainer, and the trainer to have to cough up most of the half he got, also to the farmer who probably had no idea how much his horse was actually being sold for, and me to have clear ownership, and his pedigree and all?"

"You bought Muddy from the knackers?" Rawn blinked. "Dex, he's an extraordinary horse. How much did you pay for him?"

"Forty marks. I got Spot there for sixty. I am *not* going to try and find out what *she* was doing there."

Stevan choked and Fabrigel boggled.

"You're fucking me," Pierre said. "A horse like that sells for four thousand, easy. And that was *before* a god borrowed him."

"Not with a broken coffin bone, he doesn't." Nati pointed out. "Big sweetie pie. *Obviously* Dex should own the horse."

Rawn nodded. "Obviously. I'll see to it."

About the Author

Hey, I'm a Texas gal. Okay, I wasn't actually born here, but mah Daaddy was born in Amarillo, and mah Great Granddaddy was one a them Real Old Oilmen.

Of course the rest of the family was wastrels; musicians and poets and such and moved to California.

I'm doing my best to be a typical member of my family.

I'm just not saying which side.

Excerpt from The Barton Street Gym

Joe crawled through the low tunnel. The stone, gritty and worn, was dry in the middle, damp from the bitter mist at either end. He scanned the far side. His eyes had adjusted to the constant twilight, but the occasional thin misty drizzle could hide one of the small scouts easily. Joe spotted movement to the left. An alien shape, turning around and trotting away. Long tail to balance the big head. Some sort of small dinosaur. If they ever got out of here, he'd find out what they were called.

His heart thudded in his ears—or was it a vibration in the ground? Joe shrunk back in the low tunnel. Behind him, Tommy crawled hastily in. The tan sandstone flags they lay on jumped and quivered. A taloned foot descended to meet the pavement. Joe could have reached out and touched it. The foot was scaled, with spread toes. Almost bird-like, apart from being the size of an elephant's. The ground seemed to flex with the weight. The foot lifted and disappeared.

Joe leaned forward. A hint of crushed leaves scented the chilly mist. In the dim light he could see the Tyrannosaurus Rex pacing away from them, so large it brushed the walls, disturbing the vines that grew here and there on the stones. It turned, and ducked to pass through one of the larger arches.

Straight ahead, the light showed nothing.

Literally.

Joe glanced right, then scrambled out and crossed the old flagstones to the edge. He shrugged out of his back pack. The flash was in the side pocket. Joe dropped to his belly, shivering as the condensation soaked through his clothes. They'd been conserving the power pack, so the light shown brightly down, down, down... no sign of bottom. Worse, he could see that the stone pavement they were laying on was a ledge only a couple of meters thick. Joe turned the light outward. No sign of the other side of this canyon... assuming there was another side.

No wonder the ground flexes where the T-Rex walks.

"Looks like we've found the edge of the world." He kept his voice low.

"Cut the light." Tommy's voice was a bare breath. "Let's get away from 'ere, I don't want to get trapped against a fall like that."

Tommy's implanted brain chip was loaded with a wealth of military tactics. For verisimilitude, no doubt, but it was coming in handy, here.

Wherever "here" was.

Joe pulled out his last candy bar. He hesitated, then put it away. No telling how long it would be before they found the way out of this... place. He turned and trotted cautiously in the direction the T-Rex had gone. Maybe the T-Rex—or whatever it really was—would lead them out of this maze.

And back into the real world.

***

"You sold the house?" Alice looked from her father's face to the narrow front of the old house. Men were carrying furniture out. *They didn't even tell me? What have they done?*

"We've bought into the Barton Street Gym. We'll have a dimensional cubby with our living room furniture in it, so we can have family get-togethers every afternoon, after school." Her mother looked smug and satisfied.

"But... Where am I going to sleep?" She shivered and hugged herself; disbelief fading into shock.

"Oh, Honey, that's the best news of all. They

just approved *Alert* for children ten and older. You'll never need to sleep again."

"But... " *I like my dreams. I like taking an hour to wake up on Saturday morning, snuggling with my...* "What about all my models?"

"Oh, we'll put them in storage with the rest of our furniture. You're getting a little old for dolls and toy horses."

"Mom! They aren't all plastic, you know. What about the bio-models?" She could see them both bracing their shoulders. This wasn't going to be good. She could feel herself starting to hyperventilate. *They can't have killed them, they can't have!*

"Alice." Her father was being formal. Not. Good. "I should never have bought you that first bio-model, I can't imagine what I was thinking. But when all's said and done, they are based on rats, and the humane thing to do is to put them down. I understand there's a new process that injects acrylic and they'll look just like they do now."

"No. Absolutely no. I only have four bio-models. They will come with me *alive* or I won't come at all. I will report you to child services as abusers."

They drew matching breaths. "Alice Steinway Brown, how dare you... " Her father got in first. Deep voice, towering, dark.

"You've sold my home, stolen my dreams, and now you want me to smile and say, oh sure, kill my bios, I'd love to have their murdered corpses on a shelf—*if* I had a shelf." She cast a glance at the movers. *Have they packed my room? Where are the bios?*

Alice felt like she was choking, and finally had to ask. "Have you killed them already?"

Her mother scowled. "No. I thought you'd want to pet them or something, and say good bye."

Alice closed her eyes in relief, and rubbed her arms, feeling sick. She scuffed her shoes on the familiar cracked sidewalk. *Not my sidewalk anymore. Not my flowerbeds. Not my maple tree in not-my-backyard. Think, Alice, why* must *they not harm the bios?*

Her mother sounded close to tears. "All your friends live in Gyms now."

The new lifestyle. Ah, yes, that will work. "I don't have friends. The older girls I know, who are already taking Alert don't live in Gyms, they live on the street and in the mall, and in school. They cross paths with their parents every once in a while. If I need to come to our 'dimensional cubby' twice a day to check on the bio-models and play with them, you'll be able to find me. Otherwise, why should I bother ever going there?"

That got them, she could see it their eyes, hear it in Mother's faint sigh. The bios were safe. Even if they really were just dumb animals, genetically engineered to look like dolls, their personalities and inane chatter courtesy of multipurpose nanochips implanted in their little rodent brains.

She turned and walked toward the house. "I will get the bio-models now. So no unfortunate accidents occur."

"Alice!" There was a warning growl in her father's voice.

She ignored him. *Sorry, Father, but you just blew all my trust in you to tiny little bits.*

***

"You'll quickly get used to the feeling of crossing the dimensional threshold." The fussy little manager wiped his hands together as the last of the movers left. "There now, that looks very comfortable.

All you need to remember is to always pull the d-door toward you, so you and the door are in the same dimension." He gave Alice a jaundiced look. "If you push, the dimensional shift across your arm tends to jerk you forward and off your feet. The kids laugh and call you a klutz. And anyway, we've got the doors fixed so that shouldn't happen."

Doesn't like kids, and doesn't want us playing around with the doors.

The dimensional doors were square, about two meters in each direction, with a lip about ten cems high, like a hatch in a submarine or something. You had to step over it, and if you were tall, duck a bit. She'd noticed, walking in, a couple of doors with ramps.

This floor had a corridor following the glass outside wall all around the irregular shape of the building. The "cubbies" lined the inner side of the corridor, so they had a view, some contact with the outside world, as they came and went from "home." A second corridor ringed the inside core of plumbing, wiring, elevators, stairs and whatever. Then there were "spoke" corridors that crossed from the core elevator lobby to the outside corridor. The inner corridor and the spokes held the autodiners, mini-spas, vendomarts, hair stylists, and day care centers, about half in cubbies of their own. The spoke corridors were color coded, for orientation, not décor, although they made an effort in that direction as well, with potted plants and abstract art. All-in-all it was still a big impersonal maze. *For us human rats to run through.*

"So, will you all join me at the Top Hat Club on the forty-sixth floor? Good food and an amazing view!"

"Sounds wonderful." Her mother looped her arm through her husbands.

She looks happy. Alice scowled. "I think I'll stay and get my stuff arranged." *Get the bios out of their box.*

Her father's eyes narrowed. "I think you should come along."

Alice folded her arms and stood silently. *I'm still grounded, from sneaking out to that party, so what can you do? Extend the time? Again?*